BOUND BY
GUILT

SANDRA BARD

Dreamspinner Press

Published by
Dreamspinner Press
5032 Capital Circle SW
Ste 2, PMB# 279
Tallahassee, FL 32305-7886
USA
http://www.dreamspinnerpress.com/

Bound by Guilt

Cover Art by Paul Richmond
http://www.paulrichmondstudio.com

ISBN: 978-1-62380-496-1
Digital ISBN: 978-1-62380-497-8

Printed in the United States of America
First Edition
May 2013

This is for my family, friends, cats, and dogs.

PROLOGUE

KIT hated funerals and had sworn he'd never attend another after suffering through his mother's at the age of seven. But here he was, head bowed with shame and guilt, wearing mismatching clothes, wishing he'd never set eyes on Cory. Dr. St. James, he reminded himself sarcastically as he tried hard not to squirm at the feel of the sweat running down between his shoulder blades. He didn't think he'd be able to return the shirt with sweat-stained armpits, and hoped fervently that Eddy would leave stocktaking for some other week.

Not that Eddy would fire him or anything, Kit thought. He had been at Eddy's shop, called Eddy's for obvious reasons, for two years, and he'd been very careful in keeping his social life and work separate until now. The pay at Eddy's wasn't great, but it was enough to get by, and the working hours were manageable. Kit usually supplemented his income by snagging a few lovers in his off time. He preferred his lovers male, mature, and rich—single, married, or otherwise attached. In fact, he preferred them attached. That way he did not have to drag the relationship on for long. Just because Kit's lovers were rich enough to pick up his tab, didn't mean they were good in bed, and Kit liked it short and sweet. Long-time relationships with rich lovers led to complications, and Kit wasn't looking for some fairy-tale romance where his mark fell in love with him and declared undying love.

Kit's longest relationship had been with an accountant, and that had lasted three months. By that time the guy had been on wife number four, and Kit had quit (his john, not Eddy's) when the accountant started adding up his alimony bills while in bed with Kit.

Cory, dear, dead Cory, had been something of an accident for Kit, since he had not been looking for anyone—actively searching, that is—when Kit had run into him.

CHAPTER
ONE

KIT met Cory during a dry spell in between "boyfriends." Kit didn't do any outright hooking, and one-night stands made him feel cheap. Most of the time, they expected Kit to pay for his drink and room, and Kit was not in the mood for another month of budget balancing. He had been on the lookout for someone new to support him for a bit, and in walked the perfect guy.

The first time Kit ran into Cory was at the store, as he was arranging the racks in the summer-wear collection. He had heard the door open, accompanied by the tinkle of the chimes indicating a customer, as a draft swept through the interior. It had been a particularly slow day with a grand total of five customers. Only two of the previous customers had bought anything, and Kit had been feeling lethargic from boredom.

"Can I help you, sir?" Eddy called out from behind the cash register, where he had been reading a paperback, and Kit rolled his eyes. Apparently the slow spell was getting to Eddy as well if he was accosting customers before they made it past the doorway. Or maybe Eddy was just worried he might not be able to pay the rent on the shop at the end of the month if the sales fell off too much.

"I'm just browsing." The voice made Kit pause, but he did not turn around. It was a slightly more cultured voice than he was used to hearing in the shop. "I was passing by on my way to lunch, and the green shirt on the display caught my eye."

"Christopher," Eddy called out, pretending as usual that their shop was much larger and Kit was at the far end instead of two racks away. "Can you bring up the summer collection—hunter-green number eight, please?"

Kit had to bite his lower lip to stop himself from laughing out loud. Eddy's was at best a trivial shop that sold clothes from small-timers—some unique designs but nothing to boast about. They certainly didn't have numbers for their shirts, and green was green— what the fuck was hunter green? Eddy was trying to look good because he knew Kit was listening in on the conversation and knew exactly which shirt the customer was referring to, since Kit had done the shop display in the morning.

Kit was debating the wisdom of informing Eddy that they only had one green shirt in the entire shop, and it was currently on display on their one and only unisex model, when the customer spoke. "It's all right," he said. "I'll just walk around and take a look—browse to see if something catches my eye."

Interesting voice, but might not be an interesting guy, Kit surmised as he finished arranging the blue pinafore the best he could on the mirrored drapery. He scooted down to arrange the hem in a way the lace would catch the light, and found a pair of well-polished shoes in his line of sight.

Kit looked up slowly, up the well-pressed, dark-blue dress pants, cream dress shirt, and dark-blue tie with a hint of gold stripes, held in place with a gold tie pin. Working at Eddy's meant Kit knew how to assess the value of clothes when he saw them, and this guy screamed money. Probably from the law firm across the street, by the looks of it.

As he stood slowly, brushing his hands on his clean but faded jeans, Kit realized the guy was old—well, older than he had first expected. The green shirt on display was for someone young; this guy, Kit assessed quickly, was around fifty or thereabouts, with gray at his temples and lines around his eyes and mouth. He was, however, rather good looking, and the expensive cologne he wore was enticing.

"You must be Christopher," the customer said, and his eyes smiled.

"Yes, sir," Kit answered, snapping into his sales assistant mode. The guy was just his type, rich and not young, but that did not mean Kit was stupid enough to press his luck.

"Then perhaps you can help me out," the potential mark said, appearing slightly thoughtful. "I'm looking for some light wear—for a friend… a young man about your age, perhaps a little older. I'm told I have no sense of fashion, so perhaps you could help me out."

Even as the customer spoke, his gaze roamed over Kit's body in an almost unconscious gesture that had Kit smiling to himself. He had already made an assessment about the guy—one, he was rich, and two, he was old. Three, he had a younger male "friend" for whom he was buying clothes—that screamed younger lover. A son, nephew, or brother would have been specifically mentioned as such, and the way the guy was looking at Kit said he liked what he saw. No one looked at sales assistants as though they were on sale unless interested.

"Certainly, sir," Kit said chirpily. "But perhaps, if you could bring your friend over, maybe he can pick out—"

The customer smiled and shook his head, and to Kit, it seemed that he was sad. "Sasha doesn't go out much," he said.

Oh! Well, Kit could work on such a person. Apparently Sasha didn't go out much and his lover was unhappy about it. The relationship was on rocky ground, and this gave Kit the confidence he needed. He knew from experience that any weakness could be exploited for his benefit. Anyway, Sasha sounded like a name more for an exotic dog than a person. "What does your friend look like?" Kit asked breezily as he walked over to the left side of the store, where most of the men's clothes were. "Blond? Dark haired…?"

"Sasha's a blond." The customer hesitated. "He's got these red highlights, though, and—" Kit flicked his eyes up to see the old guy blush slightly, and he made a mental note to get some highlights the next time he went for a haircut. "—perhaps a couple of shades lighter than yours…." And bleach his hair a bit—this kind of guy always went for the same type of twinks, Kit knew from experience. "A little taller than you and somewhat slimmer."

A model, then, Kit thought. Kit was proud of how his body looked. Slender, not overly muscled—not many older lovers liked bulky twinks with more muscles than they had—and he preferred to wear loose clothing to appear slimmer. *For Sasha to be slimmer, he must be fucking anorexic or bulimic*, Kit thought savagely.

Just as Kit was about to open his mouth to make a smart-assed remark, he saw Eddy making frantic gestures behind the customer's back.

"See if any of these will suit *your* Sasha," he said, pulling out a select few shirts and placing them on the dress he had been arranging. "The purple is my favorite, and this blue one looks good with almost everything." He turned smoothly as the customer perused through the selection of shirts. "Excuse me a moment, sir," he said, and strolled toward Eddy.

Eddy all but grabbed him by the collar and pulled him over the counter. "Do you know who that is?" he whispered into Kit's ear, spittle flying in his eagerness.

"No," Kit said in surprise. Not many things got Eddy this excited—unless it had four legs and a tail and was running on a race track. "Should I?"

"You should read something other than the comics," Eddy retorted, and Kit bit back the reply that he read the personal-ad section in the paper. He didn't want to abandon a potential customer for long in case he lost interest. Kit's paycheck always included a little bonus if the monthly sales went up, and he knew a buyer when he saw one. "He's Dr. Cory St. James," Eddy replied. "You know, scientist turned businessman, he owns St. James Pharmaceuticals down the road."

"You've been reading the gossip column, I see," Kit joked as he drew back. "Don't worry, I'll treat him like royalty."

He walked back to the customer, St. James, who was looking at him with an amused expression. "Problem?" St. James asked, and Kit laughed.

"Not at all," he replied. "My manager just informed me that you're rich and prestigious and if I make a sale, I'll get a bonus."

St. James laughed as well, and Kit could see Eddy cringing visibly in the corner. "I like your style, Christopher," St. James said, smiling. "So, what else do you have that might interest me?"

"I'm always willing to show you more, Mr. St. James," Kit said, tilting his head down and gazing from under his lashes suggestively. "My friends call me Kit." Eddy had said the man was a doctor, but he didn't look like any doctor Kit had seen, and anyway, it was too late to go back to calling him Dr. St. James. Kit moved to the next rack and bent down instead of squatting on his heels as he usually did to move aside the small stool in the way. It was good to show off what was being offered. Then Kit was all professional, knowing he had just about pushed his limit for the day, and switched to his sales-assistant mode perfectly.

He managed to sell five shirts, seven trousers, jeans, and enough odd ends to double his monthly check, and decided that even if St. James did not come back, he should be happy with what he had.

But St. James was back two days later with most of the clothes he had bought. It was Eddy's off day and Kit was at the store alone, which was just as well, since Eddy would have been heartbroken.

"Sasha didn't like this," St. James said, pulling out the purple shirt. "Or this...." The blue shirt. "Said it made him look like an old man...."

Fussy little bitch throwing a hissy fit, Kit thought through gritted teeth as he tried to smile. "We can't reimburse you, Mr. St. James, but we can exchange these for something else—of equal value."

"Cory, please," St. James said with a smile. "Calling me St. James makes me feel old, not that I am not." A wry grin.

Kit laughed at the joke and didn't try to guess St. James's age. "Cory it is, then," he said, letting the name drag in his mouth just to see a reaction. "Tell you what, sir, we'll be getting a new shipment next week, and you can pick out something from that. Until then, leave these here, and I'll write up a receipt for you."

"I think that's an excellent idea," Cory replied as he pulled out a business card. "My home number is on the back, my office number is at the bottom. Just give me a call when you get new stock."

Kit decided to give it a try again, just so he could get a feel for the competition. "If you could bring Sasha with you, though...," he said, letting the suggestion hang.

"Sasha is a little busy at the gym these days," Cory replied, and again there was a shadow of sadness in his face. "The pool and the gym are just about the only places he goes… so…."

Kit smiled to himself and did a little dance inside his head. Here was a guy crying for attention, and Kit was going to lavish him from head to toes. But Kit knew how to play his cards. He held back, writing receipts and smiling politely at St. James—no, Cory.

The new stock came on Monday. Kit waited until Wednesday afternoon to call up St. James. Thursday was Eddy's off day, and Kit wanted the shop to himself. Kit dialed the home number, and someone picked it up on the fourth ring.

"Hello." The voice was chocolate and honey melted together. If this was Sasha, Kit was in for a long trial. "St. James residence."

"Hi, I'm Kit from Eddy's… boutique." The voice had thrown Kit off balance, and he did not know what to say. Three words, and that voice had him panting—no wonder St. James was mad over this Sasha guy, even if he was such a bitchy little thing. "I just wanted to tell Dr. St. James"—there, Kit had rehearsed that line several times, so he knew what to say—"that the new stock he ordered is here. If he could drop by tomorrow to—"

"I'll tell him." The voice said, sounding cold, forcing Kit to speculate that his mere existence had won him the wrath of Sasha. "Anything else?"

"Uh…," said Kit, still off balance. "No, but…." He was listening to the dial tone. Stupid Sasha had hung up on him. Now he wasn't even sure if his message had gotten through.

But St. James showed up the next day late in the afternoon, just when Kit was about to give up, and was more than happy to go over the new stock with Kit. As Kit was totaling up the bill after the sales, he glanced at the wall clock and smiled. "I'm about to close up for the day, Mr. St. Ja… Cory. Care for a cup of tea?"

St. James appeared surprised but pleased. "Yes, I…." He looked at his watch and grimaced. "I'm sorry, but Sasha has an appointment—I promised to drive him there, and…."

"Just a cup of tea," Kit said, smiling invitingly. This was his first test to see if Sasha had an absolute grasp on Cory, or if Kit had a chance. "Please, I've been here the whole day without a lunch break, and I hate eating alone."

"I suppose." Cory seemed to hesitate. "Well, I guess a cup of coffee won't hurt, just give me a minute to call up James."

"James?"

"My chauffeur," Cory said as he pulled out his cell phone. "He can take Sasha to his appointment."

Success, thought Kit, as Cory took Kit to a local coffee shop. The place wasn't so flashy that Kit in his jeans and T-shirt would feel out of place, but not too grubby either. Kit's new patron paid for everything with his credit card. Kit didn't leave with Cory, knowing anything too obvious might drive him away. Cory was far too well bred to be taken in by someone who came on to him like a ton of bricks.

Instead, Kit stood on the pavement outside the café and watched Cory walk to where he had parked his car, when the waiter who had served them came to the door. "Here," the waiter said, handing over to Kit an off-white calling card. "Your friend dropped this when he paid."

"Uh," said Kit, nonplussed as he took it. "Thanks." He turned it over and frowned. The card was embossed in gold and looked expensive, and on it was a long word followed by the word "clinic." The long word did not make sense, but the clinic bit did. So did the name underneath the title, Dr. Henry Hausser—some sort of medical card. Whatever, Kit thought as he pocketed it. He'd give it to Cory the next time he dropped into the shop—and Kit was sure he would come back.

By Saturday, Kit's curiosity got the best of him, and he finally dropped a token into the payphone outside the store and dialed the number on the card. A pleasant female voice answered on the third ring. "Blepharoplasty, Dr. Hausser's office."

"Bleph—what?" Kit said before he could help it. "Is that like a curse or something?"

The girlish voice on the other side laughed, friendly and probably used to idiots calling out of the blue. "No sir, we're a medical clinic. We specialize in eyelid remodeling, but that's not the only thing."

"Like with film stars," Kit blurted out.

The voice laughed again, and had Kit been straight he'd have fallen for the faceless voice there and then. "We can't make you a star, but you'll look like one," she said, still not fazed by his questions.

"So, you're, like, a plastic surgery place?" Kit couldn't help but ask.

"That's right, sir," the girl said. "Dr. Hausser specializes in eyelid reconstruction, but we also have a panel of other talented doctors who specialize in other things."

"Such as?" Kit prompted, still curious.

"We also do otoplasty, that's ear pinning, and neck and face lifts, that's rhytidectomy, reshaping of eyes, rhinoplasty, which is basically nose reshaping and for female clients, breast enhancements...."

"So...," said Kit a little tentatively. "How much would it cost me to, say, get my nose done...?"

"Dr. Hausser is one of the most skilled surgeons in the field." Now the voice sounded more professional and less friendly. "Depending on what you need, it could vary from five to nine thousand dollars."

"Oh," Kit said, stunned. Nine thousand bucks to make a nose stick to the middle of the face. "Uh... thanks."

"No problem, sir, please call us again if you need to know anything."

Kit hung up, feeling overwhelmed but also a little pleased. He knew Cory wasn't getting his nose done; he wasn't the type. That left little mysterious Sasha... who was probably getting his face worked on so he could look like a prince, while Cory paid through *his nose* for it. Sasha was really pushing it, and from experience, Kit knew that if someone pushed his mark too much, that person risked getting dropped like a hot potato. The art of getting something was not to ask for a large amount all at once.

On Tuesday, Kit called Cory to arrange a meeting to return the business card. It was such a flimsy excuse that Kit knew neither of them was fooled by it. Cory obviously wanted to spend time with Kit, so who was he to complain. They had dinner at a slightly more upclassed restaurant, and Kit learned that, yes, Dr. Hausser's card was for Sasha, and that to eat crabs, he had to crack the shell just so.

The following week, Kit found out that red wine was to be sipped and not gulped, and it was just as heady as beer but sweeter. What did Cory call it—smoother? And that Cory was rather easy to talk to and never thought twice about picking up the bill. They never talked about Sasha, though every time his name came up, Cory would get a slightly distant look in his eye that Kit did not like. Kit, though surprised that Cory had time to spend with him that week, did not question his good luck. He was pleased with all the attention he was receiving, and it was good to know that he had lost none of his old charm. He was still able to win over older attached men, no matter how much they professed their so-called devotion to their better halves—or so Kit thought until Cory mentioned casually that Sasha was out of town that week, spending time at Dr. Hausser's clinic. Added to the blow, Cory canceled their next "date" to pick up Sasha from the airport, which made Kit realize that he had yet to overcome the greatest obstacle in his path—Sasha.

So far, Sasha never showed up to any of their meetings, not even once, and Kit had an idea that he was too busy between gym, plastic surgeons, and whatnots to actually spend time with Cory. By then, Kit was actually starting to like Cory. He was easy to talk to and fun to be with. He had been all over the world and told Kit things without making him feel like a moron. He also told Kit things about himself which Kit found endearing, like he was not a medical doctor as Kit had first thought but rather a scientist specializing in physics. His full name was Coriolis after some French guy who had figured out that a ball didn't roll straight on a turntable or something like that.

After their fifth date, Cory drove Kit to his apartment, and instead of getting out of the convertible, Kit leaned forward and kissed Cory on the mouth. Cory tasted of wine and the caramel dessert they'd just shared. His lips were firm, and for an old guy, he kissed rather well. Kit dived deeper, desperate for more. However, just as he was getting the rhythm right, Cory pushed him off firmly.

"I'm sorry, Kit, if I gave you the wrong impression," Cory said, appearing distressed. "But we cannot—I can't—you're young enough to be my son."

"I'm twenty-two," Kit replied, knowing from past experience that age was the first thing to be brought up. "And—" He slithered over to the driver's side and let his hand brush against Cory's crotch, where the bulge was obvious. "—you want me."

"No," said Cory, though his hips bucked toward Kit.

Emboldened, Kit cupped his erection and stroked it through the fabric. "Come on, Cory, I want you."

"No," Cory gasped, though Kit could see it was a struggle for Cory to refuse Kit. "Sasha.... I've got to go—Sasha is waiting for me." That name, like a talisman, seemed to give Cory the energy to move. "I'm sorry, Kit—Sasha and I are together. We haven't been intimate in some time, so...." Intimate. Kit snorted. These old guys always used big words when a four-letter word would do just as well. "I... my body responded to yours, but I think you should go home."

Kit slid back and let himself out of the car, frowning. He closed the door and walked toward his apartment, cursing his luck. He had pushed too soon. Cory had not been ready, but damn—he was close. Cory was too nice to actually cheat on Sasha, but surely—Kit didn't need Sasha to go away. He was willing to share, just as long as Cory kept him fed and well paid. Now, if he could convince Cory he didn't need to lose his precious Sasha, who wasn't even putting out after leaching all that money off Cory. Maybe if he could convince Cory that Sasha needed a long vacation at a health spa or ski resort while Kit worked his way into Cory's home. By the time Sasha came back, Cory wouldn't even remember who he was.

However, the following week, Cory didn't show up at the shop. Kit had known he wouldn't—these scenarios played out the same, and Cory was dealing with guilt just then. But Kit knew what to do. All he needed was an excuse to visit Cory. On Friday morning, Eddy gave him the perfect pretext, and Saturday found Kit on Cory's front lawn, waving a catalogue under his nose. He knew from their numerous conversations that Saturday was Sasha's pool day and Cory spent the morning at home relaxing. What he had not known was that Cory lived in a fucking mansion and had a garden the size of a soccer pitch.

"I know you're mad at me, and I screwed up, but please, Cory," Kit pleaded when Cory tried to close the door when he saw who was there. Dressed in shorts and a short-sleeved T-shirt, Cory looked relaxed and somewhat older. The hair on his arms was also going gray, and without those expensive suits to hide his flab, it was obvious he was going to get fat. Still, Kit had seen and done worse, and overall, Cory was still a good-looking guy. "Just take a look at this and pick something. Eddy will have my head if he learns I screwed up. You're our best customer and if I fuck this up I'll lose my job."

"Fine," Cory said, holding the door open. "Come in while I take a look at this."

Kit stepped into the house, which looked like a stage setup from one of those period pieces. The furniture was antique, and even the phone looked like one of those really old models with a curved receiver. The inside was grand, with high ceilings and large airy windows, but Kit was too intent on winning Cory back to worry about interior design. Plus, if he was successful, he could always look at this at leisure.

He walked up to Cory as soon as the door was closed, and pressed up against him boldly. "Missed you," he said, pressing his lips to Cory's neck.

Cory shuddered and tried to push Kit away, but his heart was not really in it. Kit could tell that much as he pressed his advantage. Kit latched onto Cory's neck while taking off Cory's T-shirt. This was not the time for niceties; that could come later. For now, he needed to stake his claim before Sasha came home and demanded a foot massage.

Cory didn't pull away from the kiss, nor the hand between his legs, and when Kit unzipped Cory's shorts and let them fall, Cory did not protest. Cory seemed to have gotten his act together by then as he pushed down Kit's jeans and fondled him between his legs as he kissed Kit hard. Kit let Cory take charge; let himself be bent over the table with his jeans around his ankles and his shoes still on.

"I've got a condom in my back pocket," Kit ground out, and Cory was quick in picking out just what Kit wanted. He was so close to reaching his goal; he could bear the discomfort of being fucked in the ass by some guy who hadn't heard of lube. Kit wasn't ready, but he was so getting fucked and—emotions were worth crap anyway. Kit was not in it for the physical pleasure, that was optional. He just had one objective: to win.

"Co... ry."

The voice penetrated their lust-addled brains where the sound of the door opening had not. It was too late to pretend they were doing anything else but *that*, but as Cory pulled back roughly, Kit gasped, feeling as if his intestines were being dragged out through his anus.

"Sasha," Cory gasped, and he tried to shield Kit with his body, blocking Kit's view of the competition, not that that would help with the situation. He pushed Kit aside, and Kit tumbled to the floor, tangled up in his jeans that were pooled around his ankles. "It's not what you think—"

Kit snorted from his undignified position on the floor as he untangled himself and began to pull up his jeans. What did it look like, he wondered as he stood up slowly, a confident grin on his face, and stopped.

The first thing he saw was the mouth. Anyone who had a voice to die for should have a mouth like that, soft and kissable, a hint of vulnerability in it. Not that there was anything else to see since the rest of his face was swathed in bandages, leaving a single opening for a bright green eye. The rest of his body was not any better. Sasha's left arm ended at the elbow—the T-shirt he wore did nothing to hide it—and his entire body weight seemed to rest on a walking stick held in his right hand.

"I'm sorry," Sasha said softly, his voice almost musical. "Therapy ended early today, so I took a taxi."

"Sasha!" Cory took a step forward.

Sasha took a step backward, swayed, and then found his balance. His shoulders were straight, but his mouth looked sad. Kit noticed it slanted down slightly on one side. "I'll leave—please, don't let me stop you." He took another step back, and Kit saw that his left leg dragged. He stared at Kit, and that mouth smiled faintly, mockingly. "You must be Kit, I've heard a lot about you."

Kit couldn't reply as he stood there, looking at the man before him. He took a step back himself and then slid along the wall to reach the front door, finished pulling up his pants, and buttoned up. He rushed outside while zipping, not wanting to deal with the fallout of his actions.

Kit could not remember leaving, he could not remember how he had gotten home, but he did remember gasping as he'd thrown himself on the bed. Sasha was a... was a... freaking cripple. Why hadn't Cory mentioned anything?

The next day, Kit hauled himself out of bed and dragged his feet to work at ten, an hour late. He was sure Eddy would blast him for leaving the catalogues at Cory's place, but there was no way he was going to get them back. But he was mistaken. "Hey, Kit," Eddy said as soon as Kit was in the store. "Did you see it—that guy, St. James... he offed himself last night."

"He what!" Kit was sure he swayed.

"He shot himself in the head," Eddy repeated. "See—" He waved the newspaper toward Kit. Then he started to read what was in it, but Kit didn't hear. All he could think of, as he leaned against the wall, was that it was all his fucking fault, and what was Sasha going to do now.

CHAPTER
TWO

DR. CORIOLIS ST. JAMES: entrepreneur, inventor, brother of (Ms.) Lux St. James and (Ms.) Candela Keyton, son of Dr. and Mrs. Gareth St. James (deceased), all-around good guy and freaking idiot for offing himself.

Kit hated funerals. He knew they were the only places everyone said good things about someone, even if that someone was the shittiest asshole. They were the place where family members tried to re-sculpt their dead loved ones into something they were not in life.

He had no idea why he was attending Cory's funeral in the first place, since, as the joke went, it wasn't likely that Cory would attend his. But Kit had liked Cory, and the news of his death had made Kit feel guilty—though he couldn't figure out the reason. While he was no fool to think that it was pure coincidence that Cory had swallowed a gun the day after—or was it the same day?—Sasha caught Kit and Cory in the front room, he could not really see the situation escalating to a suicide. Kit had never, ever caused someone to kill himself or do something drastic. Well, apart from the time when one of his past lovers had dented his BMW because Kit had given him a blow job while they were driving.

Kit's attire had already earned a few scowls from the devoted mourners. The shirt Kit had borrowed from the "to be returned—damaged" section at Eddy's was just the wrong type of black silk to wear to a funeral, with two front buttons undone and pulled apart so the tear at the top wouldn't be obvious. The slacks were the wrong shade of black for the shirt, and his dark-green shoes, which had seemed to pass muster in the dim light of his rented room by being close to a shade of black, looked unmistakably green in the bright daylight.

Listening to the mourners helped Kit identify the trio who sat in the front aisle—Cory's two sisters and one of their husbands. If Kit recalled correctly, only one of the sisters was married. No Sasha. But Kit wasn't naïve enough to assume they would accept their brother's male lover with open arms now that their brother was dead. Cory had once mentioned that Sasha never accompanied him to family dinners either; perhaps there was a reason for that.

Standing at the back, Kit glanced around, trying to catch a glimpse of the person he'd come to see, even if it was from a distance, but in the sea of black, he could recognize no one.

Thankfully, by the time Kit had gathered his wits enough to walk into the church, most of the service was over, and they were about to move the casket to the crematorium that was situated right next door. There was nothing to do as the coffin was carried out. Kit had been too late to view the body. He wasn't even sure if he wanted to see Cory for the last time, knowing the back of his brains was shot out. As he was about to follow the group, Kit realized he was not the last to leave the church. Sitting in an aisle close to the center was another figure. Slim and straight-backed, head held high.

Kit swallowed—and moved forward. He was not sure what he would say, but he did not want to linger in this place any longer than necessary. He opened his mouth to call out, but his throat was dry and he couldn't make a sound. Feeling like a moron, he stepped closer when the seated figure stood up—slowly.

Catching a sideways glimpse, at first Kit was sure he had made a mistake. This person sitting all alone was not Sasha. He couldn't remember the face, since he had not seen one, but he was sure he wouldn't forget the bandages. Now there were none, nor was there a walking stick, and this person had both hands. Kit froze for a moment as the slender man stood and started to walk toward the exit.

As he moved, his left leg dragged, spurring Kit into action. He started to walk forward, still hesitant, as the figure reached the door and walked out. Kit hurried outside and stopped short, almost running into

Sasha's back as he stood at the doorway, looking at the funeral cortege some distance away, making no move to join them.

"S… Sasha," Kit said hesitantly, and the back stiffened. Slowly, the slender figure turned, holding the wall for balance, his face blank. At the sight of Kit, Sasha's eyes flashed, and his hand scrabbled along the wall for better purchase as he straightened.

"What do you want?" The voice was still the same, but the spite in it was new—not that Kit could blame the guy. Kit could only stare at the face he had caught a mere glimpse of amidst the bandages. Sasha had arranged his hair to fall over the left side of his forehead, hiding the damage, but it could not cover his entire face. Sasha's left eyelid drooped, and his nose was crooked. His cheek was a mess of scar tissue, some shiny and taut, some pink and wrinkled; his left ear was missing a lobe, and the corner of his lip on closer inspection seemed to twist slightly off-kilter. But the overall effect was not as bad as Kit had feared it would be. Sasha's right side was unmarred, pale skin that hadn't seen the sun in a while, flesh sunken under the prominent cheekbone, and again, the same startlingly green eye. Morbidly, Kit's eyes kept straying back to the damaged side.

"I wanted… to… say… I was sorry," Kit said softly, taking a step forward. Kit had rarely felt sorry in his life, but he was here to say that. He had cried a bit when he'd realized Cory was dead. He had actually liked Cory and was going to miss him, more as a friend than a potential mark. Making amends with Sasha had seemed like a good idea in the middle of the night as he was reading the obituary with tear-blurred eyes, but now it seemed utterly ridiculous.

"Get lost," Sasha snarled, pulling back. "You'd better go—you have no right to be here."

That stung, no matter how true it was. To Kit, it was a familiar situation: he never had any right to be acknowledged by his boyfriends; he was always their dirty little secret, to be used and thrust back into the closet. "For what it's worth," Kit said quietly, looking down at the hardwood floor, "I didn't expect it to turn out this way."

"How did you expect it to turn out?" Sasha demanded as he pushed himself away from the wall and stood straight. "You little— you…." The scarred face twisted into a grimace. "Slut."

Kit shrugged. He'd been called worse and done worse. If that was the best Sasha could come up with, he had nothing to worry about. Still, his pride pricked him, and he couldn't hold back the words that sprung out of him. "Why do you think Cory came to me?" Kit bit out. "Little crippy couldn't put out so—"

Sasha pulled back his arm for a punch in such a manner that Kit knew "pwetty" little Sasha had never done anything like that before. There wasn't much force behind the swing, but when it connected with his chest, it hurt. Kit staggered back in surprise, realizing why Sasha now had two arms—prosthetics were extremely useful as weapons, it seemed. Stunned, Kit pushed back with an open-palmed slap to Sasha's chest. It was not much of a shove, but Sasha's leg seemed to fold up under him, and he fell backward, landing on his butt, hard. Both his arms hit the ground, the right silently and the prosthetic left with a dull thud.

Kit had a feeling he was the first person to ever lift an arm against Sasha, who seemed too stunned to react. Or maybe, he thought as the smug feeling evaporated, he'd really hurt the guy. Sasha looked like a walking skeleton; maybe he wasn't shatterproof. He moved out of the doorway, and stooped. "Hey, you hurt?"

"Don't touch me," Sasha spat as he attempted to stand up. His right hand scrabbled to find purchase to pull himself up, but the smooth, whitewashed wall didn't offer him any handholds.

"Fine," said Kit, drawing back. It wasn't like he was going to help the prickly bastard. Sasha's impeccable suit had dust stains on it and his hair no longer looked perfectly set. Kit gained some satisfaction in knowing that Cory's boyfriend was not as collected as he had seemed at first. It was amusing to realize Sasha could be as clumsy as Kit at times. If only Cory could see Sasha then, as he tried to get up and failed, falling on his bum again onto the hard ground. His failure to get to his feet seemed to make him angry, and cursing under his breath, face red with effort and embarrassment, Sasha pulled himself closer to the wall in crab fashion, probably ruining the seat of his expensive black suit, and started to push his body up, using his shoulder and organic arm.

There were a lot of things Kit enjoyed watching, but this sight was not one of them. "You know," he said tentatively, holding out his hand to assist him to his feet. "It's easier if I help you up."

"Fuck you," Sasha replied from between tightly clenched teeth, sounding breathless from physical exertion.

As much as Kit wanted to ignore everything and walk away, he could not. Instead, he stepped forward, grabbed Sasha by the arms, and pulled him up forcefully, unable to watch the proceedings any longer. It seemed he yanked a little too hard. All of a sudden he had an armful of black suit filled with skin and bones. Kit remembered Cory telling him Sasha was a little slender, but what he had neglected to say was that Sasha was so pitifully thin that, without his clothes, he was practically transparent. Through layers of cloth—just how many, Kit could not count, he could feel Sasha—all bones and a layer of skin to hold it together.

Sasha smelled faintly of lemon and mint, with a dab of expensive aftershave perhaps better suited for someone older and more masculine. His body felt as light as that of a small bird, all fragile bones that could snap if gripped too hard. Stunned, Kit let Sasha rest against his chest for a few seconds, but then Sasha drew back, almost snarling. Sasha staggered back and Kit expected him to fall over again, but he miraculously held himself upright, though barely.

"Don't you have a walking stick?" Kit asked as he held out a hand to steady the other man.

Sasha made an aborted gesture to brush away the helping hand, and swayed as though he were buffeted by a wind. "I don't need it," he said forcefully. "I don't need any help from anyone," he added for emphasis, and started to walk toward the pebbled path leading to the front gate.

"Uh," said Kit carefully, "I think the crematorium is that way."

"I'm not going there," Sasha replied, carefully putting one foot in front of the other as he walked down the path. "I had my time with him when he was alive. They can—can—" His voice broke off in a choked sob, and Kit realized how close to breaking down Sasha really was. Kit took another step forward and watched as Sasha made his way over the pebbles, his leg dragging a little more with each new step.

If Sasha was aware that Kit was following him, he gave no indication of it. Instead, he tottered down the slope, making an elegant figure in black despite his odd gait. Kit didn't think Sasha could hold his pace for long, and he was correct—just when the slope was at its sharpest, Sasha slipped, and Kit rushed forward to steady him. "Don't you dare try to walk down on your own," he hissed, angry at Sasha for being such a drama queen. "You can't, and you know it."

"I'm perfectly capable of looking after myself, thank you," Sasha said in a clipped tone, and tried to brush Kit away.

"Really? So you're just pretending to be a fucking cripple?" Kit snapped, having had enough of the backtalk. While it did not help him win points, it did shut Sasha up.

Though Sasha was taller, Kit was stronger, and he put an arm around Sasha's waist, pulling him closer to hold him steady. It was then he realized just how much of a strain Sasha was under. His body was trembling from exhaustion and probably also from emotional stress. Sasha leaned against Kit grudgingly, his body language screaming dislike, but Kit wasn't worried. Most people didn't like Kit; it was something he was used to, and he could deal with it. Plus, helping Sasha to the car was a way to make amends.

They made it down the path safely, and as they reached the gate, an elderly man in a black suit and peaked cap came running toward them. "Master Sasha?" he inquired, sounding worried.

It took Sasha a couple seconds to unclench his teeth and swallow before replying, "I'm fine, James. I strained my leg—that's all."

"Let me help you to the car then, sir," said James—Cory's chauffeur, Kit remembered, though they had never met. He took Sasha from Kit with a small smile and nodded. "Thank you, sir," he told Kit, looking inquiringly at him.

"It's Kit," he said. "Christopher," he added, because James had the sort of old-fashioned dignity that demanded something more than a street name.

"That was very kind of you."

Kit nodded and mumbled an "It was the least I could do" and shuffled back, feeling slightly self-conscious.

His words seemed to spur Sasha into action. He turned around sharply, and it was all James could do to prevent Sasha from falling backward. "The least you could do?" he said in a carefully controlled voice, his eyes blazing. Though one side of his face was expressionless, the other half conveyed his anger. "Don't you think you've done enough, you gold-digging tramp?" He rested his weight on James and pulled himself up, making the chauffeur stagger. Sasha took a deep breath, collecting himself visibly. "James," he said, his voice eerily calm. "Can you please pay Mr. Christopher for helping me down? Five dollars should do it. I seem to have left my wallet at home, and I don't think he does anything for free."

Seven minutes later, Kit got onto the bus heading toward Eddy's, five dollars richer. Just as well, he thought. At least he did have some cash on him now, and it wasn't likely he would see the little stuck-up asshole again. Things could have turned out worse.

TWO days later, Kit was practically on the counter, screaming at Eddy, "What do you mean my paycheck is going to be delayed? I need it to pay the rent, or I'll be sleeping on the pavement in a cardboard box."

Eddy shook his head and actually looked sad. "You know I've never done this before, Kit," he said. "I'm serious."

"But why can't you give me my pay?" Kit demanded in desperation. He was already behind in paying the previous month's gas bill, and his rent was due in another three days' time.

"You know we've had a slow month," Eddy said. "And I need to pay the suppliers, or we won't have anything to sell next month."

"But we did sell stuff," Kit protested.

"We sold stuff," Eddy agreed. "Mostly to Dr. St. James, and since he died his account was frozen, and we haven't received any payment for the things he took."

"What!" Kit groaned. "Why didn't you just call up the bank and tell them—?"

"I tried," Eddy said with a shrug. "But they told me that it was frozen at the request of the family lawyer and—"

"I'm going to kill him," Kit said, springing back to the floor. "That little—little worm—can't walk on his feet but has the nerve to...." He was sure Sasha had done it out of spite. It was obvious the skinny twerp knew exactly where Kit worked and how to get back at him. "Give me the receipts," he said. "He had his say at the funeral—"

"What funeral?" Eddy asked, confused.

"—but I'm not going to let him rob me of my pay," Kit continued. "Give it to me, Eddy—I'll sort this out."

Anger and bravado helped Kit bang on the door of the St. James residence, but when confronted by a pair of hostile eyes, he gulped and shuffled, trying to come across as inconspicuous. All Kit knew of her was what he'd learned from Cory over dinner. Lux St. James was three years younger than Cory, with his build but none of his coloring. She was dressed in black, but the veil and hat that had been prominently on display at the cemetery were missing. Her eyes were piercing gray, and when she bore down on Kit, he had to fight the urge to take a step back.

"Yes," she said, making Kit feel he were an annoying fly.

"I'm here to...." He waved the copies of the receipts and tried to form the proper words.

"Bills," she sniffed. "My brother is dead, you know," she added in a tone better suited for addressing morons, and Kit supposed his old, ill-fitting clothes gave the impression of a half-wit.

"I know," he said when another figure joined the first at the doorway. Cory's older sister, Candela, married to a famous photographer if the obituary had been correct. She looked a lot like her younger sister and about as welcoming.

"What is it?" Candela asked.

"Bills," Lux said with a vaguely insulting air. Cory had once told Kit his sisters were named after measurements of light, but in Kit's opinion neither of them was remotely illuminating.

"Let Mr. Walters handle this," Candela said, opening the door wider and motioning for Kit to enter. Kit walked into the house, avoiding the obvious spot where he had last seen Cory, and was rewarded by the sight of two men in deep conversation. One was an older man in an expensive three-piece suit holding on to a briefcase in a death grip, and the other turned out to be Candela's husband.

"Dear," said Candela, motioning to her husband. "This"—Kit was sure her vocabulary didn't include a proper word to describe him— "young man is here with some bills. If you could just let Mr. Walters handle this while we take a look at the inventory."

"Of course," the husband agreed, and the trio, including Lux, proceeded into the inner room, leaving Kit alone with the briefcase-toting gentleman.

"I'm here from Eddy's." Kit launched into his speech before his courage deserted him. "I'm here about some unpaid bills. Co—Dr. St. James usually paid by credit card, and the account was balanced at the end of the month, but the bank told us that his account was frozen and—"

"Ah, yes," Mr. Walters nodded, making no move to take the receipts from Kit. "Dr. St. James's accounts are suspended until the matter of his estates is decided by the courts."

"Courts," Kit repeated stupidly.

"I suppose there's nothing to hide, really," Mr. Walter said, giving the impression of being slightly bored and casting a look at the inner room from where conversation, punctuated by sharp exclamations, could be heard. "It'll be in the news soon enough." He took a deep breath, puffing up his chest. "The St. James family will be contesting the will left by Dr. Coriolis St. James. Until the matter is settled by the probate courts, we have requested that all his accounts are frozen."

"Oh," said Kit as his hand fell to the side, the receipts slapping his thigh with a dull thud. "Who exactly was getting the dough?"

"You mean the assets?" the lawyer said, confusing Kit.

"I do?" Kit asked stupidly before he realized his vocabulary had been corrected, and blushed furiously.

"If you have any unpaid bills," said the lawyer. "I suggest you settle them with Mr. Alexander Krylov and—" Kit frowned. He did not know anyone called Alexander. Seeing Kit's bewildered expression, Mr. Walters added, "I believe many knew him as Sasha."

"Oh," said Kit. "So—is he here?"

"Who?"

"Sasha," Kit said with emphasis. "Is he here?"

"Most certainly not." Mr. Walters sounded indignant. "He was asked to vacate the premises until the settlement of the case, and he left yesterday."

"You kicked him out?" Kit asked, wondering why he did not feel as happy as he should at the new development.

"Not at all." The lawyer seemed offended. "Mr. Krylov left willingly. The Misses St. James were very generous. They let him take all the necessary clothes and accessories with him when he left and had the chauffeur drive him to his destination."

"Makes you all regular saints, doesn't it," Kit snarled, feeling sorry for Sasha despite everything. "Where is he now?"

"I'm afraid I cannot tell you that." Mr. Walters looked smug. "He might not be my client but I do respect other people's privacy. Was there anything else you needed to know?" Mr. Walters asked coldly. "If not—"

The phone in the sitting room rang, interrupting their conversation. It was the one Kit had noticed during his previous visit, an old-fashioned one with the curled handset.

The lawyer picked it up slowly and said a careful "Hello." He seemed to listen to the speaker on the other side for a moment and grimaced. "I'm sorry," he said. "Sasha"—the name pronounced carefully as though it were some curse word—"no longer lives here." Pause. "There is no forwarding address or telephone number."

He listened for a little longer as the speaker on the other side started to sound more agitated. "Well, if his therapy is as important as you say it is, I'm sure he'll show up for it on time." More silence, then, "If he missed them, then he's probably not coming. I'm sorry I can't help you with this. Good day." A longer pause, and the conversation continued. "Yes." Mr. Walters grimaced. "If I do see him, I'll tell him that he should come. Yes, thank you." He hung up and turned toward Kit with an expression that clearly read "are you still here?"

"Paul," a soft, feminine voice called from an inner room, and the lawyer turned toward it. Why, thought Kit, couldn't those women have high, grating voices instead? "Can you come over here for a second?"

"If you'll excuse me," Mr. Walters bit out. "I think you can find your way out." He strode toward the voice, pointedly turning his back so that Kit was left openmouthed, the receipts still in his hand.

Kit started to back out slowly; he could see little use in staying. He did not think any of them would be willing to foot a bill for Sasha's clothes purchased by their dead brother anyway. He knew he shouldn't be surprised; the first thing most families did was throw out the mistress, the bastard child, and all the other dirty secrets, but Cory must have really cared for Sasha to have left everything to him. Not that he was going to get anything, by the looks of it, Kit thought bitterly.

He could see a similarity in their positions, in a way. He didn't think Sasha had the money to hire a lawyer and go against the St. James family, especially since Cory had paid for everything Sasha needed.

But the guy did need his therapy, if his leg was anything to go by, and what the hell was he thinking, not going to his therapy when he clearly needed it? Kit knew that lawyer wouldn't be passing on any messages to the former lover of Cory St. James. Still, Kit thought philosophically, it was not his problem.

Kit did not get involved. Period.

It was just a thought, that was all.

CHAPTER
THREE

KIT was sure he had seen the last of Sasha. It had been a rather colorful episode in his life, but it was over and he had learned his lesson. He would be more careful when picking up someone from now on—not that he had much of an interest in picking up anyone lately. If he were to admit the truth, the incident with Cory had shaken Kit a bit, and he did not feel confident enough to make a new conquest. Kit sometimes found it hard to concentrate while at work, and whenever a customer walked in, he would lift his head, expecting it to be Cory.

Luckily for Kit, there weren't many customers walking in. Unluckily, the store was going through a rough spot, and it was not just because Cory's credit cards were frozen. Most of the horses Eddy had bet on had lost. Though Eddy was not a heavy better, coupled with college fees for his two daughters, rent for the shop, paying the suppliers, and the shop's monthly profit dropping well beyond safe margins, the shop was struggling. They were losing out on both customers and suppliers, and on top of it all, Kit's paycheck was still late. Which would inevitably lead to some heartfelt pleading with his landlord for a bit of leverage.

"What if we have a sale?" Kit told Eddy while going through their belt collection with a frown. "We can hike up the prices a bit and put on a 10 percent discount. We can give out the belts for free to a few people—you know, the ugly yellow ones no one ever buys."

"You think it'll work?" Eddy asked, looking mildly interested, pushing aside the stack of unpaid bills he had been going through. "I thought you'd be the first to jump ship now that it's sinking."

"Been here for two years, Ed," Kit said casually. "Not the best job, but I think I'll start with a pail instead of a lifeboat." Truth be told, the clothes store protected Kit from his "other life," one which Eddy had no inkling about. Working at Eddy's meant Kit got to keep regular working hours, and his nights were free to prowl if he wanted to. Eddy didn't care if Kit had dropped out of high school or couldn't do long division in his head. More importantly, being happily married to a nurse at the local hospital, Eddy had never even looked at Kit in an "odd" way.

"Why don't you run over and get some lunch," Eddy suggested, his tone indicating he was touched by Kit's enthusiasm.

Kit rolled his eyes and refrained from pointing out that he was skipping lunch since it would make a dent in his meager savings. While lunch was out of the question, he was dying for a chance to get out of the shop, and he wasn't up to second-guessing Eddy's generosity. Pushing the door open before a customer could walk in, not that they'd had any that day, Kit dashed out onto the pavement. The afternoon heat slapped him squarely in the face, making him blink as his eyes watered. Shading his eyes, Kit looked around, and his heart stopped as his eyes rested on a familiar vehicle.

Almost against his will, Kit moved forward until he was standing next to the well-known car, recalling the last time he had been in it, crawling onto Cory's lap, trying to suck his tonsils out....

"Ah." Someone cleared his throat behind Kit, and he froze, feeling slightly disoriented. He turned around, half wondering if he would run into Sasha, and then sighed when he saw who was standing behind him. While part of him felt relieved, another part of him felt slightly disappointed. He had seen Sasha four days ago. It was not like he needed to see that snot-nosed bastard again.

"James," Kit said, finding his voice before it became far too awkward. "I... just saw a car I'd seen before."

"Mr. Christopher, wasn't it?" the old man said with a smile as he recognized Kit. "I was just dropping off Ms. Lux at the office."

"It's Kit," Kit corrected absentmindedly, then repeated, "office?" looking at the other side of the road. He knew Cory's office had been somewhere in the high-rise on the next block. It was the frontline for a string of pharmaceutical research labs located elsewhere. "So," he said unthinkingly. "They're taking it over too, huh?"

James looked at Kit sharply and then away into the distance, probably because speaking ill of his employers went against his policy. "You could say that," he said in the end.

"How's... Sasha?" Kit asked softly, looking in the direction of Cory's office. After the unfortunate day when Cory had decided to eat a gun, there had been a large number of people outside, staring at it with morbid curiosity. But that had died down and now everything seemed back to normal—if under a new management.

"I didn't think there was any love lost between you two," James observed, and Kit looked away, flushing, reprimanded.

"We aren't exactly best friends," Kit admitted with a grimace. He should leave, he knew. There was nothing much to say, really. "It's none of my business... just curious."

"Not really," James said with a shrug. "Dr. St. James' lawyer came over to the mansion. I told him he could find Master Sasha at his therapist, but he hasn't been there the entire week. There are some documents for Master Sasha, but there's no way of delivering them to him."

"What does Walters want with Sasha?" Kit asked, remembering the lawyer he had run into during his previous visit to the St. James residence.

"Not him," James said with a small, self-satisfied smile, and Kit knew the old man was enjoying himself, talking to someone who knew the situation. "Mr. St. James' lawyer... the one who drew up the will."

"Oh," said Kit, taking in the information. Having heard several people, including Eddy, speak of it, Kit understood the will Cory had left was important. However, having never inherited something and not likely to get anything from it, Kit could see very little point in pretending to be interested in it. "Well, I'll be going, then," he said weakly.

"It was nice meeting you, Mr. Kit," James asked politely. "I suppose you could also drop in on Master Sasha if you had some free time."

"I doubt it," Kit said sharply. "He and I don't exactly—"

"He had his therapy scheduled at a health clinic not far from here," James said, still smiling but obviously pushing it. "I used to drive him for his sessions before all this happened. Just two blocks away to the west side…." Kit did not wait to listen to which health clinic James was referring to; he knew exactly where it was. Good thing he was not headed that way, since his room was in the opposite direction and he could see no need to subject himself to any more torture. He sighed and looked back at the shop; he had not been out long, but he supposed the lunch break was over and he might as well go in.

"Or perhaps you can meet him up at his house," James continued. "He's not been to his therapy, from the sound of it."

"I think not," Kit said, shaking his head for emphasis. Didn't James remember how Sasha had treated Kit at the cemetery, what he had been hinting about. But Kit was thinking of the situation with the shops and the unpaid bills. If Sasha was willing to pay back at least half of what Cory owed them, Kit'd be able to pay his rent on time. Actually, Eddy had given up on those unpaid bills as a loss. If Kit could collect the money himself, he might not have to report it back to the shop. It wasn't exactly stealing.

"If you could get them to Master Sasha—I could pay you a delivery fee," James said, his eyes shining with determination. "I'd go if I could but unfortunately it's not wise for me to stray too far. I'm not sure what my new employees would think if they find out I was consorting with the enemy." The last was said with a wry grin to indicate James was only half serious.

Kit was still of two minds, but hearing the word "pay," he paused and looked at James. "How much of a delivery fee are we talking about?"

THE house Kit found himself in front of was a single-storied A-frame with a sloped roof, large windows, and plenty of attic space, at least from what Kit could see from the outside. It also looked as though no one had lived in it for several years. The prominently displayed windows were intact but hidden under layers of grime; the shingles on the roof seemed more inclined to slide down than stay on, and the front garden, as small as it was, was overgrown and neglected.

Taking a deep breath, Kit pushed the gate open. He scowled when it refused to budge more than a couple inches after emitting a high-pitched noise reminiscent of late-night horror shows. He sucked in his stomach and slid in through the gap, knowing Sasha was slender enough to fit through easily. He walked up to the front door, thankful it was not so far back from the front gate that he had to beat a path to it with a machete and a snakebite first aid box.

The garden was overrun with dying rose bushes, thick vines resembling twisted roots, and waist-high grass. The smell reminded Kit of used cat litter boxes, though there weren't any houses close by. However, there was a lack of beer bottles and used condoms commonly visible at teenage nesting grounds, which was how abandoned houses were frequently used.

Kit hesitated at the front door, wondering if James had indeed given him the correct address. He didn't actually need to give the documents to Sasha in person; slipping them under the door would have been sufficient had he been sure he was in the right place. Kit peered in through the windows to see if there was any indication of human habitation.

There was nothing much to see past the dirt-crusted windows; the interior of the house was dark and the doorstep smelled strongly of cat pee. There was not a single light visible, and the front door didn't look all too solid. Apart from the chirping of some insects in the grass, there was hardly a sound. Kit was missing his urban existence, even if it was just the screeching of tires. Wondering what sort of a person could stay in such a place, Kit lifted his hand, fist clenched, and gave the door a solid knock. The door shook in its frame and a few loose flakes of paint fluttered down, but nothing stirred inside.

Kit glanced over his shoulder at the sky, which was getting darker. He had to get this over with and hurry off to his room before the last bus. He had no idea how late buses ran along this route, and he wasn't about to find out. Trust Sasha to move to a house off the main road, probably because he was too delicate for exhaust fumes. Kit gave the door another perfunctory knock and decided he was wasting his time. He'd just leave the documents at the door and go back to his room instead of waiting until someone showed up.

Well, thought Kit with a philosophical shrug, he'd tried, and that was what mattered. James had given him ten bucks for the delivery and another five for the confirmation. Kit could live without the other five bucks, though it would have helped. Kit wasn't fooling himself into believing he had offered to do this out of the goodness of his heart. Whatever righteous indignation he had felt at the treatment of Sasha by the St. James family had been tempered by an entire day at the store helping a pudgy woman pick clothes for her grandson. Kit turned around, stuck his hands in his pockets to ward off the chill as the last of the daylight faded, and started to walk toward the gate. As he did, the front door opened slowly, grating on the floor, forcing Kit to turn around, heart in his mouth.

Sasha was dressed in a pair of loose jeans and a large, short-sleeved T-shirt that made it obvious he was one-handed. On his nose perched a pair of gold-rimmed reading glasses, which were at odds with the rest of his getup. It was apparent from Sasha's expression that the last person he wanted to see was Kit.

"Want more money?" Sasha asked coldly as he looked down at Kit from his position, two steps up. Kit was sure Sasha practiced his high-and-mighty attitude in front of a mirror. He flicked his eyes down briefly and was rewarded with the sight of Sasha's bare feet, long pale toes curling elegantly. There was something undeniably appealing about the way Sasha looked, Kit realized. It was relaxed but at the same time... sexy. This was what Cory had come home to, the narrow toes, cute gold reading glasses, clothes that threatened to slide off at whim. Kit had been outclassed from the beginning.

"As a matter a fact, I came to ask you about a number of unpaid bills at our boutique," Kit snapped back, his good-Samaritan mood vanishing instantly.

"How much?" Sasha demanded, sounding high-handed and snotty. For a moment Kit was overwhelmed by the urge to just hit the guy and get it over with. He held his emotions in check as he usually did with a particularly difficult customer by biting the inside of his cheek. When Kit hesitated to answer, Sasha stared at him through narrowed eyes and snorted. "I should ask you how you found this place," he added.

"I got the address from James," Kit said, seeing no reason to hide it. "I went to the—the St. James residence some time back with the bills, and they said you'd moved out."

Sasha's face remained impassive, and if there were any emotions below the surface at the mention of Sasha's eviction, they were well hidden. "Do you have the bills?" Sasha asked after a pause, while Kit stood waiting for a reaction.

"Yes," said Kit with a casual shrug, not wanting to admit he was fucking up the meeting. He unzipped his jacket and pulled out the envelopes James had given him, which he had carried that way for safekeeping. "I also have a few letters for you from James."

A corner of Sasha's mouth lifted, and he made a slight "tch" sound, the only indication he was irritated, then turned around and walked into the yawning darkness of the house, leaving Kit on the doorstep until he realized he was supposed to follow Sasha into the chasm. Scowling at nothing in particular, Kit stepped into the house and waited until his eyes adjusted to the gloom before walking down the corridor in front of him.

The passageway ended shortly, leading to a dimly lit room with chipped floor tiles, cobwebs in the corners, and an inch-thick layer of dust. Kit stopped at the doorway, taking in the room's dismal décor, and followed the footsteps in the dust into the next room, and promptly tripped over an empty takeout box.

The room seemed to be where Sasha had set up house. The dust appeared to have been stirred, and a naked bulb hung from the ceiling, bright enough to reveal even the corners of the room. On one side a large window overlooked the back garden, which was larger and even more overgrown than the front of the house. A single bed was pushed to one side of the room, next to a writing table overflowing with books. There were stacks of books on the floor, more along the wall, and some on the windowsill. An entire wall was taken up by a sagging bookshelf, filled with large books, which Kit was sure puny Sasha was not able to lift on his own. The floor and part of the bed were littered with boxes: large cardboard boxes used for packing as well as several takeout boxes, mostly from a local pizza place. Kit wondered how much food a guy could eat in a day. However, shifting closer, he noted most of the boxes were almost half full. Kit speculated that Sasha had nibbled at a corner and lost interest.

"Well," said Sasha, his voice sounding slightly annoyed. "If you've finished looking around, let's see the papers."

Kit wordlessly handed over the stack of letters, most of them legal material mailed to Sasha at his former address, feeling a flush flood over his face as he stood there like a fool, gaping at his surroundings. "Who owns this dump?" he asked as he took it in, comparing it to his shabby room that was a thousand times more welcoming.

"I do," Sasha informed him in an icy tone, seating himself on the chair by the table. "Are these all the bills—do you have the notices from the bank?" He pulled open a drawer and brought out a sheaf of papers, probably old bills and whatnot, to cross-reference the letters he had received. Kit had not been invited to sit down, but he sauntered toward the bed and plunked down on it noisily, giving the owner a chance to protest. There were no objections forthcoming as Sasha pushed up his reading glasses and continued to go over the papers. Kit shifted a little and the mattress dipped, causing something by the upper end to roll toward his lap. For a moment Kit stared at the object incomprehensibly before realizing it was Sasha's prosthetic arm, resembling some grisly detached limb (which it was).

Unwilling to gawk at it for long, Kit looked away, and his gaze landed on the pizza box resting near the corner of the bed. He pushed back the flap and was gratified to see several slices inside. Picking one up, he sniffed it and then proceeded to eat, ignoring his manners at the sight of free food.

Sasha turned in his chair at that, looked at Kit probably seeing him for the first time, and grimaced. "That's from yesterday afternoon," he informed Kit, then continued to watch, most likely expecting Kit to spit it out.

Kit shrugged and continued to eat. For him, the quality of food was not how cold it was or how long it had been sitting in the box.

Food was food as long as it did not give him indigestion. "Not all of us are so lucky to have—" Kit had been about to say "a sugar daddy," but even he could see the inappropriateness of his comment. "—be rich," he finished lamely.

Sasha stared at Kit for a moment, his expression closed off. "Here," he said, suddenly thrusting out a slim folded paper. "If you see James, tell him I'll be in touch with him shortly. As for your shop, I've written a check, but it won't do you any good until the end of the month. Other than that, I can suggest you go to whomever sent you and tell them I'm still alive. I'm sure—"

"What do you mean, whoever sent me?" Kit demanded as he pushed the last of the slice into his mouth.

"Exactly what it means," Sasha informed him. "You tell the sisters from hell that I'm not after their money and to leave me alone. I seriously thought they'd do better than the likes of you, though."

"James asked me to come," Kit protested angrily. "He's worried about you." Kit was slightly envious that Sasha still had people who cared about him enough to pay someone else to look in on him.

"Whatever," said Sasha, avoiding Kit's eyes. He let the letter flutter to the floor as if holding it was too much of a strain on his hand, and Kit had to scramble to catch it before it hit the ground. "You expect me to believe that?"

"I don't care what you want to believe," Kit snapped.

Sasha tsked from the corner of his mouth and stood up carefully, balancing his weight against the back of the chair. "How much are they paying you?" he asked.

"I have no idea why you think—"

"I think so because the first time I saw you, you were cheating with my lover," Sasha snapped, interrupting Kit.

"That has nothing to do with—"

"You mean you didn't know Cory was involved with me?" Sasha's voice dripped with sarcasm.

"What I knew was that Cory wasn't satisfied with you…," Kit said weakly in return.

They both paused, having come to a standoff, glaring at each other.

"I know about the likes of you," Sasha said carefully. "You people disgust me. You live off others without doing a day's worth of work and don't care about who you hurt. If you've finished eating that, you'd better leave. I'll have a check sent to your shop soon enough."

"Not like you were doing anything else," Kit said furiously. "You were leeching off Cory as well. You were living off him, letting him pay for you, and letting him take care of you—" He took a deep breath and finished the sentence. "—I needed him more than you do… did."

"You know nothing about Cory and me," Sasha snarled, letting his anger show for the first time. "I don't have to explain it to someone like you. Get out of my house."

Furious, Kit turned around, walked to the doorway, and then stopped, recalling another message that needed to be conveyed. "Um," he said hesitantly. "Sasha…."

"Yes." The voice was hardly welcoming.

"While I was at the house, there was a call for you about your therapy. They said you hadn't been there in a while and…." He turned around and stared at Sasha, hoping he would fill in the blanks, but when he was met with only silence, he shrugged. "If it's money…."

"It's paid for," Sasha said with a harsh laugh. "And not to worry, it's not Cory's money, it was from the insurance."

"Insurance?" Kit echoed blankly.

"From the accident," Sasha said with mock patience. "I think I've said enough," he added, his eyes turning hard. "Take the pizza if you want to and go."

"If you knew the therapy was paid for, why aren't you going?" Kit persisted. Sasha seemed floored by the question for a moment before he grimaced and looked away. His hand on the back of the chair shifted, and Kit could see that standing for a long time was not something Sasha could do comfortably. "You can barely stand," Kit added.

"I…." Sasha seemed to hesitate. "See little point in going."

"But you can't stay like this forever," Kit protested, shocked by the idea. Anything that was paid for was worth using. He could see that Sasha didn't truly understand the concept of not having anything. The waste of all this food was a good example.

"I see no reason as to why my life is of any interest to you," Sasha said coldly.

"Because… because…." Kit tried to find a reason. "Because you're here because I… I… messed it up."

"Because the world centers on you," Sasha said with a sneer as he let go of the chair and staggered forward, dragging his leg.

"No!" Kit snapped. "But maybe if Cory and I hadn't—" He hesitated. "If we hadn't…." How was he going to word it?

"You've done enough…. I can do without your interference."

"Well," said Kit at a loss of anything to do. "I'll be going then—uh—thanks for the check."

He walked out of the house, clutching the leftover pizza slices in a box, feeling a headache build inside his skull. Kit pointedly did not think of Sasha living in a filthy mess, looking like a walking corpse. It wasn't his responsibility to take care of Sasha, really.

CHAPTER
FOUR

"OOOH, Daddy, look!" squealed the bleached-blonde teenager, and Kit winced. He was surprised someone actually wanted to buy those hideous yellow belts. But Kit assessed the girl as he would a potential customer and could see why she might be attracted to such hideous merchandise. All her clothing choices were just wrong for her, and as someone who worked in a clothing shop, Kit wondered if she had dressed in the dark. The girl with bad taste in accessories wore a short halter top, low-slung high-cut shorts, ankle boots, and double-ringed earrings in the shape of miniature handcuffs. If she had not been accompanied by an older man who had done nothing but talk on his cell phone since entering the shop, Kit would have mistaken the girl for an underage hooker. He'd come across a few during his time on the road, and they'd dressed the same.

"Yes, yes," said the father distractedly, nodded to the girl, and continued with his conversation over the cell phone.

The sale sign had attracted curious passersby who wanted to have a look, but not buy. Most seemed interested in browsing, which translated to pulling everything off the racks and leaving clothing lying about haphazardly, burdening Kit with the job of putting it all back in its place. Kit was seriously starting to think the sale wasn't worth the trouble after all. They hadn't sold anything worth writing home about, and his feet were killing him. And it was supposed to be Kit's off day.

However, the girl turned out to be a buyer, and a wild one at that. She picked out a lot of things off the racks, seemingly at random, and placed them on the counter. She tossed back a strand of overly bleached hair and looked at her father, who was still in the middle of his conversation, then rolled her eyes. "Dad will pay for them," she said, and waited for a reaction. Seeing none, she turned her attention to the partially open doorway and scowled. "Tell him I'll be outside."

Kit looked at Eddy, who was hurriedly bagging the merchandise before anyone changed their mind. The father finally wound up his conversation and snapped shut his cell phone. He looked around in confusion until his eyes settled on Eddy. With a hesitant smile, the older man approached the checkout counter and took in the stack of bags waiting to be paid for.

"What did she buy?" he asked wearily; he'd probably had the same conversation before. He pulled out his credit card well before Eddy could answer him, and from the corner of his eye, Kit noted it was a platinum card with the name Daniel Nash embossed on it.

Mr. Nash did not blanch at the sight of the final price. Kit was sure he could very well afford it. However, Mr. Nash looked at the mountain of colorful paper bags with "Eddy's" embossed on them, and appeared to be slightly put out. "Can you spare your assistant for a bit?" the man asked Eddy apologetically. "My office is on the other side of the road, and if he can help me carry all this over...."

"Of course," Kit said readily, knowing he'd be tipped generously for that. He quickly gathered up the packages and then looked at Eddy for approval, though he knew Eddy was hardly in a position to protest. After all, the guy had bought more than their last five customers put together, and they needed it.

"She's probably at the gaming parlor down the block," Mr. Nash informed Kit in a weary voice. "She's just thirteen, even if she doesn't look it." When mentioning his daughter's age, Mr. Nash glanced at Kit sideways to assess his response to the information, probably prepared to warn away a potential suitor. Kit shrugged and looked ahead, biting back the comment that he didn't think any protective father should let his daughter dress like an easy fuck. Where he came from, girls dressed that way when they needed attention, sometimes the wrong type.

"She stays with her mother," Mr. Nash said in a subdued voice as they waited for a lull in the traffic to cross the street. "My ex-wife."

"Ah," said Kit uneasily. In his experience, mentions of ex-wives were followed closely by a dissection of their unsatisfying marital sex lives and a hand on the upper thigh. Luckily for him, the traffic broke up as the lights changed at the intersection further up the road, and the conversation came to a halt as they walked across the road.

The inside of the building was as hot as the outside, if not hotter, and Kit blinked at the stuffiness. "AC's been down the whole day," Mr. Nash said with a shrug. "Cassie was complaining about it earlier, so I had to drag her outside for a breather." The elevator was even more stifling, but it got them to the fifth floor, where Mr. Nash's office was. By then Kit had labeled Daniel a total loss. The man wasn't interested in Kit at all, making Kit feel both disappointed and relieved. He needed to make some money, and Mr. Nash was the right type, but Kit just didn't feel up to it, not yet.

After making sure the packages were safely stored, Kit pocketed his generous tip and headed toward the elevator, where a man in a blue coverall was putting up an out-of-order sign. "Sorry, pal," the workman said, not looking sorry at all. "Need to switch the power off to fix the AC."

"How long?" Kit asked more out of habit than anything else, since he knew such things took time. In his apartment, it took weeks to fix a broken light fixture.

"Might take all day," the workman informed him with a shrug, indicating it was none of his business, and Kit grimaced, rationalizing that it could have been worse. The elevators could have gone on the fritz while they were about to come up, or more annoyingly, while they were inside. It was just four floors. Kit lived on the eighth floor of his apartment building, and the only elevator in his building had stopped working somewhere around the time the Second World War had ended.

The stairs were right next to the row of elevators, and Kit jogged down easily to reach the next floor. As he was about to proceed down, he noted a slender, well-dressed man with his back to Kit, jabbing at the call button impatiently.

"It's out of order," Kit said offhandedly. "Might take all day, not much use waiting for it." He was about to continue on his way when the man turned. "You," Kit said, a little surprised. "What are you doing here?"

"I should probably ask the same," Sasha said dryly, his voice sounding as hypnotic as ever. "I seem to run into you every time I turn around."

"Not that often," Kit said, unwilling to just walk by. What was it about Sasha that just made him want to stand there and push a few buttons? "It must be every other day that we meet."

Sasha pointedly ignored Kit's witty comeback and turned, taking the walking stick from under the armpit where he had tucked it to press the elevator button. He started to walk carefully, balancing himself slightly awkwardly, toward the door on the far side that read "Fire Escape."

"You know, there is a perfectly good staircase right here," Kit couldn't help but mention. Sasha continued his leg-drag walk as if he was deaf. It was a little odd to see Sasha walk. He'd lost his arm and the use of his leg on the same side, forcing him to hold his walking stick on his good side, which made balancing difficult. Sasha appeared to have left his prosthetic at home, and the folded long sleeve only made it appear worse.

"I think someone's still not going to physiotherapy," Kit muttered under his breath, just loud enough to be heard, but again, it seemed Sasha was one of those people who'd rather pretend they had a hearing defect than give into the baser pleasure of snapping back a rude remark. Kit narrowed his eyes and cleared his throat loudly, but Sasha continued to ignore him. Perhaps Sasha really did have a deaf ear on top of it all, Kit though vindictively, stung at being so thoroughly ignored.

Still, Kit was curious as to why Sasha would use the fire escape when there was another, better staircase close by. He also wanted to know why Sasha was in that particular building when Cory's office was located farther down the block.

He followed Sasha casually, hands in his pockets, making no move to hide himself. Sasha reached the fire escape door, gave the handle a turn, pushed the door open easily, and looked over his shoulder at Kit, visibly annoyed.

"Are you following me?" he asked, sounding irritated.

"I suppose I am," Kit admitted with a lazy grin he knew would aggravate the other man. "What's the secret behind the door?"

"Will you go away if I tell you?" Sasha asked, his head bent, his back to Kit.

"I might." Kit didn't even know why he was annoying the crap out of Sasha, just that there was something about the stubborn pride behind those snappy answers that prompted him to provoke more of them.

"I don't do stairs well," Sasha said in a low voice, his back still turned to Kit as he pushed the door open wider to reveal a brightly lit, well-maintained flight of steps. "I feel more comfortable if there's no one watching me."

Kit nodded, waiting for Sasha to limp to the steps and decide what to do with the railing and the walking stick, since he had only one functioning arm.

"I could help you," Kit offered slowly.

"You could also push me down and break my neck," Sasha said without pausing his slow and painful descent.

"And what's in that for me?" Kit said with mock carelessness, though he was getting a little miffed by the number of sharp retorts from Sasha. He knew Sasha didn't like him, hated him perhaps, but Kit was willing to put up with that. Not that he wanted to get into Sasha's good graces; that was next to impossible, but Kit didn't prey on marks with the intent of hurting anyone. It took up far too much energy and distracted him from his goal of earning a little money to keep himself going. Kit had made a grave mistake when he'd gone after Cory.... He'd gotten somewhat attached, and Sasha had been an important part in Cory's life. Maybe he was, in his own way, making amends for what he'd done to Cory and Sasha.

"I'm not paying you for helping me down," Sasha said as he navigated onto the next step. Kit calculated that, at the rate Sasha was going, he would reach the ground floor somewhere in the next century.

"We are both heading the same way," said Kit as he walked up to Sasha. Kit was shorter, which made it simple for him to slip a hand around Sasha's waist and grab the stump of his left arm and place it over his own shoulder.

Sasha stiffened but didn't try to pull away or struggle, probably aware of the danger of falling down the staircase, should he be released all of a sudden. "Let go of me," he said in a carefully controlled voice, expecting Kit to obey his command.

Kit didn't bother replying, taking a page out of Sasha's book.

Sasha had lost even more weight, something Kit hadn't thought was possible. Though it was a hot day, Sasha's skin felt cool and dry. Instead of sweat, Sasha smelled faintly of the same cologne he had worn at the funeral, more suited for someone older, not that Kit knew exactly how old Sasha was. His slight frame and the vulnerability inherent in his situation made him appear younger, but looking at him closely for the first time, Kit realized he might be anywhere from a couple of years older than Kit to his early thirties.

"Let's get down before we all die of old age, shall we?" Kit said cheerfully. "Unless you want to stay there until they switch on the elevators."

"No," Sasha said in a strangled voice, most likely forcing his words through clenched teeth. "That's fine, let's just go." It gave Kit the impression Sasha didn't want to stay in the building a moment longer than necessary, though why he was there in first place was a mystery.

"So," he said as he practically lifted Sasha and placed him on the first landing. "What were you doing there?"

"I went to see Cory's lawyer," Sasha said in a clipped voice, probably wishing he were elsewhere and not having this conversation with Kit. "You should know; you did bring me the documents."

"Well," Kit asked as they started down the next flight, wondering how Sasha had imagined he could manage this on his own. "How did it go?"

"Why are you so interested?" Sasha asked suspiciously.

"For your information, I'm not being paid by Cory's sisters," Kit said before Sasha could end the question with an accusation.

Sasha stiffened and turned to face Kit angrily, and Kit wondered what had pissed off Sasha this time. "Don't you dare call him Cory," Sasha hissed angrily. "Just because he... he...."

"Was my friend," Kit supplied helpfully, wondering just what it was with Sasha and his hang-ups with such things. Now they were getting back to *that* topic, but it wasn't as though they had actually been having a conversation before.

"It doesn't give you the right to talk about him. He wasn't your... yours," Sasha bit out furiously.

Kit knew he didn't mean anything to the men he seduced—it was just a question of money—but sometimes it hurt to be reminded of it. For a moment, Kit contemplated leaving Sasha to deal with the steps on his own, but he was unwilling to admit defeat. Were he to let go of Sasha now, it would mean the little prick had actually gotten to him. Kit sighed and looked at Sasha, who was staring at him, eyes blazing. They were standing close enough that Kit was once again reminded of just how fascinating Sasha's eyes were, very, very green and framed by long lashes, and he was able to smell Sasha himself over the cologne. It was probably not the best thing to observe in such a situation, but he wasn't about to let the twerp wind him up.

"Maybe not," Kit said gamely, forcing Sasha to take another step. "But he did have a much better time with me." Even as he said it, Kit knew he couldn't have won over Cory. Cory wasn't the type to leave Sasha or kick him out of his house. Kit would have lost to Sasha, whether he'd fucked Cory or not, but he wasn't going to admit that.

"So much so, he killed himself," Sasha said, his lips drawn back to a snarl. The comment shook Kit more than he wanted to admit, and he looked away quickly, his hand tightening around Sasha's slender waist. Kit did feel guilty, but he wasn't going to give Sasha the pleasure of knowing he'd scored a hit. Kit carefully controlled his emotions and managed to look at Sasha, fighting the urge to spit into his eyes. Sasha no longer looked like the polished young man Kit had met a few minutes ago at the bank of lifts. He looked more alive when he was angry; his eyes seemed to blaze with life, and his cheeks had bright spots of color burning in them. When Kit didn't answer, Sasha's expression turned wary, and he slowly pulled back—as much as he was able to in Kit's grip. "There is no need to stare," he said stiffly. "You've seen it all before."

It was then that Kit realized he was facing Sasha's bad side, and Sasha had assumed Kit was staring at his scarred face. "Funny," Kit said. "I didn't even notice it." And it was true. While the scars were still there, they faded into the background when speaking to Sasha.

Sasha apparently took Kit's reply as sarcasm, since he reared back abruptly, not unlike a person struck physically. "Do I have to put up with your incessant chatter as well as the humiliation of letting you practically carry me down?" Sasha growled, looking away, and for a moment his face revealed something close to despair.

Kit wisely kept his silence, knowing anything he said would be misinterpreted. However, he could not help wondering about Sasha's physical state. "Are you going to therapy?" he asked. "Your leg seems worse than last time."

"It's none of your damn business," Sasha hissed, but this time there was less fire in his words.

"It'd be a shame to just let yourself go," Kit said conversationally, as they continued their descent. His hands were feeling tired now that he was supporting most of Sasha's weight, and the slender body no longer felt as weightless as it had in the beginning.

"I'm going," Sasha replied, glancing away. Kit could see a lie a mile away, and this was one of them, but he let it go. It wasn't like he was Sasha's mother or anything.

"So," he tried again, curiosity getting the better of him. "What did your lawyer say?"

Sasha remained silent as they made it down three more steps, pretending to concentrate on finding his footing, but finally he looked at Kit and sighed. "You can tell them if you want to, it's not like it's a secret. He told me the St. Jameses don't have a leg to stand on."

"Can you afford it?" Kit asked, ignoring the first part of the sentence.

"He's the company lawyer, paid for by the company, which is technically in my name now," Sasha said with a shrug, probably implying that paying a lawyer was something needless.

"And if he loses?" Kit asked.

"He says he won't," Sasha said. "Says there're no loopholes. He and C—Cory'd thought of this exact scenario when they were drawing up the will…." He hesitated and looked at Kit. "Not the part where he k-kills himself, but the fact his family will try to fight it."

"That's good, isn't it?" Kit asked as they reached the landing. He let go of Sasha and leaned against the wall, panting. Who'd have thought that hauling a guy down a couple flights of stairs was as exhausting as a regular workout? He sometimes helped out old Mrs. Peters, who lived on the third floor of their apartment and had arthritis, but this was worse. Mrs. Peters smelled of sweat and mothballs, not aftershave, and Kit did not feel her body pressing against his, shoulder to shoulder, hip to hip. It was almost intimate, and that unnerved him. He could feel Sasha's body heat, or rather the lack of it, through their double layer of clothes, and though Sasha seemed unaware, Kit was very conscious of it.

He could see why Cory had remained with Sasha even after a disfiguring accident. There was something about Sasha that made Kit, who actually hated his guts, want to hang around. His voice, his calm demeanor, though that was only skin deep, as Kit was starting to discover, and despite missing an arm and having one side of his face resemble a melted wax figurine, he was still worth looking at. It was the way he handled himself, Kit thought, watching Sasha catch his breath, leaning against the railing. He was balancing on his good leg, the other slightly bent so as not to put any weight on it, his walking stick propped up next to him while he brushed his hair back with a sweep of his long fingers. As he did that, Sasha let his head fall back, exposing his neck, seemingly enjoying an invisible breeze, and Kit suddenly found his chest contracting.

"Uh," Kit said as casually as possible, striving to inject some normality into their situation. "Why don't you wear your arm?"

"It needs adjusting," Sasha replied. Apparently that question didn't annoy Sasha.

"Oh," said Kit, encouraging him to speak as he approached him, and this time Sasha willingly leaned against Kit so they could continue.

"The doctors tell me my muscles and tendons are still shifting as they heal. It'll be some time before I'm comfortable using it," Sasha replied.

Kit searched for something else to say, but his inspiration seemed to have dried up. He also had a feeling Eddy wouldn't be too pleased with him for taking so long to drop off a couple bags at a building across the street. "Oh, look," he said with relief. "We're almost there."

Kit let go of Sasha as soon as they reached the ground floor, making Sasha stagger before he could regain his balance. Sasha steadied himself with his walking stick and looked at Kit with a weary gaze. "Thank you," he said carefully.

"No problem," Kit said as he started toward the shop. He felt slightly cheated by the experience. While Sasha had answered all of Kit's questions, he hadn't paid any attention to Kit. He hadn't asked Kit what he had been doing in the building or anything personal. Kit was sure if he had caught his lover cheating on him, he would have at least tried to find out something about the competition. Sasha didn't deem Kit worth questioning, seemingly having made up his mind about Kit beforehand.

Kit took a few more steps forward and looked back to where Sasha was standing by the curb, waiting, most likely, for a taxi. He couldn't imagine Sasha taking a bus, no matter how broke he was.

"You know," Kit said, since he really couldn't keep his mouth shut. "That's the shop where I work… where I met Cory." Why he said it was beyond him, and from the expression on Sasha's face it was obvious he didn't know where Kit was heading either.

Sasha regarded Kit, probably willing him to say something more, and when he didn't, nodded and said, "I'll be by to pay those bills, once this is cleared up." Then he calmly turned around, and almost like magic, a taxi came to a halt in front of him.

Sasha was one of those people for whom the world stopped, Kit thought grumpily as he stomped back into the shop. He couldn't figure out why, but those parting words left Kit feeling robbed. He had been hoping for something more climactic. The point of riling up Sasha was to see a reaction, and not getting one was disappointing.

His bad mood continued for the rest of the day, and by the time the shop had closed, Eddy shooed him out eagerly. The morning heat had transformed into a soft drizzle by late evening. The weather matched his mood perfectly, Kit thought as he reached the building where his room was.

The pile of soggy material on the pavement in front cheered him up momentarily. It usually meant some poor bastard who was late paying his rent had been evicted. Kit's smug feeling remained until he discovered the "poor bastard" who had been evicted was himself.

CHAPTER
FIVE

MRS. PETERS had been kind enough to save some of Kit's belongings, but most of his stuff had been nicked. His mattress was a total loss, having been gutted by some individual probably in search of valuables hidden within.

He didn't have enough money to make a down payment for another room, or to even get a cheap room for the night. He could understand the landlord's reasoning; he had put in a one-week security deposit at his former room when moving in, and since he was a week overdue on his rent, he had been kicked out. It didn't make him feel better, knowing the proprietor of the building could not afford to be lenient when there were plenty of residents who had wriggled out of paying their rent in the past. Gazing up at the window that belonged to his old room, Kit could see a light, which meant it was already rented out to someone else.

While Mrs. Peters had been sympathetic, she had not invited him to stay the night. There was hardly enough space in her cramped apartment with four of her grandchildren, let alone an extra guest. He fingered his pocket—three bucks, not enough to get him through the week unless he planned on sleeping in the bus stop and eating off the garbage.

Kit thought over his options. He didn't think Eddy would put him up for the night. Crashing his boss's place in the middle of the night because he had been kicked out didn't bode well for future employment. While Eddy was late paying him his salary, Kit knew

Eddy would pay eventually, and he didn't want to lose out on that altogether.

Then there was a homeless shelter down the road, run by a group of women wearing religious attire that resembled white bedsheets. However, Kit knew the shelter catered mostly to the street people, and he wasn't one of them. The drizzle was turning into an outpour, and Kit knew the place would be packed to the ceiling with street bums. He didn't relish the thought of staying in a place filled with unwashed bodies, keeping a close eye on his belongings in case someone ran off with them. While Kit was not that well off, he'd heard of people getting knifed over a pair of shoes at the shelter, and he didn't want to risk that.

That left him with the option of moving in with his friends. There was only one problem—Kit did not have any friends. At least, not the kind that would put him up for the night, and maybe a little after that. Kit knew it would take at least a week for Eddy to balance his account, and until that time, he would have to find a place to crash. In the meantime, he needed to eat, travel to work, and buy new bedding.

Kit threw the garbage bag, into which Mrs. Peters had stuffed his belongings, over his shoulder, and frowned. Well, he did know someone, and he was pretty desperate.

It took Kit over an hour to trudge up the road to Sasha's place. By then the last bus had run, and he'd walked what felt like a hundred miles but was probably much less. Kit was soaked from head to toes. His shoes made a squishy noise every time he put his foot down, and his jeans were so waterlogged they weighed a ton and a half. Kit pounded on the rickety front door for a good five minutes before it was wrenched open by a disgruntled-looking Sasha dressed in sweats and a long-sleeved loose sweater. Again, his gold-rimmed glasses were perched on his nose, and his feet were bare.

He stared at Kit for several seconds before speaking carefully. "Let me guess. You killed someone and stuffed the chopped-up remains in that bag."

Kit looked at Sasha for a moment, wondering what to make of that quip. If it had been anyone else he would have put it down as a joke, but with this guy, he never knew.

"It's my stuff," he said with fake cheerfulness. "It's your lucky day, I'm moving in with you."

There was a two-second pause, and the door shut so quickly Kit didn't even have time to blink.

"Hey," yelled Kit, pounding on the door with his free hand. "Open the door, asshole."

The door was inched open again, and Sasha stood behind the gap warily, one hand on the door, ready to push it closed in a second. "Go away," he said. "I've had enough of you."

"I'm not joking," Kit said desperately. "I got kicked out of my room. I don't have a place to stay."

"And you thought of me," Sasha said dryly before moving to shut the door.

"Come on," Kit said desperately. "I don't have anywhere else to go. You have a pretty huge place, and it's mostly empty, so it's not like you can't spare the space. I'm getting soaked, and it's cold out he—"

"Too bad." Sasha was a cold-hearted bastard who deserved everything life had dished out at him.

"Just for a night," Kit lied. He wasn't beyond groveling when needed. It wasn't anything he hadn't done before. He knew that pride didn't fill an empty stomach. "Please, just…."

"I believe there is a place down the road where if you stand long enough on the pavement, other people take you into a room," Sasha said, his eyes narrowing cruelly. "I hear they pay you by the hour."

"I'm not some cheap hooker, you little shit," Kit snarled angrily.

"Now, now," Sasha said, smirking, pleased with his ability to get a rise out of Kit. "Is that the way to speak to someone who might offer you shelter for the night?"

"Does that mean you are going to let me stay?" Kit perked up at that.

Sasha seemed to consider the question for several seconds as the rain died down, allowing the wind to pick up. "No." The jerk smirked, seemingly having the time of his life and then slammed the door shut.

Kit stood there, stunned for a moment, fuming at the indignity. He hadn't really expected Sasha to take him in, but to tease him like this and then let him down, all the same? How dare that little cripple do that to him?

"Hey," Kit shouted over the rising wind. "Hey…." He looked around for inspiration. It would have been easier if there had been neighbors. He had experience creating commotions that had embarrassed the occupants so much they might have been forced to wear paper bags over their heads to step out onto the front porch. Trust Sasha to live in a remote corner of the earth where there were no people around. "I'm going to sit here until you let me in."

The door opened immediately, making it obvious Sasha was on the other side, probably with his ear pressed to the door, listening to Kit spluttering. "I'm calling the police," Sasha stated, now serious and angry.

"Just you try," Kit said, smiling defiantly despite the sudden panic. "I'll tell them we live together and we had a fight and you kicked me out."

Sasha actually snorted at the suggestion and turned up his crooked nose. "Do you really think they'd believe something as preposterous as that?"

"Who knows," Kit said, smiling through gritted teeth that were starting to chatter. "You want to bet on that?" He really hoped Sasha wouldn't call the police. "It's not like I have anywhere else to go."

Sasha seemed to consider Kit's declaration, and Kit decided he was considering all the trouble he'd have to go through if he were to call the police. He proved Kit right by speaking softly. "You really don't have anywhere else to go, do you?" Finally, grunting, Sasha stepped back so the doorway was clear. "Just for the night," he said with a scowl.

Kit wasn't about to push his luck by making a smart remark. He silently brushed past Sasha's slender form into the welcoming, dry hallway. He dropped the garbage sack containing his entire life onto the floor and did a foot-stamping-body-hugging dance to get warm. He was turning into a block of ice and was likely to come down with something, though it was very rare that he got sick.

"You're soaking wet," Sasha observed, standing two feet away, as if it were a communicable disease.

"It is raining outside, in case you haven't noticed," Kit snapped back as he dropped his wet jacket onto the floor next to his clothes sack. Sasha seemed to take in Kit's appearance with a slightly speculative look, and then nodded to himself, seemingly coming to a decision.

"Hn," he grunted. "Bathroom's through there," he said with a nod of his head, "first door to the right." Then he turned around, a little too gracefully for a crippled guy, and walked down the hall, leaving Kit feeling stunned by the sudden change of tone.

But Kit was beyond questioning the change of heart. He toed off his sneakers and skidded across the dark hallway and through the room, which appeared to serve no purpose whatsoever, through Sasha's bedroom, and finally across the disused, dark living room with furniture in dustcovers. The first door to the right revealed a rather bare but surprisingly clean bathroom.

Kit stripped off his wet clothes, stepped under the shower, turned it on, and almost groaned in pleasure. Hot water, Sasha had hot water. He closed his eyes and threw his head back, enjoying the very rare pleasure of showering with anything other than tepid leftovers from the bottom of the water heater. After a few seconds, Kit opened his eyes, old habits forcing him to get the best out of the water before it ran out. He reached for the shampoo that rested on a small ledge running around the shower cubicle at shoulder height, and flicked open the cap. It smelled nice but felt empty.

Shrugging, Kit twisted open the top of the empty shampoo bottle and held it under the showerhead until enough water collected in it, shook it until the water sloshed around hard, and emptied the contents onto his hair. There, more than enough suds to wash his hair, and maybe even his upper body. Kit rinsed it off as quickly as possible and finished his shower in just under five minutes.

Pushing the sliding door open, Kit stepped out of the steaming cubicle and almost ran into Sasha, who was standing outside.

"What?" Kit said as he grabbed the doorframe to keep his balance. Instead of answering, Sasha deliberately dropped his gaze and flicked over Kit, appraising his body.

While Kit was accustomed to people looking at him, he was not used to the unashamed way Sasha scrutinized him. Kit tightened his grip on the doorframe to stop himself from reflexively clasping his hands in front of his crotch. He had no size issues, but really all this staring was starting to make him feel uncomfortable.

"Like what you see?" he asked with a cocky grin, masking his sudden shyness.

In reply, Sasha looked back up at Kit's face, his expression closed. "I brought you a new shampoo," he said, holding it out. "The one in there was all used up."

"I'm done," said Kit, reaching for a towel from the rack and tying it around his waist without giving the impression of being a prude. "Finished looking?"

"That was fast," said Sasha, ignoring the question.

"Where I come from, we bathe fast since there's always a long line outside," Kit said flippantly as he walked out of the bathroom, brushing past Sasha.

"You use public baths?" Sasha asked, sounding shocked as he followed Kit out of the bathroom.

"In my previous apartment," Kit explained, a little pleased that Sasha wanted to know something about him. "Each floor has a toilet on one end and a shower on the other. And when someone flushes, we all get cold water."

"Hmm," said Sasha as he carefully stepped into the living room after Kit.

Kit looked around the semidark living room, lit only by diffuse light from Sasha's bedroom. During his hurried track through the house in his wet clothes, Kit hadn't noticed how cold the living room was. Not freezing cold—more like the cold that seemed to seep into abandoned rooms. He could see doors leading off to the side and back, and a large french window overlooking a part of the overgrown garden. Sasha's house either had an odd structure or he used a side entrance instead of the main door. Kit would have loved to explore his surroundings a bit more, but was apprehensive of wandering around a strange house in nothing but a towel while being stared at in turn by the owner of the aforementioned towel. Kit walked back into the hallway where he had dropped his clothes bag, and rooted through it in search of something to wear.

Kit managed to unearth a ratty T-shirt and a pair of sweats; all his "good" clothes appeared to have been stolen, maybe by Mrs. Peters' grandchildren for all he knew. Opting not to wear his wet shoes, Kit wandered back into Sasha's room, at a loss for anything else to do.

He was prepared for another confrontation. It turned out to be rather anticlimactic. Sasha was seated at his table, reading a thick textbook intently. He ignored Kit completely, and not knowing what to do, Kit sat back on the bed. Kit pushed Sasha's prosthetic arm aside and nudged open a pizza box that sat on top of the pillow. The box revealed almost four and a half slices of uneaten pineapple pizza, warm and appetizing.

Kit looked at Sasha to gauge his reaction, but he continued to concentrate on his book, turning pages occasionally. Kit decided it was as much of an invitation to eat as he was going to get. He gobbled down three slices in quick succession before lying on his side, feet still resting on the floor, his eyes fixed on Sasha for a response to his actions.

It seemed Sasha was truly enraptured by whatever he was reading, since he didn't even glance up when turning a page, and Kit finally gave up on trying to provoke his current landlord.

"So," said Kit, and had to fight back a yawn as he spoke. "What're you reading?"

"Basic animal science," Sasha said shortly and continued to peruse the book.

"Oh," said Kit, yawning widely. He was more tired than he wanted to admit, and wasn't up to a long conversation. He continued to pay attention to Sasha, who seemed to be in a world of his own. Slowly, Kit's vision grew blurred and shadowy as the events of the day caught up with him.

Kit woke up with a start and realized he had fallen asleep staring at Sasha. His legs were stiff, meaning he had been asleep for some time, perhaps an hour or so. He looked at the study table to see if Sasha was still there, and was startled when his eyes fell instead on a big ginger cat staring at him with a pensive expression on its face. Kit sat up straighter, yawning, and realized the room was as cold as a meat storage locker because one of the windows was open. Sasha stood by the open window with the remains of the pizza in his hand, feeding it to a mean-looking gray cat. There were more cats on the windowsill, Kit noted—about six or seven, by the looks of it. He remembered the front garden had smelled of cat litter when he had first arrived, but hadn't attached much significance to it. *What do you know, Sasha has a thing for cats*, Kit thought with amusement, though the thought wasn't interesting enough to force him to stay awake.

The next time Kit woke up, the room was dark apart from a faint beam of light coming in through the doorway. The window was firmly closed, and Sasha was missing altogether. Looking at the open doorway leading into the living room, Kit assumed that Sasha must have gone to the bathroom. After lying on his side for a few minutes, Kit got to his feet and shuffled sleepily to the doorway. From there he could see the living room with the furniture resembling oddly shaped ghosts. Sasha sat on the windowsill, his forehead pressed to the grime-encrusted windowpane. From this angle, Kit could not see whether Sasha was asleep or just staring outside intently. However, Kit felt strangely reluctant to disturb him, and not knowing what to do, he wandered back into the bedroom and returned to his previous spot.

Oh well, Kit thought as he lay on the top of the bed, drawing up his legs this time and placing his head on the pillow and closing his eyes. If it was the only bed in the house and Sasha wanted to sleep in it, Kit was sure Sasha would inform him of it clearly. The bed didn't smell like it had been slept in; it smelled slightly of dust and pizza. Not that Kit minded it very much.

The next time Kit woke up, it was morning. For a moment he lay on the bed, trying to remember where he was. He was not the type to get up in strange beds, especially not with a severed arm pressed to his chest. Kit sat up with a strangled yelp, pushing back hastily before he remembered where he was and that he'd been hugging Sasha's prosthetic arm the entire time. Ew.

There was no sign of Sasha in the room, and a quick peek into the living room revealed that the windowsill was bare and the bathroom door was open. Kit shuffled into the living room, pulling up his sweats as he did, and looked around to make sure Sasha hadn't collapsed behind the sofa. The space between the sofa and wall turned out to be bare, but it revealed a false fireplace mounted on the wall. Above the fireplace was a wooden mantel on which a few dust-covered photographs were placed in a neat row. Curious, Kit picked one up and wiped away the layer of grime obscuring it.

It revealed a group of people in slightly old-fashioned clothes sitting stiffly on straight-backed chairs. Kit took in the elderly couple, probably in their early fifties, with a toddler balanced on the woman's knee and three young men standing around them. Their family resemblance was unmistakable; the young men all sported the same facial features as Sasha, though their cheekbones did not stand out as prominently and none of them looked emaciated.

The older couple was probably their parents, Kit decided, and the toddler must have been their grandchild, though it was impossible to tell which of the sons was the father. Or why the toddler's mother was conspicuously absent. The other photos were of the older boys in graduation cloaks.

Kit wondered if the toddler in the photograph had been Sasha. He was getting bored just studying all these old photos full of people he didn't know. He made his way back to the bedroom and looked into the adjoining room, just in case Sasha was there wielding a poker and waiting for him to step out.

Seeing no one, Kit walked up to the study table and picked up the book Sasha had been reading the night before. It turned out to be a medical textbook with illustrations of cross sections of animals. *What do you know*, thought Kit, setting it back in its place. *Little Sasha likes to torture small animals in his spare time and is taking lessons on it.*

As he was about to move away, Kit noticed a piece of paper, folded in two and placed on the edge of the study table, with "KIT" written on the top fold. Picking it up, Kit was surprised to see Sasha's handwriting was not as neat as he had imagined it to be. In fact, some of the letters looked downright childish, resembling the work of a five-year-old with shaky fingers.

"Going out," the note read. "Expect you gone when I come back. Shut the door when you leave, it'll lock behind you."

While the note was not worth pondering, Kit realized he should hurry if he was to make it to work, especially since he now had a longer way to travel to the boutique than before. Hurrying to the bathroom, Kit found a spare toothbrush in the cabinet under the sink next to a bottle of aftershave with an unfamiliar label. Sniffing closely, Kit recognized it as the one Sasha usually wore. On the label, someone had jotted down, "To my princess, happy birthday. Love, Mom." It was dated the previous year. Kit didn't think Sasha was borrowing someone else's aftershave, and it certainly wasn't Cory's, whose mother had died a long time ago. The message was confusing, to say the least. However, dwelling on such things wasn't productive, and Kit was already late.

Kit rushed to get dressed, picking out a pair of jeans and a crumpled shirt from his meager collection of clothes. His shoes were still dripping wet, but Sasha's feet were only a size larger than his and an extra pair of socks took care of it. There was nothing to eat in the bedroom, and Kit was in too much of a hurry to see if the house actually had a kitchen. Instead, he rushed out after making sure he had enough pocket change for the bus. As he shut the door behind him, Kit wondered why Sasha had left Kit in the house alone, especially since he didn't seem to trust Kit.

Perhaps there was nothing worth stealing in there, Kit thought with a shrug. Anyway, Sasha knew he was coming back; it wasn't like he had anywhere else to return to, and all his clothes were still inside the house. If nothing else, he had to return Sasha's shoes; it would be a shame if the guy missed them.

Kit made it to Eddy's five minutes late, breathing hard from running from the bus stop. He thrust open the door, rushed inside, and skidded to a stop when Eddy jerked his head up, startled, from the cash register. "I didn't think you were coming in today. You're usually here before I open up."

"Which is why you should pay me, you know?" Kit said as he sauntered toward the register. "Good help is hard to find these days."

The guilty expression on Eddy's face made him pause. "Don't tell me," Kit said with a scowl. "You weren't even thinking about paying me anytime soon."

"It's not what you think," Eddy said with a pleading look. "I wish I could, really." Eddy looked down at the till and then sighed. "But see, it's not going to be easy—I was thinking of closing the shop for a while and—"

"A while!" Kit exclaimed shocked. "You're going to screw me over. Man, I know we've had a rough time, but I haven't even looked around for another job 'cause I thought you'd come through."

"It's not the shop," Eddy said, appearing apologetic. "It's Clare.... She's in a bit of trouble and Janice wants to go see her."

Clare was Eddy's eldest daughter, who was in her second year at college, and Janice was Eddy's wife, a nurse at the local hospital. Briefly, Kit wondered what sort of trouble Clare had gotten into. Perhaps she was pregnant. Girls always seemed to get pregnant at the wrong moment, or maybe it was something serious, like a botched-up abortion, or....

"Clare's failed two of her papers and Janice thinks she's depressed...," Eddy went on, and Kit's sympathy went out the window. He saw little point in college and papers. Then Eddy finished rummaging through the bottom drawer and pulled out two fifties and a ten. "Here," he said. "Think of it as the pay for last week. I'll have the rest when I get back. I'm going to look into a few things while I'm over there to help out with the business."

"You could leave the shop open. I'll take care of it while you're gone," Kit offered hopefully. Hell, if Eddy gave him the keys, he could sleep in the back room; there was even a sink and an emergency toilet, which they shared with the building next door.

"Not a chance," Eddy said with a shake of his head. "Without the new stock, you'll be stuck with the old stuff, and we both know it's not worth opening the shop for. If I close the shop, I can at least write it off as a tax loss."

"Come on, man," Kit said in desperation. "I got kicked out of my place yesterday for not paying the rent and…."

"Oh," said Eddy, actually looking sorry. "Where're you staying now?"

"I crashed at a"—he could hardly call Sasha a friend, but how exactly did he describe their relationship?—"friend's place but can't stay there for long."

"Just until I come back," Eddy said, looking relieved that Kit had a place to stay and he wasn't burdened by the guilt of Kit sleeping on the pavement. "It's just for a week at most, and after that I'll give you a raise."

"Like I believe that," Kit grumbled, though he remembered the last two times Eddy had promised him a raise, he'd actually gotten it.

"Think of it as a holiday," Eddy added. "You get a week off and you get paid for it."

"It'd serve you right if I actually found another job while you're off on your second honeymoon," Kit scowled, but realized he was tempted. Hell, with the money he had and by staying at Sasha's, he might be able to make it through the week. Jobs didn't grow on trees, and he hadn't been on the job market for a while. It wasn't as though he had anything much to list on his résumé as work experience or education. He would take the break Eddy offered and look around for a job. If Eddy came through after a week, then Kit had a job. If not, he hopefully would still have a job.

If he could just convince Sasha to let him stay for a week.

CHAPTER
SIX

KIT scowled as he stepped out of the shop, looking over his shoulder at Eddy, who was doing some last-minute tidying up for the day. Or for the week. Or whatever. They had closed the boutique before the usual time since Eddy wanted to make an early start the following day and was reluctant to leave Kit alone in the shop. Not that Kit really wanted to stay there, since they'd had another slow day. Maybe they should think of opening something that would draw in customers, Kit thought, something like a bar or a strip club.

Kit glanced up at the clear sky and then at Eddy, who was hanging out the notice, which read "Closed for restocking" on the door. "So," Kit said a little hesitantly. "Do I call you up in a week or do I just drop in on you…?"

Eddy paused for a moment. "Do you have a phone where you're staying?" He knew Kit hadn't gotten around to buying a new cell phone after his last one had been smashed under the heel of an angry bartender.

"There might be," Kit said with a shrug. "I don't know the number."

"But you do have my home number," Eddy said. "Just give me a call and leave a message. I'll just call you back at that number."

Kit could very well imagine Sasha allowing Kit to use the phone and then taking messages from Eddy for Kit. Yeah, right, the guy acted like he was royalty half the time. He'd probably tell Eddy to stuff it, only in politer terms. Kit nodded in agreement, though, since there was little else he could do. If Kit could convince His Highness to let him stay, then using the phone would be simple enough.

Still, Kit thought as he started walking toward the bus stop, *there has to be a way....* He stopped, grimacing. Distracted, he'd been about to walk in the direction of his former lodgings when he should have been heading the other way. There was still enough time to kill before he felt hungry, and the sky looked clear. Satisfied, he started to stroll in the opposite direction, head down, hands in his pockets, thinking over his options.

He could get Sasha to let him into the house, at least to collect his stuff. He wondered if he could plead with Sasha to let him stay for another night. He couldn't exactly force himself on Sasha the way he'd done the day before. There was a limit to using strong-arm tactics, and he didn't think Sasha would be so generous the second time around.

He had enough money to rent a room in a cheap motel for a day or two, but that would be a risky venture since he might need money afterward. He could also sleep elsewhere, roughing it, so to speak, but those days were over and Kit wasn't willing to revert back to what he had been. That didn't leave him that many options though, and....

Kit looked up to take in his surroundings, and frowned. He'd strolled past a block or two, lost in thought, and was now standing in front of a rather small but popular gym. The sign read "Absolute Physique—A Full-Body Workout," and underneath it read in smaller script "Licensed physiotherapists." Even if the sign had been absent, Kit would have known this was the gym Sasha frequented, especially since James had mentioned it. There was no guarantee Sasha was still inside, but Kit decided to check, just in case. He didn't have a key to the house and didn't like the idea of waiting outside for His Royal Highness to return.

The entrance was set a little way back, with a staircase leading up to it on one side and a wheelchair ramp on the other. Men and women, dressed in business suits as well as sweats and other casual clothing, strolled in and out of the open doorway. Some carried gym bags while others were empty-handed.

Sure that he would not stand out too much, Kit bounded up the steps, taking them two at a time, and past the open doorway into what appeared to be a reception area. The girl at the reception wore a T-shirt with the gym logo in the center, a name badge on her chest, khaki shorts that went down to her mid-thigh, and purple sneakers. She had the well-scrubbed, healthy air sports fanatics seemed to encourage.

There were doors marked "weights," "indoor tennis," "pool," and "changing room," but nothing about physiotherapy. Wondering if he had come to the wrong place, Kit walked up to the girl, making sure to smile but not too much.

"Can I help you?" the girl, whose name badge on closer inspection read "Jean," asked as he reached her, and Kit guessed she knew enough to recognize someone out of place.

"I'm looking for a friend of mine," Kit said. "Sasha—" He racked his brain trying to recall the name Mr. Walters had given Sasha, but could not remember anything past Alexander. "Comes here for therapy—walks with a limp…." Kit wondered if he should stress the facial damage as well, or if it would come across as morbid and very un-friend-like of him.

"Ah," said the girl with a nod, looking curious. Kit bet Sasha didn't have that many friends dropping by during therapy.

"Is he still here?" Kit asked to get over the awkward pause, in case the girl decided to inquire about the nature of his relationship with Sasha.

"Hold on," she said, and walked up to a wall phone, picked it up, dialed four numbers, and spoke to someone on the other end. Kit watched with narrowed eyes, wondering if he should just give up on the idea and leave while he could, though he did not think he was doing anything wrong by being at the gym. As he was weighing the benefits of walking out again before he drew undue attention, Jean finished her call and walked up to him. "Through here," she said, opening a door marked "Private," positioned discreetly next to the receptionist, with overgrown palm fronds all but hiding it from sight.

"Er," said Kit hesitating a bit. What exactly had he gotten himself into?

"Just tell Ann I sent you," Jean said and gave him a wave to usher him through.

With a mental shrug, Kit walked through the doorway into a well-lit gym area much larger than he had expected, fully packed with all sorts of odd equipment. Most of them had hand railings on either side, and Kit was intelligent enough to figure out this area was probably used by patients with physical disabilities. Standing at the base of the staircase with non-slip grip-encased railings on either side was a tall woman dressed in a similar fashion as the girl at the reception. At the sight of Kit, she strode toward him, holding out her hand.

"Jean said you were a friend of Sasha's," she said, getting to the point directly. "I'm Ann."

"Kit," he mumbled, a little stunned, wondering if he should tell her he and Sasha were not exactly friends. He held out his hand and bit back a wince as his fingers were crushed in a bone-crunching grip.

"We don't usually let visitors into this area," Ann continued. "Most patients value their privacy, but luckily for you, Sasha is my only charge right now."

Ann referring to Sasha as her "charge" made Kit think of a five-year-old. Which brought up the question of just how old Sasha was, but Kit dismissed the thought as irrelevant. He had more pressing matters to worry about, such as why he had been summoned into the inner sanctum by a woman resembling a B-movie Amazon.

"It's just that...." Ann paused for a moment. "Well, I know Sasha doesn't have any family close by, and with the death of his... uh, uncle, he's been—"

"Uncle," Kit snorted. "Cory was hardly Sasha's uncle, unless...." He drifted off, seeing Ann's face. "Oh, sorry, right, you mean his... uh... uncle...."

"Right," said Ann in a tightly controlled voice, making Kit aware he had fallen from grace in her eyes. "Anyway, I've run out of options, and I'm grasping at straws." Her tone indicated just how much of a "straw" she thought Kit was. "You're the first person other than Dr. St. James to show up here to inquire about Sasha, and, well...." Ann seemed to have some form of internal struggle, and finally came to a resolution. "Well, why don't you see for yourself," she said, indicating a side of the gym.

Kit moved toward the indicated place and found himself looking into another part of the gym, which seemed to be made up of shallow swimming pools. They all seemed to be thigh-deep, with metal railings set in the middle to assist those who might want to wade up and down, "might" being the key word. Sasha stood in the middle of the pool farthest from them, wearing a pair of shorts and a T-shirt, holding on to the railing for balance, looking....

"What's he doing, posing for a photo shoot?" Kit asked before he could curb his tongue.

Surprisingly, Ann didn't seem to find his outburst irrational. "Exactly," she said. "I just can't get through to him. He just shows up here and does one lap and then goes away. I have no idea why."

"Is he always like this?" Kit asked carefully.

"He was never one of those motivated patients who make it out of the wheelchair when the doctors say they'll never walk again, but...," Ann said with a shrug. "I've seen people recover from worse injuries, and his leg isn't as badly... but since Dr. St. James...."

"Stupid crippy," Kit mumbled under his breath. So typical of Sasha to behave in a way that would cause problems for everyone, including his therapist.

There was a long silence, and he turned his head around to see Ann glaring at him, face red, lips drawn back in a snarl.

"What did you just call him?" she forced out through gritted teeth.

"N-nothing," he stammered, startled. "I just—"

"Did you just call him crippy?" she practically roared, and Kit stepped back, startled.

"I—"

"You called him something extremely offensive," Ann snapped, visibly struggling to control her temper. "That just isn't done, not here, not anywhere."

"It's not like I called him that to his face," Kit mumbled defensively.

"That doesn't make it right," Ann told him. "Just because a person is disabled doesn't give you the right to call him some derogatory term, whether you're his friend or not."

"We aren't exactly—" Kit broke off, embarrassed, not wanting to bring up his relationship between Sasha and him. Instead, he took a deep breath and tried to explain to Ann that he hadn't meant to be deliberately offensive. "When I was at the orphanage, there was this kid without an eye, and we called him One-eyed Wonder, and anyone who was crip—disabled was Crippy One, and so on. It wasn't like we were being offensive, it was just the way we called each other." He grimaced at the memory. "Being politically correct was the least of our problems there." It wasn't much of an apology, but he wanted to let Ann know it was just an insult for him, like "asshole" or "idiot," not something— well, in Sasha's case he had been angry and it had gotten personal—but not something he'd given a lot of thought to. Perhaps he had been rather insensitive with his use of insults.

"Just remember that word isn't to be used in polite company," Ann told him, less severely than before.

"What do you want me to do?" Kit asked Ann, feeling guilty at his part in the entire mess and eager to change the subject.

"Talk to him," Ann said casually. "It's not as if I didn't try that either, but since you're his friend—I was thinking of calling his parents"—which was news to Kit, since he hadn't known Sasha's parents were alive—"but since you're here…." Kit groaned. It must be his lucky day; he got to give Sasha a pep talk.

"Well," said Kit before Ann could add something else. "No time like the present."

He slid open the partition door and walked into the pool area. Belatedly, he wondered if Ann had wanted him to have a talk with Sasha just then or later on, but by then it was too late. Sasha had heard the door slide open and had looked up from his posing.

Kit walked up to Sasha around the pool edge, taking his time, formulating a plausible excuse for his presence. He needn't have bothered trying to start a conversation since Sasha beat him to the punch by scowling at Kit and demanding, "What are you doing here, now?"

Kit came up with and discarded several excuses as to why he was visiting Sasha during therapy. He didn't think "I was worried about you" was too believable. "You have the house keys," Kit said simply. He didn't think Sasha was stupid enough to fall for anything else.

"I expected you to be gone by now," Sasha said dismissively, glancing away. "I left money in the top drawer. You could have taken it and disappeared."

"I didn't look," Kit said through gritted teeth as he took in the implied insult. Sasha'd expected Kit to snoop in his study table, take the money, and run. It was an admirable assessment; had Sasha given Kit the money willingly, Kit might have returned for more, but had Kit left with the impression he had stolen the money from Sasha, he wouldn't have been able to return. "Why are you telling me that now?"

"If you weren't stupid enough to take it then, you won't take it now," Sasha said derisively and turned away. Perhaps because Kit was there and he no longer had an excuse to stand around, he took a few steps forward, balancing himself on the railing with his good arm.

Kit stood for a few seconds to see if Sasha would add anything new, but he seemed content to let it hang. Finally, Kit could not curb his tongue anymore. "I will be staying for a while with you," Kit finally declared. "For a week—until my boss comes back."

"You have a boss?" Sasha seemed amused with the comment and stopped his walking to turn toward Kit. "You mean your sugar daddy?"

"You have the nerve to talk about it?" Kit said derisively. "People here seem to think Cory was your uncle. How pathetic is that!"

"I know," Sasha said, startling Kit. "These people here are all muscles and not much brain." He tsked and scowled.

"Ann said she didn't know what to do with you," Kit offered. "She's worried about your lack of progress."

"She doesn't have any right to complain about anything," Sasha said with a snort. "She should mind her own business instead of throwing scum like you at me. What did she think you would do—motivate me to strangle you?"

Kit rolled his eyes. "You know, I don't think they actually intend to hurt you."

"Why should you care?" Sasha tossed over his shoulder as he took two more steps forward.

"I don't," Kit stated. "But you're not exactly helping yourself by acting like a brat."

"Again," Sasha said in a mocking tone. "Who are you, my mother?"

"Definitely not," Kit shot back. "But what's with you? You've got people worried about you but you don't seem to care."

"And why should I care about anything," Sasha said flatly. "I'm done speaking to you, just go away."

Kit stood by the side of the pool for a few seconds to see if there were any more comments to be thrown his way, but there seemed to be none. He knew he should just let it go and leave, but a stubborn part of him was unwilling to. Plus, Sasha still had the house key, and Kit had no other place to go. He looked at Sasha, who'd stopped walking and had resumed standing in the water, resembling some mannequin. Again the unfamiliar feeling settled in his chest like a small flutter. The way Sasha stood in the water, the way his head tilted to a side, the way he held his body so still....

"Hey," Kit called out. "Um, uh... Sasha...." He waited a bit, but there was no acknowledgement. He looked toward where Ann was supposed to be, but she was nowhere to be seen. He supposed he should leave, but something close to anger was starting to build up in his chest, especially since he was being ignored. "Hey," Kit called out louder, but there was no response. He stood there for a few seconds, but Sasha seemed to have turned into a wax figure.

Then, with an internal shrug, Kit stooped down and undid the shoelaces and removed Sasha's shoes, which he'd been wearing the entire day. Next the double layer of socks, which he stuffed into his shoes, and he rolled up his jeans. Next, steeling himself, Kit stepped into the pool and was surprised by both the water temperature and the feel of the bottom of the pool. The water was warm enough to feel comfortable, and the bottom of the pool was not slippery tile as he had first imagined, but made of some rough material that gave a better footing. Sasha got to do all the easy shit; having to walk up and down a hot-water pool was his day's chore, and he still complained about it.

As Kit waded toward Sasha, he discovered the pool to be deeper than he'd first expected. He was soaked up to midthigh despite having rolled up his jeans. He couldn't very well stride against the water despite the sure footing, but he did manage a firm walk.

Kit walked right up to Sasha, ducked under the railing, and stood in front of him. "What's your problem?" he demanded without waiting for Sasha to make the opening move.

Sasha gave him a dispassionate glance and then looked away, pretending it was normal to have people standing in his face in the middle of the pool. "I don't know what you mean," he said calmly. By now Kit was learning a bit about Sasha and could recognize the shut-off look Sasha was fond of in uncomfortable situations.

"I mean," Kit said forcefully. "I mean…." He faltered as his words dried up. As always, something in Sasha stirred up his impulses, but Kit didn't know what. He stood there as he tried to form the words to describe why he was feeling so angry at Sasha. "Why don't you do your therapy?" he asked finally. "Don't you want to walk?"

Sasha closed his eyes briefly and then looked away at the far wall. "Sometimes, I think, I'm not supposed to," he said finally, in a low voice.

"Not supposed to do what?" Kit demanded. "Walk?"

"Yes, that too, among other things." The tone was flat and emotionless.

"What's with you?" Kit asked, pulling back a little, stunned by the answer. Sasha's apathetic state was getting to Kit. How dare Sasha just stand there and say he didn't care about anything? Sasha had more in life than Kit had ever had, damaged body notwithstanding, and he just didn't seem to care. Sasha had a dead lover who'd left him a fortune, a house to himself, people to worry over him, from his late lover's driver to his therapist, and the sort of charisma that didn't go away with age or injury.

"You wouldn't understand," Sasha said, finally focusing on Kit. "Get out of my way."

"You want to die 'cause Cory did? Is that it?" Kit queried, something inside him snapping. "No wonder Cory killed himself. He probably couldn't put up with you any longer."

Kit wasn't even looking at Sasha when he said it, so he didn't see the punch until he fell back into the water. Kit emerged from his unexpected submersion, holding his cheek and coughing. Sasha packed a mean right hook when he wanted to. Kit opened his mouth to shout back, but even as he did, Sasha hit him again. This time the punch was aimed to his chest, and Kit blocked it, jumping back awkwardly. The second punch wasn't as powerful as the first, and anyway, it was easy enough to dodge a one-handed guy.

"You know nothing about Cory," Sasha growled as he stepped forward. "How dare you say something like that? How dare you come into our house and mess with his head and kill him, then stand there saying such things?" Sasha, angry, was a force to reckon with, and Kit prudently took a step back. "You little tramp, coming to my house, looking like a drowned rat, eating my food, trying to be—making me feel guilty about you—" Sasha took a deep breath, probably to brace himself for the final words. "—trying to be friends with me, you little shit!" Wow, thought Kit, Sasha knew four-letter words.

Kit knew he should retaliate. He wouldn't normally let someone punch him and call him a little shit and get away with it, but as Sasha vented his feelings, Kit realized he couldn't muster up the anger needed to strike back. Perhaps it was because he'd been instrumental in Cory's death. And he *had* barged into Sasha's life, into his house, and into his private moments. He deserved the punch. That didn't mean he was going to keep his mouth shut.

"Fine," he said, throwing up his hands. "Cory died, deal with it. If you think I killed Cory, just let it be so, but let me tell you, I didn't put a gun to his head." Kit didn't want to hit the guy. Sasha couldn't handle a good punch from him, not in the state he was in.

However, Kit didn't have to hold back for long. As intense as Sasha's emotions were, they seemed to burn out fast, leaving Sasha heaving for breath. He might as well have run a mile. Then, realizing he was losing momentum, Sasha made one final leap, taking both of them down in the pool, him on top of Kit. The water felt warmer than Sasha, whose breath smelled of cinnamon.

Kit sat up in the water with Sasha panting on top of him, and tried to speak. "Look," he said firmly. "Cory killed himself, remember? I just wanted to steal him away from you." Which probably was not the sanest thing to say at the moment, but he was tired of living with the guilt. He was no more guilty of having killed Cory than he was of Sasha's scars, he told himself firmly. "There's always a choice, and you know it."

There was a long pause, and finally Sasha moved, hooking his good arm around the railing and pulling himself up. He didn't speak, but his eyes remained fixed on Kit, who was still seated in shoulder-high water. They were both wet. Sasha's white T-shirt clung to him like a second skin, and Kit could see the outlines of his ribs through it. But there was also something else about Sasha that made Kit's breath catch in his chest and his fists clench as he fought the urge to trace those ribs. He decided it best to remain seated in the water until Sasha composed himself, in case Kit felt like doing something stupid.

It took Sasha only a couple of seconds to regain his usual poise. Sasha's gaze was starting to unnerve Kit, who was about to spout some inane line about life just to fill the silence when Sasha finally spoke.

"I killed Cory," he said softly.

Kit sat there with his mouth open in surprise, a chill running through him though he was sitting in warm water. "You shot him?" he asked in a half whisper, afraid to say it aloud.

"Of course not," Sasha said, and the spell was broken.

"Then what?" Kit demanded, finally getting to his feet and brushing at his sodden clothes. Two sets of clothes soaked through in two days; it was practically a record.

"I left him," Sasha said finally. "That day, after I caught him with you… I packed my bag and left. He was drinking, he always drinks when he has a problem. I took a taxi and went to my house and the next day in the morning James called me and… said…."

"So," said Kit forcefully. "You didn't kill him." Kit knew that if he were to argue further, he could say Sasha had left because Kit had been with Cory, and that in turn meant Kit had killed him, but he did not want to bring it up. Anyway, it seemed Sasha wasn't done speaking.

"I sometimes wonder," he said softly, "if Cory would have done *that* if I'd been there." He broke off and looked away at the far wall, probably thinking of all the what-ifs. Then he turned his attention to Kit again, and his expression returned to normal—well, normal as far as Kit was concerned.

"I don't get it." Kit knew the intelligent thing would be to keep his mouth shut, but he had long since forfeited his common sense in exchange for speaking his mind. "I know you had your problems"—if there was another way to refer to Sasha's injuries tactfully, Kit couldn't think of it—"well, before Cory—uh—killed himself, so I don't see why you have to pay for it now. Still do." Kit understood guilt, but to him, it was something that happened to other people and not him. It was very frustrating to see people wallow in guilt when they could just fucking pick themselves up and get over it. Like he did. "He's dead," Kit said finally. "You're not, and I think you have to live for yourself and not anyone else. I don't think Cory wanted to be remembered as your burden."

There was a long pause, and finally Sasha snorted. "Let's get out of the water," he said flatly. "I'm getting wrinkled."

CHAPTER
SEVEN

KIT was given a gym T-shirt and a pair of sweats by a sports instructor called Jim, who was built like a professional boxer. Grateful that he had at least taken off his shoes before his impromptu plunge in the pool, Kit emerged from the changing room, drying his hair with a gym towel. Sasha was nowhere to be seen. Kit knew he'd been in the next stall, changing. It was likely that Sasha took longer to dress, with his handicap and all. Kit put aside the towel and almost swore when Ann seemingly materialized in front of him.

"So," he said, seeing no point in stalling. "You must have figured out that we aren't the best of friends."

"Perhaps you *are* the sort of friend he needs," Ann said without hesitation. "Most people would cut him a little slack because of his condition, but you don't. I think Sasha is just too used to other people going easy on him."

"I'm sorry I couldn't help," Kit said, at a loss for anything else to say. He didn't think Sasha was the type people took pity on; he seemed more the type people customarily deferred to without even knowing they did.

"You've helped enough," Ann said with a shake of her head, and Kit was not sure if she was being sarcastic or not. "I was eavesdropping on you two, and now I know his problem. Maybe—"

"You aren't going to tell anyone, are you?" Kit demanded. He had known Ann was present in the background, but for her to admit to listening in on their argument... she must have been feeling really exasperated with Sasha's self-inflicted lack of progress.

"Of course not." Ann looked offended. "Whatever I learn about my clients is confidential." Ann squared her shoulders and looked at him straight in the eye. "You need not worry about such things."

"Fine," said Kit, mistrustful, though he assumed her overly formal way of phrasing the last sentence was meant to convey her sincerity. "Does this confidentiality extend to me as well?"

"Of course," Ann said readily, and Kit accepted it at face value. There was nothing else to do.

"Just one thing...." Ann seemed to hesitate, and Kit frowned, wondering why Ann, who had been so sure about everything before, was now wavering. "It's about Dr. St. James...." She looked at him and sighed. "When I referred to him as Sasha's uncle...."

"Yes," Kit asked pointedly. She could not be in so much denial that she was ready to misinterpret what she had heard about them.

"I know it's not true, and everyone talks about it, but when they first came for therapy, the way they behaved...." Ann paused as she tried to find the right words. "I really thought they were father and son, the way they acted toward each other."

Kit opened his mouth to ask for an explanation, but at that moment the changing room door opened, and Sasha emerged, dry, properly dressed, balancing on his walking stick, and looking like a model who'd just stepped out of a fashion magazine. *He probably manicured his nails as well,* Kit thought spitefully as he took in Sasha's appearance.

They both ignored each other as much as possible, Sasha barely acknowledging Kit, who in turn looked away as they walked out together. Sasha stopped a taxi without a word and continued to ignore Kit when he got into the backseat next to him.

The taxi ride was rather dull. So dull, in fact, that it felt almost like an event in comparison when Sasha sneezed. Twice. Sasha's sneezes were also polite, Kit observed. They were neither loud nor startling; they sounded almost like those sharp hiss noises cats make when upset. Not surprisingly, Sasha also carried a white handkerchief he carefully wiped his nose with—it would probably be a sacrilege for the guy to actually blow his nose on a disposable tissue like anyone else—and then carefully re-pocketed it. Kit was mildly amused that Sasha was developing a cold after having been partially submerged in a pool of hot water, while Kit was in perfect health, though he was the one who had gotten soaked in the rain the day before.

Once they reached their destination, Sasha paid for the taxi and didn't make any snide comments when Kit followed him into the house. Half an hour later, Kit sat on the bed, Sasha had retreated to the bathroom, probably to blow dry and restyle his hair, when there was knock on the door.

Kit stared at the bathroom, willing Sasha to emerge, but he seemed to be taking his time, forcing Kit to finally answer the door. It was a pizza delivery by a Pizza Hut boy who informed Kit there was an order for pizza to that address, paid for a week in advance. Kit didn't offer to tip the boy. He wasn't sure if he was supposed to, and anyway, he didn't have the money to spare.

Kit carried the steaming box back to the bedroom and deposited it on the bed in the exact position it had been the day before. Sasha emerged ten minutes later, having showered again and changed his clothes, smelling faintly of fabric softener and shampoo.

"Pizza," Kit said, breaking the silence. Sasha merely grunted and sat at the study table. Kit noted he didn't seem to have much difficulty walking around in the house; perhaps his leg acted up when he was outside. Sasha nibbled at a slice of pizza while Kit practically inhaled his share, then lay back on the bed as Sasha resumed his usual practice of reading a book at the table.

The silence between them, though not uneasy, didn't invite conversation, and Kit couldn't think of anything to say. He found the stillness between them disconcerting. He would have preferred to talk, but they had come to a somewhat tentative understanding at the gym, and he didn't want to ruin it with a few misplaced words. When the felines started to line up on the windowsill, Kit fell asleep, wondering if he should say something about Sasha's cat obsession or whether that was a taboo topic as well.

When he woke up, as with the night before, Sasha was missing, and Kit was sure his housemate had gone to his perch on the windowsill in the sitting room. He was about to let it go as another eccentricity he could not handle, but then he heard the high, sharp sounds of someone sneezing from that direction. With a roll of his eyes, Kit sat up in the bed. It really was none of his business or his concern if His Lordship were to catch a cold, but he still stripped the cover off the bed and carried it off to the sitting room.

Kit found Sasha, as predicted, exactly as the day before, with his head pressed against the glass. This time, though, he was sure Sasha was awake, since he looked up when Kit shuffled into the room. Kit hadn't bothered to change from the clothes he had gotten from the gym; he didn't have that many clothes to change into, and the ones he was wearing were comfortable enough to sleep in. In contrast, Sasha had changed into a pair of sleep pants and a large sweatshirt that should have been warm.

But then Kit remembered how Sasha had felt when he helped him down the stairs. Sasha had felt cool; his body was always cold, and maybe it was just that. Still, he hesitated to approach the figure draped across the window, even when he had been spotted. Finally, realizing he couldn't stand at the doorway holding a bedcover the way a child might walk around with his blanket, Kit approached Sasha and held it out to him.

"Here," he said. "Put this over your shoulders."

Sasha took it wordlessly, but he did not drape the bedcover; instead he bunched it up on his lap as though he had no idea what to do with it. Short of inviting Sasha to bed with him, there was nothing Kit could do, and he wasn't sure how that would go over between the two of them. He turned back and took a couple steps toward the bedroom.

"Thanks." The word was spoken in a low voice, almost inaudible, but Kit froze in his tracks. He turned around slowly.

"Why don't you sleep?" Kit asked the question he had been dying to ask.

"I don't sleep much." It was not much of an answer, but Kit let it slide.

"You don't eat either," he said instead.

There was a snort from the window, and the figure shifted. In the faint light it was hard to see exactly what Sasha's expression was. "I hate pizza."

"Then why do you…?"

"I don't cook, and it's easier than choosing take-out," Sasha said calmly, not that it helped make sense of the whole situation.

Kit took a few more steps into the room and sat on the sofa hesitantly. The dustcover smelled of mildew and mothballs, but it was comfortable. He could sense Sasha was in a mellow mood, probably a few steps away from falling asleep with his face pressed against the window, and his guard was down.

"So," he said slowly. "What's out there?"

"Nothing." That took long enough.

"Why don't you sleep on the bed?" Kit offered. "I'll take the sofa." He was certainly short enough to fit on it comfortably.

There was no reply. Kit had not been sure what to expect, but the offer had been genuine. The sitting room was not that cold, and he could wrap himself in a dustcover if needed. Additionally, it was Sasha's home, and he didn't want to evict him from his own bed. Not that it had been slept in recently.

"I'm fine," Sasha said with a huff, most likely annoyed by Kit's persistence.

Kit looked away in silence, unwilling to get up and go to the bedroom, not sure if he should stay, and just as unwilling to start a conversation in case he put his foot in his mouth. He settled back and pulled up his legs; his toes were starting to feel cold. He wanted to break the silence. Kit was usually not comfortable around others unless they were talking. He looked around to see if he could pick a safe subject to comment on, and in the diffuse light streaming in from the bedroom, he spotted the photos resting on the mantel. He crouched on the sofa and grabbed the one closest to him. It turned out to be the family photo.

"Who's this?" Kit asked.

The question snapped Sasha out of his musings, and he uncurled from the windowsill carefully. Kit watched as he put his good leg down first, braced himself against the wall, put down the other leg, and sort of swung to the sofa. Sasha fell onto the sofa lightly, making the maneuver appear easy, though that probably had something to do with his lack of weight. Kit froze for a moment, unwilling to believe His Royal Highness had deigned to grace Kit by sitting on the same seat as him.

Kit waited as Sasha sat properly, the bedcover still held in his fist, and took the photo from Kit, their hands brushing lightly. Sasha's hand felt cold to the touch, almost frozen. Kit looked up sharply at the contact, but Sasha seemed distracted by the photo. Sasha continued to study the snapshot for a long time, and Kit was about to give up on ever getting his answer, when Sasha spoke softly.

"They're my parents," he said, indicating the old couple. "I'm the one sitting on their knees."

"Your parents!" Kit exclaimed, then bit back the rest, in case he sounded offensive.

"They were rather old when they had me," Sasha said with a shrug. "I suppose you could call me an accident." He snorted in the semidark and shifted so his shoulder touched Kit's. He waited for Sasha to draw back, but Sasha did not seem to notice the physical contact, so he relaxed slightly.

"I can relate to that," Kit offered into the silence. "Being someone's… well, not an accident in my case, more like a mistake."

"Though if you listened to my parents," continued Sasha, as if he had not heard Kit's comment, "you'd think they'd never had a single slipup." Kit couldn't see the photo in the dark but could very well imagine it, the way those people were seated, all stiff and straight backed. "I think mom was hoping for a girl, probably the only reason they didn't get rid of me."

Kit remembered the aftershave in the cabinet under the sink. "No wonder she calls you princess."

Sasha turned his head in the dark, and Kit grinned, though the expression on the other man's face wasn't welcoming. "Hey, it was right in front of my face," he said, protesting against the unspoken accusation. "It wasn't like you were hiding it. Plus the aftershave doesn't suit you," Kit said finally.

"I know," Sasha said with a half laugh. "I think she buys the same brand for every man in our family."

Kit slid back into silence, feeling somewhat more comfortable now that they were actually conversing without insulting each other. The luminous hands of the wall clock read three in the morning, though it could be mistaken. Sasha didn't seem the type to go around replacing clock batteries or dusting rooms. "So," he said sleepily, biting back a yawn. "Where are they now?"

"In a better place."

"Sorry," said Kit settling down, yawning again. Glancing at the time seemed to have made him sleepy.

"They're in Florida," Sasha said wryly, and Kit had to smile at that. "Along with two of my brothers."

Kit yawned again and settled further into the comfortable, if somewhat dusty sofa. "Those guys in the photo," he said. "Your brothers?"

"Hm," confirmed Sasha as he untangled the bedsheet Kit had brought for him, and then draped it over his shoulders. He looked speculatively at Kit, and for an instant Kit was sure Sasha was about to share a corner of the cover with him, but the offer didn't materialize.

Kit wondered if he should ask Sasha about his family, but didn't think it was worth the trouble to pry. He tried to imagine what it was like growing up as a child of elderly parents, both past their prime. He glanced briefly at the photo still in Sasha's hand and then looked away. Wondering if he had overstepped his welcome, Kit started to unwind his legs so he could head back to the bedroom. He needn't have worried, since Sasha seemed to be in a very talkative mood. At least as talkative as could be expected of a person who was always so silent.

"My parents weren't exactly ready for me," Sasha said with a shrug, carrying on with the conversation. "My brothers were the ones who took care of me, but even they were too busy."

Kit wondered if he should ask Sasha more about his childhood. After all, there were so many directions the conversation could take, but he hesitated to ask questions in case they brought up the issue of Cory. The last thing he needed was to spoil the mood.

"Is that why you stayed back when they moved to Florida?" Kit asked, hoping it was a safe question.

"Something like that," Sasha replied readily. "I was at the local university at the time."

"Oh," said Kit, wondering about that. Sasha didn't act like a university student, and he had a vague idea that most of them were younger—not that he was aware of how old Sasha was, and he was not bold enough to ask that. Still….

Perhaps because they were both treading on uncharted territory, Sasha seemed to go silent, but he didn't get up, and Kit found himself feeling reluctant to do so. He wondered if Sasha had stayed with Cory because he was the parent that Sasha had never had, but then he rolled his eyes mentally at the speculation. He was thinking like an idiot. Perhaps he was hanging around Eddy because he needed a father figure. Now that was ridiculous.

He sighed and closed his eyes briefly to think about it, and the next moment was jerked awake when the person whose shoulder he had fallen asleep against sneezed sharply. Kit had been resting in the crook of Sasha's neck, his mouth just millimeters from the spot where the neck met the shoulder, in an awkwardly intimate position. Had it been anyone else, Kit would have considered nuzzling, perhaps leaving a hickey, but this was Sasha, not some random guy who'd let Kit sleep over.

Kit pulled back, startled, unable to believe he had fallen asleep on Sasha's shoulder and already missing the feel of his bony headrest. Sasha smelled clean and sharp, and felt warmer. Kit edged away a little sleepily and looked at Sasha, who didn't react to his movements apart from one brief glance in his direction. His Royal Highness had been awake the whole time; at least aware enough to know that the person he disliked strongly had been drooling on his shoulder, and he hadn't pushed Kit away. With an internal shrug, Kit leaned back into the sofa, close to Sasha but not so close that he'd accidentally use Sasha's shoulder as a headrest again, and shut his eyes again, inviting sleep.

If Kit had been expecting a complete change in Sasha's personality the next morning, he was disappointed. He woke up alone on the sofa with a crick in his neck and the bedsheet draped over his knees. The note Sasha had left for Kit on his study table read "Gone to meeting with lawyer" instead of "Get out" as Kit had half expected it to. A quick look confirmed the stack of papers that had taken up a side of the table, as well as Sasha's gym bag, which he had last seen on the floor near the bed, was gone. The key was still in the door, which meant Kit was going to be alone the entire day, if nothing else.

Kit found out the meaning of the term "stir crazy" a few hours after he had crawled out of the sofa. The house had little in it worth exploring. It was huge, and there were a lot of rooms, but all of them were empty. The only things worth noting about the other bathrooms were that they all had running water. The kitchen proved to be as empty as the rest of the house. Kit managed to unearth more pills and gels to rival a small pharmacy, ranging from painkillers and muscle ointment to unmentionable capsules with odd coloring in one of the bedroom drawers, but he supposed that, given Sasha's current physical state, it would have been stranger if he'd found nothing.

By the time Kit had explored the house, he was starved, and there was nothing to eat in the house except for day-old pizza, which he was frankly getting sick of, and a leftover stick of celery in the fridge. Kit considered going out to pick up something to eat, and then came across the familiar problem of not having any money to buy food with—at least not on a long-term basis. He called Eddy's house for the umpteenth time and left a message on the answering machine while chewing on a slightly funny-tasting slice of pizza. Eddy hadn't called him back, even though he'd left his number—Sasha's number—with the previous message, and he repeated it just in case Eddy had missed it.

Debating the wisdom of spending his last bit of cash on something to eat, Kit remembered that Sasha had told him there was money in one of the drawers in the study table by the bed. Kit hesitated over taking the money and finally concluded he wasn't really stealing, simply using it for both of them. He was just going out to do some shopping.

CHAPTER
EIGHT

"YOU cooked," Sasha observed. He sounded neither astonished nor pleased, instead acting as though the wind had been knocked out of his sails by the discovery of Kit in his seldom-used kitchen next to a bubbling pot.

"I heated up some soup and made mac 'n' cheese." Kit looked at him from the side of the kitchen, trying not to sound smug. "It's not like I made a seven-course dinner." It was Sasha's money that he had used to buy the ingredients, and he was trying hard to show his "landlord" that he could be of some use around the house.

Sasha grunted, probably because he was expressing himself more than he usually would through his facial expressions.

"I had to borrow your money to buy food," Kit said in the ensuing silence.

Sasha nodded dismissively, his jaw working silently, an indication that he wanted to say something but did not quite know how to put it into words. From Sasha's closed-off expression, Kit couldn't figure out whether he was pleased or pissed. "I'm going to take a shower," Sasha said instead as he turned away from the kitchen and limped into the adjoining room, leaving Kit with the boiling pot.

Sasha ate more than Kit expected him to. Compared to the amount of food Kit ate, it was relatively nothing, but more than he usually would if he had been served pizza.

"I take it you don't cook," Kit observed as they sat at the round kitchen table.

"No," Sasha said pointedly, sounding annoyed, most likely blaming Kit for breaking his concentration.

"Uh...," Kit said, wondering just what he had said that was so negative. "Okay."

There was a two-minute silence during which Kit served himself another plateful of food and Sasha seemingly discovered the meaning of life on the bottom of his soup bowl.

"How did the meeting with your lawyer go?" Kit asked, finding the silence uncomfortable.

"Fine," Sasha snapped.

"Did you go to the gym today?" Kit asked, trying to get over the hostility.

"No," Sasha practically snarled. "When are you moving out?"

And they had been getting on so well, Kit thought, floored by the unexpected question. "Soon," he said with false cheer, his appetite deserting him completely. "Give me a couple of days."

"You said it was for one day only," Sasha reminded him.

"Well, I told you before," said Kit with a shrug, pushing his plate away. "My boss is away for a bit and—"

"You have a boss!" Sasha sounded derisive. "Is that what they call pimps these days?"

Kit stood up, pushing back his chair hard, making it scrape along the floor with a loud screech. "What the heck crawled up your ass and died?"

"Nothing," Sasha said, a tad too quickly for it to be believable.

"Well, it's as if you've had a change of personality since yesterday," Kit observed.

"Just because you get to push me around a bit doesn't mean you get to move in with me," Sasha spat out as he pushed his half-eaten plate of food away.

"I'll be gone in a couple of days," Kit reasoned calmly enough, knowing he was in a better situation than he had been on the day he had begged for entrance while standing in the rain. He was actually in the house, so the chances of him being kicked out were slim. And Sasha hardly looked physically capable of doing that, no matter how much he tried to act otherwise.

"I've had enough of you," Sasha continued. "You, with your pretty-boy face and your boy-next-door charm, you seriously think you can win me over the same way you did with Cory?"

"Is that what this is about?" Kit asked as he moved toward Sasha. He was not sure whether he wanted to crowd the annoying little Royal Bastard or hit him in the face, but just then, he needed to move. Kit wasn't the brightest crayon in the box, but after years of working as a sales assistant and his *other* activities, he had an almost instinctive ability to read people.

Whatever was bugging Sasha, he was taking it out on Kit whether he deserved it or not. It reminded him a little of one of his former marks, Andrew, who'd been rather unpleasant to be around when the stock market was on a low. Still, this was Sasha, and Kit didn't think His Royal Highness was the type to throw a fit just because he'd missed the bus.

"Is this about something your lawyer said?" Kit asked softly, wondering if he was going about it the wrong way. There were only two ways to deal with it: he either lost his temper and shouted back at Sasha, giving him exactly what he wanted, or he held his temper in check and waited out Sasha's emotional outburst.

There was a long silence as Sasha took in the change of tone. He looked at Kit slowly, tipping his head back, his hair falling away from his face, letting the shadows play across his sharp cheekbones and high forehead.

"We went over all the provisions Cory had left for me in his will," he said, then abruptly turned away.

Kit remained silent, not sure as to what to say at the mention of the big pink elephant that they both had in common. Cory was the one subject he was unwilling to bring up at the moment.

"What you said about guilt," Sasha said softly. "I wonder how much of it is true."

"What did I say?" Kit asked, a little puzzled. He was sure he had not said anything memorable.

"We all carry our guilt around," Sasha said instead. "We shape our lives with it."

"Are you talking about yourself?" Kit asked, half afraid something would break.

"Me," Sasha said agreeably, "Cory, everyone." He sighed. "It's hard to let go of it."

"Guilt?" Kit repeated slowly. He wasn't really big on the guilt thing; that was like getting immersed in all the philosophy of life stuff, and as far as Kit was concerned, shit happened. Not that he was callous, but Kit had long decided he would not let things like remorse and conscience get in the way of his normal life. And it wasn't like he was a con man cheating fragile old ladies out of their savings…. The people he usually targeted could very well afford to give up a few bucks.

"Never mind," Sasha said as he pushed his chair back and stood up carefully, letting his good arm take his weight before he found his balance and walked toward the kitchen door.

Kit stood there for a moment, indignant His Royal Highness had not offered to clean up the kitchen or at least clear his plate. It wasn't as if Kit had just volunteered for the post of resident maid. Just because Kit was crashing at his place rent-free didn't mean he'd agreed to pick up after Sasha. He grabbed both their plates and was about to throw away the leftovers when he paused, recalling something Sasha had said a few moments ago.

"What was Cory guilty of?" he asked loudly, knowing Sasha could hear him very well.

For a moment the retreating back stiffened, but Sasha did not turn around. "Running away," he replied without turning around. "Cory ran away from everything. If things got complicated, he simply drank or walked away. Even at the end." Sasha's voice sounded angry. "He took the easy way out, leaving me to deal with the mess."

Kit didn't know what to say to that as he scraped the leftovers into a container and put it into the fridge. The washing up, he decided, could wait another day. At least it would give him something to do during the morning, and maybe if he left the kitchen fast enough he might get Sasha to expound upon his half-assed answer.

However, when he got to the bedroom, Sasha was clearly not in a speaking mood, having sat down at his customary spot at the table, though he wasn't even pretending to read his books as usual. He pointedly ignored Kit as he walked around the room, picked up the ratty sweats he wore to bed, and left for the bathroom to change. A bathroom with a hamper full of dirty clothes, soapsuds blocking the shower drain, and a toothpaste tube half squeezed out.

Someone was throwing a typical teenage tantrum over something. Kit wondered if all these talks Sasha had with his lawyer about Cory were the cause. Perhaps Sasha needed to talk to a shrink first, or perhaps Kit just needed to move out of the house. He brushed his teeth, showered, changed, and walked into the bedroom, where Sasha was polishing his walking stick.

Had it been anyone else but Sasha, Kit would have joked about wooden props and, well, things would have progressed, but in Sasha's case, there probably was no subterfuge. The guy seemed to be totally incapable of it. Kit looked pointedly at Sasha and then gave up and got into bed, pushing aside the prosthetic arm to make room for himself.

"Come to bed." Kit couldn't believe he had said that. Apparently neither could Sasha, since he froze in midsweep and then turned his head slowly to look at Kit, probably to make sure he was not dreaming.

"There should be enough room for both of us if we don't roll around much," Kit continued quickly, since there was no way he could take his words back and he had no idea how his mouth functioned independently from his brain anyway.

Sasha continued to stare.

"No sex," Kit added a tad hastily. Yes, now that would go well with His Royal Highness. "You don't sleep at all, it can't be good for you. Just...."

"How did you meet Cory?" Sasha asked abruptly.

Well, now that was something Kit would have loved not to talk about. Still, it was hard to ignore such a direct question. "He came to the shop I work in to—" Kit smiled ironically at the thought. "—to buy you some shirts."

"That's it?" Sasha said, putting aside his walking stick.

"What did you expect?" Kit asked, puzzled.

"He didn't meet you somewhere else?"

"You mean some sleazy bar or a strip club?" Kit said a tad sarcastically. "No, I don't think Cory had the time to even bother with all that shit. He was either too busy in his office or too preoccupied with worrying about you to do something like that."

"And he accidentally stumbled into you," Sasha said with bitterness. "How long were you fucking him?"

What was this, confrontation day? Kit was more floored by the question than by the use of the word "fuck," which seemed out of place with Sasha. "We were not," Kit said abruptly. "What you saw... was the first time... sort of...."

"Sort of...?" Sasha pressed the point, seemingly incapable of letting it go. Kit sat up in bed, feeling wide awake and uncomfortable. He was sweating so hard his T-shirt was soaked, and he didn't think it was because of the heat.

"You walked in on us," Kit snapped. What else was there to say? "I spent all that time trying to get Cory to just squint at me sideways, to stop pushing me away every time I tried to put a move on him, and then just when I get his fucking dick out of his pants...." Perhaps it was time to change tracks before it got too distracting or Kit revealed more than he should. "So, what exactly are you trying to pin on Cory? What would you rather he had done?"

From the startled look Sasha gave him, Kit realized His Royal Highness had not been aware his intentions were obvious. As though Sasha could hoodwink Kit when Kit was the master of manipulation— well, sometimes. "Why does it sound to me like you desperately want to prove that Cory cheated on you?" Kit wanted to ask whom Sasha had been screwing around with for him to need to justify his actions, but he did not think Sasha was the type to even think about masturbating when he was feeling bored, let alone cheat on Cory.

Sasha got to his feet abruptly—well, as abruptly as he could— letting the walking stick fall to the floor, and limped toward the connecting door, snapping off the bedroom light as he did, leaving Kit with his mouth open. That went well, Kit thought, a little hysterically.

What had he been thinking… or what had he not been thinking? So His Royal Highness had had a bad day, and his talk with his lawyer had dredged up some memories. What had gotten into Kit to invite Sasha to bed, though technically it was Sasha's bed, and things were oh so complicated? Why couldn't he keep his mouth shut?

Kit shuffled around a bit, trying to get comfortable, not that he was feeling sleepy. He should probably leave the house and its crazy-ass owner as soon as possible… not that he had many options.

Kit sat in the semidarkness, eyes fixed on the thread of light seeping through the connecting door, wondering what to do. He heard the toilet flush and the sound of the automatic washer running in the background when the bathroom door opened. Sasha had decided to do his laundry, which reminded Kit that he had exactly three changes of clothes with him, and two of them needed to be washed. And if he were to start work soon, he would have to buy some more clothes. Or borrow some of Sasha's, assuming they actually fit him. Cursing himself for not thinking of it earlier while he had been alone in the house, Kit closed his eyes. Maybe, if Sasha were to disappear the following day, Kit could actually root through the clothes rack to see if there was anything worth wearing. He settled back into the bed and closed his eyes. There wasn't much he could do for the present situation, and thinking about such things was never his strong point.

"Move over."

Kit's eyes sprang open, and he sat up on the bed so fast he felt dizzy. "What…?" he said semicoherently, staring at Sasha, who was standing next to the bed in what Kit had dubbed his nightclothes. "You're actually…." Kit shut his mouth before he could fully insert his foot into it, though it might have been too late for that.

Sasha didn't reply, and Kit scooted backward until his back was pressed against the wall, leaving enough space for another person to lie on the bed. The bed was rather small, ideal for a couple who wanted to sleep cuddling or spooning; Kit was not planning on doing anything that involved bodily contact.

Sasha wordlessly sat on the corner of the bed, then swung his feet up carefully, balancing his weight as if afraid he was going to fall over.

Then he lay on his side with his back to Kit, leaving a couple inches of space between them.

"If I'd known it was this easy to get you into bed, I'd have...." Kit snapped his mouth shut, unable to believe he had said that. He really would have to watch his mouth.

There was a snort from Sasha but no snappy comeback. Kit relaxed a little and pushed off a bit from the wall, since his back was protesting at his uncomfortable position. Lying on his side facing Sasha's back felt awkward. Kit didn't know what to do with his arm. He couldn't keep it on his hip while sleeping, since that was uncomfortable, but moving it a couple inches would mean brushing against Sasha.

Sasha, who smelled like soap and toothpaste and fabric softener, and something altogether elusive that had his nose twitching and his body begging to get closer. Damn.

"So," said Kit, trying to keep himself from making another foot-in-the-mouth mistake. "How did you meet Cory?" Great, that's the way to connect with someone, bring up the common points. Kit was sure, had Sasha been the violent type, he'd have killed Kit on the spot.

"He came to our university as a guest speaker," Sasha replied softly. "It was some boring topic like the industry and science and not many people attended."

Kit lay facing Sasha's back, his mouth hanging open in surprise. He hadn't expected Sasha to answer the question, let alone give an explanation.

"But you attended it?" Kit persisted, now that his bedmate was actually speaking.

"I sat in the front row and even asked some questions," Sasha replied, sounding slightly amused. "Afterward, there was a complimentary tea and he approached me, told me just how impressed he was by the questions and my—" He gasped out what Kit thought was a wry laugh. "—intellectual prowess. Invited me to dinner."

Kit wanted to ask more, but he wasn't sure what, and he knew he had pushed the limit beyond the point where Sasha would consider it acceptable. Instead, he settled down as comfortably as possible, convinced he wouldn't sleep a wink.

IT WAS one of those dreams where Kit knew it was dream, since his mother was there with him. They were in their last home together, mismatched furniture and the odd brown carpet that did not quite hide all the dirt, but they were together and that was what mattered. There was a persistent knock on the door that Kit knew was the police. They had come to tell him his mother was dead and to take him away. As his mother moved toward the door, Kit, in his seven-year-old body, moved to intercept her.

"Don't answer the door, Mommy," he said, though his logical mind told him it was all screwed up. His mother shouldn't even be in the room; that day he had been with his babysitter, Auntie Marie from upstairs, and she had left a couple hours before, when Kit's mother had failed to show up after work at seven as she usually did. Still, if his mother didn't open the door, the police wouldn't be able to tell him she was dead, and they would be safe, together, inside their one-bedroom apartment.

"Don't open the door, Mommy," he begged, wrapping his arms around her waist. "Don't open the door...."

Kit jerked awake with a start. His face was pressed against Sasha's neck and his hands were wrapped tightly around Sasha's slender waist, almost crushing him against Kit. And astonishingly, Sasha was rubbing his forearm calmly, acting as though it were the most normal thing to do.

"Awake?" Sasha asked when Kit drew in a deep breath and pulled away a little, his arms still wrapped around Sasha's waist.

"Uh," Kit said confused. "What...?"

"You were having a nightmare of some sort."

"Oh," Kit said, aware that his entire body was plastered against Sasha's in a not very platonic manner. He wasn't hard—the nightmare had taken care of that—but now that he was awake, his body was responding enthusiastically to the presence of another warm—well, relatively warm—person pressed against his front. Sasha's body was cooler than his, and he smelled so inviting, Kit wanted to go back to his original position with his nose buried in Sasha's hair. "Sorry," he mumbled, pushing himself away, though that was the last thing he wanted to do. "I didn't mean to wake you up."

"I was going to get up anyway," Sasha said, his voice surprisingly gentle, making Kit wonder if he had spoken aloud while dreaming. "I have to feed the cats."

"Um," said Kit, waking up a little bit more. "I cancelled the pizza order for today, so…" He sat up, pushing Sasha down as he tried to sit up as well. "There's some leftover pasta in the fridge…. I'll get it and put in on the sill."

"I can get it," Sasha persisted.

"I need some water," Kit said, wanting to put some distance between him and Sasha until he felt more like himself. He slid off the bed and dragged his feet toward the kitchen, looking at the wall clock as he did so. 3 a.m., not bad. At this rate he was going to be an insomniac like Sasha. The cats fed with the leftovers, not that Kit really wanted to throw away good food that could be eaten on another day, Kit slid back into the bed awkwardly, wondering if he should move to the sofa or whether Sasha would, as he usually did.

Sasha appeared to be asleep, though it could have been wistful thinking on Kit's side, since as soon as he lay down, Sasha spoke abruptly. "How old arc you?"

Kit froze, trying to make out Sasha's features in the semidarkness and failing. "Uh, what?" he said confusedly. "Twenty-two," he answered with only a pause.

"Thought you were younger," Sasha grunted, and he moved a little, trying to get comfortable.

"How old are you?" Kit asked Sasha. Not that it was the sort of conversation he wanted to have with someone in the middle of the night and all, but really, it seemed only fair, since he'd been asked the same question.

"Twenty-eight," Sasha replied, and Kit kept his mouth shut. Trying to gauge Sasha's age was an impossible task. It was not just the damaged face that made the guessing difficult; it was also his demeanor and the air of superiority that he cultivated. If he'd ever had to guess,

Kit would have put Sasha in a range from twenty to thirty to be on the safe side.

"Your mother…," Sasha said softly, and Kit cursed himself. He was unable to keep his mouth shut, even when dreaming, and it was starting to become an annoying habit. "How old were you in the dream?" Which had probably been the question Sasha had wanted to ask in the first place.

"Seven," Kit snapped abruptly. That was something he didn't want to talk about. "Can we not talk about this now?" he added for good measure, just in case Sasha did not understand subtle cues. "Can we just sleep? I think normal people do sleep at this time of the night."

Sasha grunted in reply, and since there was no further conversation forthcoming, Kit assumed it meant he had taken Kit's message to heart and decided to shut up for the night. Now he probably thought Kit was some clingy kid with a nightmare problem or a mommy complex, and really, Sasha should learn to keep his bloody mouth shut. But the dream was far too fresh in Kit's mind, and he wasn't used to keeping it all bottled up.

"It was just stupid," Kit said, far too loudly in the silent bedroom, unable to put into words the frustration and despair he had felt at the time of his mother's needless death. "She worked as a waitress at a restaurant downtown. She didn't even work nights 'cause I was home and she couldn't leave me alone. And then one day she just didn't come back. Then the police came knocking and—" Kit paused to swallow the lump in his throat. "—they said she'd just dropped dead in the restaurant while working. Had been complaining of a headache the whole day but no one had really given it much thought and then… it turned out a blood vessel in her brain had burst—they called it something, an anne-somethingy and…."

"Aneurysm," Sasha said softly. He turned around awkwardly until he was facing Kit, and sighed. "Try to get some sleep," he said simply. "Perhaps that wasn't the best topic to bring up."

Kit opened his mouth to say he couldn't go to sleep for the simple reason that he was far too wide awake and would sit up on the sofa all night, when Sasha turned over to his former position with his back to Kit with a grunt. That was just great. Ask Kit something he didn't want to drag up and then act like it was nothing. Typical of His Royal Highness who had the sensitivity of a…. Kit froze as Sasha maneuvered himself stiffly until he was facing Kit and awkwardly patted his shoulder. "Just go to sleep."

There was a touch of something in that voice that had Kit suddenly moving toward Sasha, seeking comfort. "Some of us have work to do," Sasha added, rearranging himself so he was facing away from Kit again, and the spell was broken, leaving Kit staring at the back of Sasha's head.

CHAPTER
NINE

Kɪᴛ came awake with a start and sat up in bed, wondering what had woken him so abruptly. He automatically put out a hand to stop himself from toppling over Sasha, but that side of the bed was empty. He turned his head to confirm Sasha hadn't fallen off the bed when he noted Sasha was still in the room, standing by the table and looking as startled as Kit felt.

"What…?" Kit started to say, but Sasha made a slashing motion with his hand, bringing the question to a halt.

"Someone's at the door," he said in a low voice, almost a whisper.

"Who is it?" Kit asked, speaking in an equally low voice as he swung his legs off the bed, though he had no idea why they were whispering.

"You stay here," Sasha snapped as he strode toward the living room in a brisk limp, probably not even realizing he walked quite well when he forgot about his leg.

Kit got off the bed, pushing the cover aside, and got to his feet, feeling wide awake. Sasha didn't receive a lot of visitors, and since the sun was barely coming up, it was too early for it to be a casual caller. He walked up to the bedroom door and peered into the living room just as Sasha pulled opened the seldom-used front door. He stood blocking the door, regarding whoever had knocked for a while before stepping back reluctantly to let that person in.

It turned out to be two people, both of whom Kit recognized immediately. The first to step into the house was Cory's sister, though at the moment Kit couldn't remember which one she was, closely followed by a man whom Kit knew to be their lawyer.

The two visitors regarded the living room with an air of disdain and seemed to sniff in contempt at the interior. She pointedly looked over Sasha, who was still dressed in his nightclothes, which, in Kit's opinion, though far too baggy, still managed to look good on him.

"Mr. Alexander Krylov," the lawyer spoke carefully, with the air of someone addressing a moron.

Sasha didn't bother replying. He walked up to a stuffed chair and sat, his face blank. He seemed to be aware of the twin sets of eyes fixed on him, since he limped rather heavily, and Kit had to clutch the doorway to stop himself from dashing out. Kit didn't know why those two were here, but he didn't think Sasha would be pleased if Kit were seen by the visitors, especially since Kit was in his bedroom. Still, Kit was dying to know what the whole thing was about, and he wasn't above eavesdropping.

There was a momentary confusion as the two visitors were thrown out of their stride by the cold reception, but they rallied, sitting on the sofa, facing Sasha, probably under the impression teaming up on him would help them gain more ground.

The woman, Kit could not remember her name, opened her mouth to speak, but the lawyer beat her to it. "We're sorry for coming here unannounced. We would have called ahead but your number is unlisted and…." Kit slipped back into the room so he was not visible from the sitting room, but was positioned just right so he could continue to eavesdrop. There were only three voices to listen to; Kit could follow the conversation easily.

"What do you want?" Sasha, it seemed, was abrupt and rude with everyone, not just Kit.

"We have come to discuss with you the conditions of Dr. St. James' will," the lawyer said, apparently untroubled by Sasha's lack of manners. Not that they had any to talk about either, Kit thought spitefully.

"What about it?" Sasha demanded flatly.

"You do realize that you don't have the money to see this through to the end?" the lawyer demanded.

"And at the moment, we are keeping this as low-key as possible, and even then company stocks are falling. My brother's untimely death created a lot of unforeseen problems." The woman spoke. "If the press gets a hold of the news that we have a legal dispute, the major shareholders will sell—"

"What do you want from me?" Sasha interrupted her unhurriedly. Kit gave the guy points for guts, wishing he could see the actual expressions of the people involved.

"Surely, you don't think that you can win against us in court." The lawyer, whose name Kit could not remember, spoke.

"Mr. Walters." Sasha did not have Kit's erratic memory when it came to names, or perhaps he was better acquainted with the St. James' family lawyer. "If you did not think there was even a remote chance of me winning, you would not be here." Wow, Sasha knew how to kick butt when he wanted to.

"But surely you cannot comprehend the expenses…," the woman spoke.

"I know," Sasha stated. "That is why I'll be selling the company once this is over."

"Don't you dare…," the woman snapped, her façade of disinterest shattering at the statement. "I know my brother had problems and his—" She paused for a moment, perhaps seeking the correct words, and Kit wished he could see her face. "—lifestyle was questionable at times, but…."

"Candela!" The lawyer spoke in a low voice, almost a warning, and Kit squirmed in his need to take a peek.

"Oh, what," she snapped, sounding more agitated. "We all knew my brother was happily married before all this with *him* started." Kit could not see, but her tone sounded as though it should be accompanied by a pointed finger. "It was just a fleeting fancy, and if he hadn't died he would have…."

"I'm not here to listen to your delusions." Sasha's voice could have cut glass and was as effective as a knife across the throat in silencing the two people.

"No need for that, Mr. Krylov," the lawyer said in a cutting voice that was so unlike his earlier soothing tone, it was obvious he was now in battle mode.

"Then let's stop beating around the bush, shall we...?"

"We want to settle this out of court," the lawyer continued. "You will be given a substantial sum of money and your medical expenses will be paid by the company as usual. But you will give up your claim on the will and give over your shares of the—"

"You seriously think I'm going to do that?" Sasha snapped. "The only reason you're here is because you don't have a leg to stand on...."

"The only reason we're here is because you'll have to sell the company even if you win against us, since you'll have to pay your lawyer," Candela snapped. "My brother's company, which should rightfully belong to the family... something you have no right owning."

"Why don't I make it clear?" Sasha said carefully. "Get out of my house."

"My brother was delusional," Candela continued in a last-ditch effort. "He wasn't in his right mind. Otherwise he wouldn't have taken up with you. I don't know you personally, but I know about the likes of you. You were too young for Cory, you were just so wrong. Admit it, you would have left if he hadn't died. He could have done better."

"Leave," Sasha said in an icy tone. "Now."

Luckily for Sasha, the two were far too civilized to say, "Or what," which was what Kit would have said. Especially since the only other option Sasha had was to call the police, which he was unlikely to do. Instead, there was a rustle of clothes, and... Kit had not been aware the sofa creaked that much, which meant they were getting up. However, it seemed that Mr. Walters could not help but make a parting dig as he left.

"Please, don't bother walking us to the door," he said smoothly. "Like you said, we might not have much to bring up against you in court, but in your case, you don't have a leg to stand on either. You should remember your involvement with Dr. St. James has already cost you an arm and a leg."

Kit did not know what to make of it, but when he strolled into the living room, Sasha was seated in the chair, his face drawn and his hand gripping the armrest so hard his knuckles shone white in the morning light. He looked up at Kit's entrance and scowled at him. "I take it you were listening," he said bluntly.

"Yes." Kit could see no point in pretending otherwise.

Sasha heaved himself out of the chair with some difficulty. As he dragged himself on his bad leg toward the bathroom, Kit wondered if he should say something, but in the end decided he should simply go and toast the bread he'd bought the previous day in case either of them felt like breakfast.

After Sasha had emerged from his long retreat in the bathroom, Kit took his turn and ended up not only emptying the automatic washer, but also sorting its contents out into two piles. At least Sasha had been considerate enough to throw in Kit's dirty clothes along with his, and Kit's problem of what to wear was solved.

By the time he returned to the kitchen, startling a large tabby sitting on the kitchen table, Sasha was burning scrambled eggs. It was sort of amusing to watch Sasha as he made a half-hearted attempt at cooking. The rigid set of his shoulders and back did not invite any comments. Kit sat in the same place he had the previous night and waited until Sasha slapped a piece of dark-brown toast and some egg with black clots of burnt matter on a plate, and shoved the whole thing in front of Kit. The cat jumped off the table at the noise, hissing in fright, and took off through the open window. Sasha pulled out the chair next to Kit and sat down heavily with his own plate, which held a considerably less-burnt potion of egg and toast.

"How come your eggs aren't as black as mine?" Kit quipped before he could rein his tongue. Sasha regarded Kit coldly and then swapped their plates silently, ignoring Kit's comment. Kit regarded the unappetizing mess on his plate and sighed. It wasn't really worth the trouble. They could have had day-old pizza and still survived.

He forked a piece of egg into his mouth and grimaced before trying another mouthful. He'd had worse, and this food was at least warm and didn't have pieces of plaster like the food at the orphanage had, so he was not about to complain. Swallowing hurriedly, Kit glanced up to see Sasha regarding him with a slightly amused expression, and put down his fork warily. "What?" Kit asked in the silence.

"You might want to hold the fork further down. It's not a shovel," Sasha replied, and Kit felt his face burn with embarrassment.

He remembered Cory gently chiding him about his lack of table manners and teaching him the proper way to select which knife and fork to use with each course, though it had been some time back and Kit hadn't been taking notes. However, as he regarded Sasha holding his fork in his hand gracefully, he had to admit his roommate had better skills with silverware than Kit did, even with one hand. It was not the highlight of the day to be put down about his lack of—what did they call it—breeding, not having attended some preppy school where they taught people how not to stab themselves with forks and all. He shoved his plate back though he was still hungry and regarded Sasha with a scowl.

"Oh, fine," said Sasha, returning to his food. "I was just trying to make conversation." Kit continued to scowl. "Just eat it. I put up with your slurping yesterday, didn't I?"

"That's supposed to make me feel better?" Kit asked, feeling insulted. Even knowing Sasha was getting back at him for having eavesdropped on the conversation between him and the duo that had shown up this morning, it still stung.

Sasha didn't answer as he tapped the toast with one of the prongs of the fork; it made a sound similar to metal hitting wood. He sighed and pushed his plate back.

"So what are you going to do?" Kit asked, more because he wanted to change the subject than anything else. Well, he was also curious as to what Sasha's next move would be.

"About Cory's sister and the family shark?" Sasha said with a shrug. "Nothing. They don't have anything to use against me. Otherwise they wouldn't have bothered to come here in person."

"You seem certain," Kit said. "Why don't you call your lawyer and tell him about this, just in case."

"I'm seeing him tomorrow," Sasha shrugged. "It can wait."

"If you say so," said Kit with pretend nonchalance. It was really not his problem, but still…. "You know, what Cory's sister—"

"Candela."

"—said about Cory being married before…." Kit tried to formulate the question that had been bothering him since he'd heard the conversation. It wasn't that he didn't know gay men sometimes married; he just didn't think Cory had been the type, and Sasha was definitely not the type to sleep with a married guy. After all, it took one to know one.

"Delusions people live with," Sasha said with a small bark of a laugh. "Cory married once when he was twenty-two, to a fellow researcher. They were married for six months. She's happily married to someone else now with five kids and doesn't even figure in his will. Candela was just grasping for straws when she brought up that one, and even she knew it."

"She made it sound like you were a…."

"Money-grabbing gold digger who'd move on to the next guy as soon as I got money." Sasha gave a deprecating laugh, and stared at Kit as if he had lost his mind. "With me looking like this? Even Cory had a hard time looking at me."

"But before—" Kit wanted to say "the accident," but he didn't know for sure and he did not want to ask. "—this… you must have… had someone." He was just curious about Sasha.

"There wasn't anyone," Sasha said sharply. "I think the reason I went out with Cory at first was because he was the only one who'd ever directly asked me out. Even then, when we first started, I knew it was the wrong choice. Cory was just not my type. He was too old for me and he had so many hang-ups. When he asked me to move in with him and make it permanent, I knew I had no choice but to break it off. I was going to break it off…." Sasha's eyes took on a slightly unfocused look; probably he was remembering something, and as much as Kit wanted to know what had happened afterward, he did not think it was the right time to bring it up. Instead, he tried to change the subject casually, since Sasha was in a talkative mood, which did not happen often.

"You mean there was no one before Cory?" Kit asked, injecting just the right amount of disbelief to stir up the other.

"Well." Sasha actually looked uncomfortable at the question. "There were a few... two guys... I did mess around a bit...." Kit had an idea that Sasha might be speaking about his childhood discoveries. "But actual sex...."

"Was with Cory only," Kit could not help exclaiming. "Man. You're practically a virgin."

Sasha drew back as if struck, and for a moment, a faint red color bloomed on his cheeks. Kit didn't think Sasha was angry. Rather, he was dying of mortification. "There weren't any guys falling over themselves to approach me," Sasha said defensively. "And it wasn't like I knew exactly how to make a pass at another guy."

Kit could very well imagine Sasha sitting in a gay bar and no one approaching him. It wasn't because Sasha was ugly, but because of his attitude. Kit was finally beginning to understand that Sasha, despite appearances, was somewhat shy, and that translated into aloofness. Sasha had an unapproachable air about him, the way a royal would have bodyguards to keep people at a distance. Kit knew of people like that, guys others looked at but were too scared to approach in case they fell short of the guy's expectations.

"It's called the Ice Prince syndrome," Kit said with a grin. "You know, you have that air that says, 'Worship me but don't touch me.'"

This time Sasha looked stung; Kit might as well have doused him in cold water—perhaps such a comment was not appreciated.

"I mean...," Kit said, backpedaling rapidly. "If I saw you in a bar, I wouldn't come near you because you appear so standoffish...."

Still not helping. Kit could see Sasha didn't understand what he was trying to say, and he was making it worse.

He tried a different angle. "It's not like you aren't good-looking...," he said, but Sasha seemed to take it as sarcasm, drawing back and pushing away from the table. As Sasha stood up, Kit stood as well and walked around to confront Sasha face-to-face.

Sasha made to brush past Kit, but Kit stopped him, placing himself squarely in Sasha's path. "Will you listen to me?" he said as he tried to get Sasha to look him in the eye. He lifted his hand and touched Sasha's face on the "good side," forcing him to face Kit, and opened his mouth to explain what he had implied when he saw the look in Sasha's eyes. Those eyes said that whatever Kit was going to say would not make any difference to Sasha. He wouldn't even bother listening. Kit drew a deep breath, lifted himself up onto his toes, and did the only thing he could think of: he kissed Sasha.

He had been dying to do it since the day he had laid eyes on those soft lips.

The kiss started out as tentative, but as Kit delved deeper, he didn't meet any resistance; Sasha opened his mouth, welcoming the intrusion. Sasha's mouth was as cool as the rest of him and tasted of coffee, burnt eggs, and something so intoxicating, Kit knew it had to be Sasha. Kit placed a hand on Sasha's shoulder and his other arm around his slender waist, pulling Sasha closer until they were plastered together. The kiss progressed from tentative to almost savage. Sasha's tongue pushed against Kit's insistently, his hand holding onto Kit's upper arm to keep his balance.

Surprisingly, Sasha's too-thin body was not as off-putting as Kit had originally assumed. His body, as usual, was surprisingly cool, but somehow when their hips met, Kit knew certain parts of Sasha were very fired up. He sneaked a hand down to Sasha's waistband and let the tips of his fingers rest there, allowing Sasha to feel his touch but not actually wandering farther down as he wanted to. It was up to Sasha to decide how far he wanted to carry this, and Kit didn't think either of them was prepared to go all out. Knowing Sasha as he did, Kit didn't think the next step would be a tumble into bed. Sasha was just not the type.

He pulled back carefully, keeping a hand on Sasha's waist to keep his balance, and looked up, unsure as to what he would see. Sasha's face was blank, his mouth was slightly open, his eyes were glazed, and he was breathing hard. Kit took a careful step back and let his hand slide free of Sasha and fall to his side.

"You've made a point," Sasha said softly, sounding slightly breathless, and Kit sighed.

"It was more than making a point," he said.

"What?" Sasha demanded as he took a step back.

"Why is it so difficult for you to realize that you are… cute, no matter what you think?" Kit said forcefully.

"Cute." Sasha sounded insulted.

"Good-looking, sexy… whatever…," Kit tried again.

"What…?" Sasha started to say when they were interrupted by a knock on the door.

"They're crawling out of the woodwork now, aren't they?" Kit said dryly. He had no idea what Sasha'd been about to say, but glad the conversation was cut short. Kissing his current "landlord" was not a good idea, especially since he was a touchy person. Kit knew better than to go around lip locking with people just because he wanted to.

Kit watched as Sasha turned around and walked to the door, probably as glad to get away from Kit as he was. After all, it would have taken a dead man not to notice Sasha had reciprocated with equal enthusiasm. He waited in the kitchen until he heard the front door open, and a brisk female voice said, "Alexander, isn't it? Did my sister pay you a visit earlier and make it worse?"

CHAPTER
TEN

KIT was almost glad of the interruption, since he had no idea as to what he should do or say in such a situation. He had just kissed His Royal Highness, and it was almost unreal, when he thought of it. Even though the kiss had been only a few seconds ago. He couldn't even believe that he had done that… and there was an orange tabby eating the leftover eggs from their plates on the kitchen table. Really, where did Sasha manage to find these cats? Half of them appeared to be about the same size as small dogs. Kit moved carefully so he would not startle the cat—he didn't know what sort of violence cats were capable of when disturbed, and looked out the kitchen door, carefully keeping below eye level. Sasha was, again, seated on his usual chair, facing Cory's sister number two who was seated, as usual, on the sofa. This time, though, Sasha was facing the kitchen door, and Kit stepped forward boldly to listen in on the conversation.

"… Candela has always been the headstrong one in the family," the woman was saying, so Kit was sure he hadn't missed out on much.

"Lux," Sasha said firmly. Kit was surprised by just how familiar Sasha sounded with Cory's sister, whom Kit guessed was in her fifties. Then again, Sasha had had a lover who had been twice as old as he was, and Lux was Cory's younger sister, Kit reasoned. "Why did you come here?"

"Because my sister decided to jump the gun and visit you. I wanted to see if I could smooth things over," she replied unhurriedly. Kit gave her points; she was far more collected than her sister.

"I'm not about to give everything over to you just because you want me to," Sasha replied with a shrug, indicating that it was the least of his problems. "As you can see, I'm not brain damaged despite all those rumors."

"Which reminds me," said Lux as she reached into her handbag. "I brought your mail.… You know, we keep receiving these phone calls and letters for you, only it's like you've dropped off the face of the earth. No forwarding address, phone number unlisted.…"

Pushed off the earth was more like it, Kit thought. Sasha remained impassively silent. Lux pointedly pulled out some envelopes from her handbag and reached forward pretending to hand them over to Sasha. She stopped just out of reach so that Sasha would have to lean forward to grab them, and Kit knew Sasha was not about to do that. For a moment there was a silent battle of wills before Lux decided to retreat to the sofa, keeping the collection of letters on the armrest. Being close to her, Kit could see some of the letters had been opened, but at least she had been thoughtful enough to bring them over.

"They're mostly from a clinic," she said, acting as though there had not been an impasse several seconds ago. "I thought you might want them.… After all, the company is still footing your medical expenses.…"

"Your point?" Sasha said coldly as he looked up briefly at Kit, and then away.

"Nothing," Lux said with a sigh. "You seem to be doing well now."

"Better than I did when you kicked me out," Sasha replied, and Kit gave him a thumbs-up over Lux's head.

"It was not your house to start off with," Lux stated.

"It wasn't yours either," Sasha replied, and then turned away. "Are you going to tell me how delusional your brother was as well?"

Lux looked away, turning her head sideways, and Kit braced himself to duck in case she glanced over her shoulder, but she did not. "I'm not going to say that," she finally admitted. "He was old enough to know what he wanted to do, and if he wanted to support you for the rest of your life, it was his choice," she said. "Especially since we all admit that he was a part of what happened to you."

"That was an accident," Sasha said firmly.

"Which he felt responsible for," Lux added.

"What do you want?" Sasha asked again, not letting her change the subject.

"You are going to see this to the end, aren't you?" Lux asked seriously.

"I wasn't going to," Sasha said, then looked up suddenly, straight at Kit. "I was going to let it go, but a person advised me to keep living."

"I admit Cory's lawyer is very loyal to him," Lux said, misunderstanding Sasha's declaration.

"I think you should leave," Sasha said abruptly. "I was in the middle of something important when you came."

Kit paused, his eyes wide, looking at Sasha over Lux's shoulder. Lux nodded and sat back, squaring her shoulders, readying herself for battle. "I'll say my piece then," she said. "I wanted to tell you to consider what you are doing right now. You might be holding a winning hand now, but that doesn't mean you know what you are doing. You don't know the first thing about running a company, and this is not something you can do by trial and error. On top of it, I hear you will be going back to your studies, and this is a full-time job."

Sasha opened his mouth to speak, but Lux held out her hand in a gesture of silence. "Hear me out," she said firmly. "You might want to let that lawyer run it for you, but you know as well as I do that everyone serves their interests first. What I'm asking of you is to think it over. If you want to have the cake and eat it, you must be aware of a lot of facts."

"I was not planning on hanging onto the company," Sasha said as Lux paused to catch her breath.

"Selling it," Lux scoffed. "Do you have any idea on how to do that? What are you going to do, put an ad in the business for-sale section? What about the board of trustees?"

"I didn't know there was a board of trustees," Sasha admitted wryly, and Lux froze for a moment before standing up. It was obvious she didn't need to add anything more to the conversation, and Kit admired her guts for that. Sasha stood up as well, without any hesitation, though he did use only one leg. Kit knew Lux had scored a direct hit where her sister seemed to have failed. Additionally, if she had come to get the scoop on things, it would be obvious to her that Sasha was clueless about a lot of things and was letting his lawyer handle the burden.

Kit ducked back into the kitchen as Lux started to turn around, and remained there until he was certain she was out of the house. He was sure the "important thing" Sasha had referred to had something to do with the kiss they had shared, and he was not about to bring that up. Kit planned on holing up in the kitchen until Sasha came back in and confronted him. After two tail-flicking contests with the napping tabby, Kit calculated enough time had passed for Sasha to walk Lux all the way up to the end of the driveway, where her car must have been parked. He heard the front door open and the uneven sound of Sasha's footsteps. He stood expectantly, waiting for Sasha to enter the kitchen, but all seemed quiet in the sitting room, and it slowly became obvious that Sasha wasn't about to return to the kitchen anytime soon. Wondering what had engaged Sasha's attention, Kit walked up to the doorway and peeked out.

Sasha stood in the living room by the sofa, leafing through the letters Lux had brought with her, looking slightly pissed off.

"Problem?" Kit asked as he stepped out, curiosity getting the better of him.

"You could say that," Sasha said with a frown. "I'm going to make a couple of calls. Do you think you can hold back on your eavesdropping urges and do something useful for a change?"

Kit stepped back, stunned, then shrugged. Sasha had always been direct with his words, and Kit was starting to get used to it.

"I think I'll just listen in on your phone call," he said with a grin. "It's not like I don't do that already."

"It's to my clinic, where they're doing the—" He paused and gave Kit an unreadable look. "—face reconstruction," Sasha finished with a shrug. "They send letters, not e-mail or anything, and this letter is a week old. I need to confirm with them that I'm coming in for the rest of the procedure and my allotted…."

"Rest of the procedure for…." Kit trailed off.

"Me," Sasha said, touching his damaged side in answer. "But before that...." He frowned, appearing to contemplate an issue. "I think I might visit my lawyer after all."

"You might drop into the gym as well," Kit suggested. Sasha looked at Kit searchingly, so he tried to add something sensible. "You do go past that place," he finally managed.

"Fine," Sasha said finally, a slightly amused expression on his face.

While it had been a good idea at the time to encourage Sasha to go to the gym, since his leg needed to be worked on or whatever, Kit regretted suggesting that while he waited for Sasha to come back. In a way, it irritated Kit that he was actually looking forward to Sasha's company; after all, he knew they weren't the best of friends or anything even remotely close. Sasha wasn't exactly known for his art of conversation, though the two of them were having more and more conversations and they were getting to the point they could relax without trying to kill each other.

Still, it made Kit nervous as he waited for Sasha to come back. He wondered if he should cook dinner. He hadn't said anything about cooking, but since he had the previous day, he wondered if Sasha expected him to do so again. Or maybe Sasha would eat out and come back, or maybe he was expecting pizza as usual. Or maybe Kit should cook for himself—but what if Sasha came back while he was eating and.... Kit was ready to slam his head against the wall in frustration.

He rummaged through the clothes cupboards, rearranging a place for his stuff and also searching for anything hidden in Sasha's underwear drawer. He rooted through the house until he had uncovered a seemingly century-old straight porn magazine collection, probably belonging to one of Sasha's brothers, and discovered that Sasha did not have any condoms stashed anywhere in the house (or lube, but there was enough stuff that could be used) and also that the only TV in the house did not work. Startled, Kit dropped the magazine he had been holding, appropriately called *Girls of Glitter*, since the models were wearing very little apart from that, when the phone rang, breaking the silence.

He rushed for it and stared at it for a while, wondering whether he should pick it up or not. The phone was a museum piece, not even a cordless. It was probably something left over from Sasha's parents' days; it had chunky keys and did not display the caller's number or caller ID, nor did it record incoming messages. Just as he was about to let it ring until whoever was calling gave up, Kit remembered he had given the number to Eddy. He snatched up the phone hurriedly. "Yeah," he gasped out.

There was an odd silence on the other side; then a familiar voice demanded, "Chicken or beef?"

"What?" Kit spluttered. "Sasha, what...?"

"I'm picking up some takeout, unless you have already had dinner or...."

"Chicken," Kit said hastily, trying to bite back a smile spreading over his face. It wasn't like he had any reason to smile. It was stupid. Sasha probably remembered Kit when he'd gone to buy dinner for himself.

"Good," said Sasha, sounding as emotionless as ever. "Cats like chicken too." And then he hung up abruptly.

Kit blinked and then put down the receiver, giving up the effort to hold back his smile. There was no reason for him to be excited about the prospect of eating takeout. Okay, so he was always hungry and didn't go out much, but that didn't mean he was starved. Though he was curious about what Sasha was going to bring, anyway, and how long it would take for His Royal Highness to come back home. Maybe Kit should have told Sasha to buy some condoms while he was at it.

Sasha showed up thirty minutes later with containers full of some Chinese takeout with an unpronounceable name. Later, while they sat eating spiced chicken in noodles, odd orange-colored stuff, and seafood stew, Sasha continued to instruct Kit on his table manners.

"Hold the chopsticks like this," Sasha told him. "One is stationary, the other moves. Keep the stationary one on your middle finger and support the back of it with base of your thumb."

"Huh," said Kit as the piece of fried crab stick dipped in some sauce fell back into the little tub, splashing the front of his T-shirt with red splotches. He scowled at Sasha for distracting him before putting down his container and pulling up the front of his T-shirt so he could lick the spillage. After all, his clothes had recently been laundered, and Kit didn't wash his clothes unless it was absolutely necessary.

"Like this," Sasha said, holding out his own. "Only the second stick is mobile. Grip it with your thumb and free fingers." He was eating his dish with grace, probably born with a pair of disposable chopsticks between his fingers. Kit tried to imitate him, but failed as a chopstick rolled free of his grip and fell onto the tabletop. Sasha made a sound of frustration and leaned forward as if to adjust Kit's grip, then seemed to change his mind at the last instant. He drew back and pointed toward the kitchen drawer with his chin. "Take a fork and just eat."

Kit opened his mouth to point out he did not mind touching Sasha, but knew such conversation led to a lot more talking, which in turn meant they ate less. Chinese takeout, though unfamiliar, was far too delicious to be wasted.

Kit expected Sasha to bring up the kiss they'd shared that morning, but Sasha remained silent on the topic. While he was grateful in a way, Kit was dying of suspense. He wished Sasha would just get to the point… or maybe he was waiting until bedtime, which was sort of worse.

Kit paused for a second and looked sharply at Sasha, who, luckily for Kit, was staring out the window at a panther-like black cat that had seemingly materialized on the sill. Were they still sharing a bed, and did that kiss mean more? *Damn*, Kit thought in frustration. He had fucked people with less thought given to the act. He could not figure out exactly what was wrong with him. Why was he thinking about one measly kiss and worrying about sharing a bed with some guy with an attitude problem?

The sharing-a-bed problem materialized after dinner, when they'd finished feeding the leftovers to the multiplying population of felines. After changing in the bathroom, as customary, Kit slowly made his way to the bedroom. Sasha was already there, picking up his nightclothes to take with him to the bathroom.

"You know you can change here," Kit said suddenly, feeling the need to speak. "You must have changed here before I dropped in. I can go to the sitting room while you change."

Sasha froze and turned around slowly, looking at Kit with a frown. He narrowed his eyes, contemplating something before he nodded in understanding. What Sasha had understood, or thought he had understood, was beyond Kit's comprehension. "Why don't you…?" Sasha said, and then he stopped.

"Leave the house and leave you alone?" Kit finished wearily. "Yeah, I've heard that before and…."

"I was going to suggest…," Sasha started, then stopped again, his face taking on a more thoughtful look. "Never mind," he said with a shake of his head. "Same sleeping arrangements as last night or should I expect more?"

"You want a written invitation?" Kit asked at a loss of anything else to say. "Wait… more?" he added, catching onto the last word a little too late.

"I was asking whether you wanted to…." Here Kit watched as a distinct blush rose onto Sasha's pale cheeks, which was in his opinion totally out of place with his self-assured pose. "If you…." He sighed and glanced away for a moment. "At the risk of sounding like a girl, I should say, you kissed me in the morning."

"I don't kiss girls," Kit said before his brain caught up with what Sasha meant. "Sorry. I meant, I know." Kit wondered where this was leading.

"I…," Sasha started and stopped, his eyes fixed on Kit, and Kit realized Sasha was waiting for him to make a move or say something. While this was not the best possible time to do anything, Kit was feeling distinctly speechless as he walked over to Sasha. He reached with both his hands and cupped Sasha's face, again marveling at just how cool it felt as he stood on his toes for the kiss.

Sasha allowed the kiss briefly before pulling back and breaking away, leaving Kit feeling confused. "Should I have done something else?" he asked, wondering if he sounded as needy as he felt.

"No," said Sasha as he tried to step away. "I don't think this is a good idea." He looked meaningfully over his shoulder at the bed that was two steps behind them.

"Why not?" asked Kit and gave Sasha a push, making him stagger back and sit heavily on the bed. The next move would have been for

Kit to sit on his lap as he had done with his "picks," but he didn't think Sasha's leg was strong enough to take his weight. Kit was afraid of coming across too forward or too cheesy. Not everyone wanted to be treated like a porn star.

He chose to sit next to Sasha on the bed, a little closer than he normally would. Kit desperately needed to know if Sasha had any condoms stashed on him if they proceeded any further, but was unwilling to break the mood.

Sasha made to move back, but Kit leaned forward for a kiss, which helped Sasha change his mind, and they met halfway across the bed. Sasha, Kit discovered, was an excellent kisser when he put his mind to it. It was not that Kit had never been kissed, not that the sort of people he fucked were really into kissing, but with Sasha it was an all-new experience. He nibbled Kit's lower lip, sucked it gently before venturing further in, with sweeps of his cool tongue that made Kit's toes curl. Sasha shifted forward, pushing Kit so he was forced to lie back on the bed, and Kit was more than ready to let him take the lead. Apparently Sasha was very used to taking command, since he used his hand to pull Kit's T-shirt up and over his head expertly.

"You top?" Kit asked before he could help it.

"Why, don't I look it?" Sasha asked with a dose of irony in his voice.

"No, just that...." Kit tried to think of a way of pointing out that, in his experience, older guys who shacked up with young men didn't expect the young men to top them, when Sasha smiled slightly.

"Cory was a total bottom," he suddenly said, making Kit wonder if Sasha had any mind-reading powers. "I was uncomfortable with the situation since he was old enough to be my f—" Sasha broke off and looked away, and Kit figured that if he didn't act fast, the mood would be broken.

He pushed his T-shirt aside and pulled Sasha down for another kiss. Sasha returned it enthusiastically, diving into Kit's mouth, his hand supporting the back of Kit's head. Kit let himself drown in the kiss as his hands reached for Sasha and pulled him firmly on top. There was a moment when they both struggled to pull their legs up off the floor without breaking the kiss before they finally solved the problem and Kit had a solid, if somewhat skinny, body pressing him down into the bed. Kit moved his hips experimentally, letting his erection brush against Sasha's thigh. Though they were both almost fully dressed, Kit knew Sasha could feel the hardness through the layers of their clothing, and he knew if he shifted just right he would be able to feel whether Sasha was reciprocating.

Kit slid an arm down toward Sasha's waistband, but Sasha moved just then, almost accidentally—maybe he was moving a tad too fast. After all, His Royal Highness was almost a diva. Instead, he reached for the edge of Sasha's sweater and tugged it up.

"No!" Sasha pulled away so fast Kit was sure he heard the air move.

"What," said Kit, confused. "What did I do?"

"Nothing," Sasha said as he relaxed a little, though he appeared embarrassed by the outburst. "It's just that I don't like anyone to see...."

"You know," said Kit, wondering how to phrase the sentence "people don't fuck fully clothed" into something Sasha-presentable when Sasha sighed and looked away.

"Just don't say anything," said Sasha as he sat back and tugged off his sweater skillfully in a single move, using his good arm.

"Oh," said Kit, half sitting up, as he took in the sight. "Wow."

Kit reached for the silver scars on Sasha's "bad" side, as he had started to call it. The scars started from his upper arm—or what was left of it—up his shoulder, made their way across the side of his chest, under his armpit, and ended somewhere under the waistband of his slacks. Even more shockingly, Sasha's ribs stood out, his breastbone stuck out, and Kit swore he could see Sasha's backbone right through his stomach. He knew the guy was skinny, but knowing and seeing it were two different things. If Sasha had sat on the street corner with his shirt off, someone would have called an ambulance, and it wouldn't have been because of his scars. While Kit didn't like fat men (though he did let them fuck him), Sasha was at the other end of the spectrum. Kit's first impulse was to run to the kitchen to feed him.

Sasha bunched the sweater in his fist in a self-conscious gesture, holding it across his chest, looking embarrassed. "You asked for it," he said as he glanced away, and then after a brief look down, started to put the sweater back on.

"Don't," said Kit, reaching out and clasping Sasha's hand. "I'm sorry... I don't know what to say but...."

"But it seems to have killed the mood," said Sasha, gesturing toward Kit's crotch. "I know. Cory had the same problem when I came back from the hospital. He would get all apologetic after I took my clothes off and would try to pretend he really wanted me, but you could see that he was feeling guilty as hell and that was the only reason he was hanging around."

"I'm not Cory," Kit protested sharply. "And anyway, I think the mood was lost when you said no and pulled away and I... I can count your ribs from across the room."

"I know you're not Cory," Sasha snapped back, ignoring the rest of the sentence. "But the thing is, I don't think you'd want this to continue any more than...."

"I want it to continue," Kit said, reaching out and touching the scars. The skin felt smooth, almost silky, and so fragile he was sure if he pressed down too hard, his fingers would break right through. He had thought scars to be ugly and, well, dark, but Sasha's were strange and uneven. He wondered if the skin there would taste differently, if it would feel different to the tongue, but didn't think it was the right time to try something like that. He sat up straight and looked at Sasha. "There, now I've seen your scars and the world didn't end. What next, you missing a ball or a part of your dick as well?"

Sasha looked away for a second, and Kit could see a faint smile curving his mouth. "No, I can safely say I'm still fully functional down there," he said. "It's just an arm and a leg."

"You know," said Kit as he reached out and caught Sasha's face, forcing him to look into Kit's eyes. "There're always these half-assed things... like that you were in an accident and you were with Cory and he felt guilty... but I want to know just what the heck happened."

"You mean you don't know?" Sasha appeared surprised.

"I don't know," Kit said with emphasis.

"Took you long enough to ask," Sasha said without much drama. "It's the first thing most people ask."

"I've been known to wait for the right moment," Kit said flippantly.

Sasha sighed as he let his shoulders slump, then started to get off the bed, dropping his sweater to the floor as he did. "You want the long story or the short one?"

"The full story?" said Kit, standing up. "Can't you just, you know, tell it while on the bed or something?"

Sasha grimaced. "I'm going to need help with this. Perhaps a little Dutch courage?"

"Is that a saying from where you come from?" Kit asked, though the saying was somewhat familiar.

Sasha stopped slithering off the bed to stare at Kit with a puzzled expression. "What?"

"Er…," said Kit, wondering what he had said wrong. "Well, you know, I know you can't be from around here because you have this weird name and what you said, Dutch…."

"You thought I was from…." Sasha looked like he did not know whether to laugh or to cry. "Well, that's interesting." He looked at Kit and sighed. "Both my parents were of Russian descent but I was born and raised here." He stared at Kit for a little longer and rolled his eyes. "I know I don't have an accent or anything but… do you do this intentionally because someone told you sounding like an airhead makes you look cute—it doesn't, by the way—or are you just naturally stupid?"

Kit couldn't figure out what he had said wrong to receive the wrath of Sasha. "What," he said with a scowl. "Russia is… like close by, isn't it?" he asked.

"Oh yes, and its capital is called Dutch," Sasha said sotto voce. "Now I really need a drink," he murmured, getting off the bed completely. "Good thing I planned ahead for this. Where is my gym bag?"

CHAPTER
ELEVEN

THEY wound up on the sofa, a bedsheet and a bottle of clear liquid between them. He watched Sasha break the seal expertly, holding the bottle steady between his knees, and then tip back the bottle and take a sip, and pass it on to Kit.

"Vodka." Kit had never tasted the stuff straight; it had always been mixed up with something or another, but he did know enough to recognize the "burn." There was a slightly lemony flavor to it, a sweetness at the back of his throat as the liquid burned a path down to his stomach.

"Limonnaya. Polish, though most people think we discovered this," Sasha said as he took a swig out of the bottle and passed it back to Kit. "I'm committing a deadly sin by drinking out of a bottle like this, but who cares."

He glanced at Kit, a sort of sideways glance with a look that said he considered Kit not to know any better, and for a moment, Kit was tempted to get up and walk away. Kit was used to insults; he had no choice but to get used to them in the company of rich old men who tended to see him as merchandise and handled him accordingly. But getting the same treatment from Sasha was somehow different. He had been kissing the guy not five minutes ago, and now Sasha was being mean to him.

Sasha must have noticed Kit's look, for he bumped his elbow gently against Kit's rib cage and shook his head. "That was uncalled for, I apologize," Sasha said in his cultured voice. "I hide my insecurities by making other people feel bad. Hit me on the head if I do that again." Kit opened his mouth to mention it was the first proper apology he'd received from Sasha, when he realized the arm that had bumped his ribs ended two inches below the elbow. Sasha's amputated arm had never been out in the open since Kit had entered the house. Sasha changed in the bathroom, showered alone (it wasn't like they'd ever showered together), and wore long-sleeved sweaters or shirts with sleeves long enough to cover his stump.

Kit reached forward slowly and touched the stump. Up close, the skin seemed to have been pulled up around the end, and there was a ragged line near the edge. Sasha was silent as Kit felt the thick scar, waiting for a reaction. Kit looked at Sasha's face and saw through the mask of disinterest. His anxiety was noticeable. "Did it hurt?" he blurted out.

"Not really," Sasha said, reaching for the bottle and pulling it free of Kit's grasp. "I think everything else hurt more."

"You were going to tell me how it happened," Kit said slowly. He looked quickly at Sasha, whose head was tipped back as he swallowed the contents of the bottle, and added, a tad hastily, "Or we could just get drunk, if you don't want to talk about it." Which was complete bullshit. Kit really, really wanted to hear all about the accident, but he didn't want to force Sasha, who was behaving in a more human fashion than he'd ever done.

"Admit it," Sasha said as he handed the bottle back to Kit. "You're dying to know every single detail."

"I am," Kit admitted. "But I can wait."

"I don't normally talk about it," Sasha said with a shrug. "That's why I brought the drink, loosens the tongue." However, he didn't start to talk straightaway, as Kit had hoped he would.

"So, do you want to drink more before you tell me your life story?" Kit asked, holding out the bottle. Really, there was waiting and then there was *waiting*.

"No," Sasha shook his head, refusing the offer. "I just don't know where to start," he said finally.

"Well," said Kit, trying hard not to sound like he was probing. "You once mentioned Cory asked you to move in with him and you were going to turn him down. But you didn't, right?" he said. "At least, I don't think you did…."

"No," Sasha agreed with an odd twist of his neck, which made him look like he was trying to both shake his head and nod at the same time. "I didn't."

"Well, you aren't exactly the person to hold back when making a conversation," Kit said pointedly, and Sasha had the grace to acknowledge it with a grimace and a slight tilt of his head. Again, Kit wondered if Sasha had ever modeled, since every one of his gestures seemed perfectly choreographed. If Kit didn't know better, he'd have guessed that someone had instructed him on just how much he had to turn his head to get the right effect.

"Cory asked me to move in with him during a dinner we had at The Twister." Here Sasha paused and looked at Kit, daring him to say he did not know what The Twister was, but Kit nodded. Hell, everyone knew what The Twister was, and none of Kit's "picks" had ever taken him anywhere close to that place. If Cory had taken Sasha there before they had made some regular arrangement, Sasha must be pretty hot in bed. Not that, Kit thought wistfully, Sasha ever did anything subpar.

"Anyway," said Sasha, continuing, "it was far too grand a place for me to tell him that I wasn't planning on a long-term relationship with him. He was too old for me and didn't last that long in bed." He gave a derisive snort. "His favorite movie was *Pretty Woman*, for crying out loud, and we used to watch it every other week for fun." Kit had no idea what Sasha was referring to, but he didn't think it was a movie about anything blowing up. "Cory was very nice, I know, but really, in bed, he was such a bore. He just laid there and seemed to think of his company while I…." He broke off and looked at Kit as if to see if he was listening. "I thought I could do better, even though…." Here Sasha reached for the bottle, then broke away to finish the sentence. "Well, I never did and never will, I guess."

Sasha held up his hand to silence Kit, who was about to tell Sasha he still looked stunning with his scars. Kit bet Sasha must have been gorgeous without them. If Sasha had wanted to, he could have had anyone, in Kit's opinion.

"Back on topic," Sasha continued. "I didn't turn him down then, told him that I'd think about it, and I think Cory thought I was going to say yes. He invited me to this outing with him the next day. To one of his labs out of town. We were going in one of his new cars, a stupid antique he was proud of, some right-hand drive car he rarely drove. He thought it'd be fun to drive down and, after he'd settled the business there, take some time off, enjoy, and drive back late."

"Enjoy what?" Kit asked, wondering. It wasn't like Cory needed to take Sasha to a wayside motel to fuck if he was taking Sasha to The Twister. That place always had photographers from celebrity rags outside, just in case someone important walked by, and Cory wasn't exactly Brad Pitt. And really, Kit couldn't see anyone being stupid enough to take His Royal Highness to a cheap motel unless they wanted to be beheaded.

"Some theme park, I think," Sasha said with a wave of his arm. "Anyway, never got to see it because Cory got held back with some problem or another, and by the time it was over, it was too late. We decided to drive back because I had lectures the next day and Cory had work."

Kit peeked at Sasha, whose face appeared so drawn out just then it looked scary. "That's when it happened," he guessed.

"Cory took a company car from the car pool," Sasha said, his voice devoid of emotion. "He later said it was the car, but really, I think he fell asleep behind the wheel. I don't know, I wasn't watching him. I was pissed at having wasted my day lounging about while he was attending all those meetings, when I could have been doing something else. In hindsight, I shouldn't have gone with him since he thought it meant I wanted to move in with him. I just wanted to find the right time to tell him without sounding ungrateful, because Cory is... was this really great guy."

Sasha dropped his head, almost folding himself in two, and Kit put a hesitant arm around his shoulders. When Sasha didn't try to break free, Kit grew bolder, pulling Sasha closer to him. Sasha let Kit stroke his shoulder comfortingly.

"It was hot, the air conditioning wasn't working, and I had the window rolled down, arm on the door, looking out, so I didn't even see what happened. One minute we were cruising along, sort of fast but it was night and the roads were clear, and in the next, I remember, the car sort of swayed, the tires screeched and slammed hard into a... wall... I think it was a wall, just ploughed through it, really." Sasha's voice seemed to dry out, and Kit didn't even ask him to go on. Wordlessly, Kit took another mouthful of the vodka, and balanced the bottle on his knee while holding on to Sasha with his other hand. Sasha leaned back toward Kit, shivering slightly, probably freezing in the cold air.

Sasha hadn't bothered to put on his sweater again, and the bedsheet they had dragged with them was bundled up in a corner. Kit hastily put the bottle down, took the bedsheet, and wrapped it around both of them, making sure Sasha was covered. Sasha had so little insulation on him, Kit wasn't surprised that he seemed to get cold at normal room temperature.

"So it was a car crash," said Kit without much inflection. He had figured out it was some accident and Cory had been involved. Somehow that knowledge was so anticlimactic, he wondered if it was worth hearing. But at least he knew why Cory had felt responsible for the accident.

"That's not the best part," Sasha said ironically as he almost unconsciously leaned against Kit, seeking warmth. "Where's the bottle?" he asked, and Kit picked it up off the floor and handed it over, wondering whether Sasha was going to get drunk before he finished. Sasha wasn't exactly a heavyweight, and didn't look the type to hold his drink. Kit hesitantly wound an arm around Sasha's shoulders and was surprised when Sasha didn't protest.

"What happened next?" Kit asked, despite his promise to himself that he wouldn't probe. He was far too interested in knowing what had happened for him to just wait it out.

"I must have passed out," Sasha said as he rested the bottle on his knee. It tilted dangerously, and Kit grabbed it before the contents spilled, and waited. "When I came to, I was stuck." He gave a half laugh, half groan, and Kit tightened his grip on Sasha's shoulder, hoping that would help. "My seat belt had twisted itself and I couldn't get it open, my arm had gotten caught between the car and wall—didn't even hurt but I couldn't get free. I turned around to look for Cory and he wasn't in the car. I couldn't even see properly, the car had hit the wall so hard on my side, it was torn open like a tin can and the metal and glass'd just ripped half my face off. Cory was standing outside, five feet away, not a scratch on him, telling me to get out."

There was a long pause, and Kit decided to wait it out. "He'd jumped out."

"I couldn't even understand what he meant," Sasha continued with another half sob. "I could smell the gasoline leaking then, I was stuck and couldn't get out and Cory was standing clear, just apologizing to me. I knew I couldn't get the damn seat belt off with one hand but if he could just get in…." Sasha broke off again, but continued in a low voice, "I screamed to Cory. I was so scared—didn't want to die and he was just there, too scared to come near in case the car caught fire, even when I was still trapped inside."

"It did catch fire," Kit surmised slowly.

"The driver of a truck passing by saved me," Sasha replied shortly. Kit's sentence had summed up the entire incident. "They have these fire extinguishers with them all the time, I suppose, and he was able to put out the fire and pull me out." He looked out the window again, though his body pressed against Kit hard. "I don't remember anything about it. When I came to it was almost three weeks later." Sasha paused and looked at Kit, then seemed to realize he could elaborate on the point. "They kept me on pain medication. I think I came to once in a while, but mostly I can't remember anything apart from flashes of pain and the sleep. I mostly remember Kevin… my brother screaming his head off at me, telling me how I should be more careful because my father had just undergone a bypass surgery and didn't need to be bothered and…."

"Supportive, wasn't he," Kit said sarcastically.

"He was being himself," Sasha said mildly. "I don't think they… my family… wanted me anyway, and everything I did just seemed to cause them more and more problems. Kevin's a broker and was probably annoyed I'd dragged him away from all his clients. Then he met Cory and figured out who he was and freaked out."

"So you moved in with Cory," Kit asked, knowing he was jumping the gun but still curious.

"Something like that," Sasha said. "It wasn't as if I had a choice. When I came to the next time, there was this doctor telling me I had lost my arm, that I might not walk again, that I needed skin grafts and I needed this and that and... I was all alone. No one to... I didn't think I could survive by myself."

Sasha was getting sloppy, acting slightly drunk, and Kit kept the bottle away from them. Perhaps they both had had enough.

"Then Cory showed up, eaten away by guilt, and offered to pay all my medical bills." Sasha looked around for the bottle, saw it on the floor, and motioned to Kit to pass it to him. "I hadn't even thought of the hospital bill until then, and all of a sudden I might as well have to sell my kidney to pay for it. The insurance covers only so much. Cory was there with the money, and he was under the impression I'd already agreed to move in with him, so it was bad of him to turn me down now that I was a wreck and he felt responsible. I suppose...."

Kit took the bottle despite his earlier misgivings, and took a swig of it to keep the story going. He didn't even feel the burn this time, and decided he was also on the way to becoming comfortably drunk.

"It was guilt all over," Sasha said. "I wasn't the person Cory wanted. I was damaged and he was too decent a guy to turn me away, so he hung on." Sasha gave an odd laugh. "Hell, we both hung on. Cory couldn't bear to look at my body, but once in a while he would feel I needed to be told I was appreciated—I felt I needed to put out something because he was there paying for my therapy and my skin grafts so I would try—but only when I was high on my painkillers and...." He shook his head. "After a while we gave up. I was going to leave him...," Sasha said softly. "But I didn't know how and... he was so guilt ridden. I don't think he wanted to let me go... it was... hell until...." Sasha looked at Kit. "You came along and messed with our life."

Kit didn't point out that it was messed up either way, and he was not fully responsible for the whole thing. It was just not fair, but he didn't think Sasha was in any frame of mind for cohesive arguments. He turned to Sasha to call it a night. Sasha had turned his head, almost tilted over backward, and was watching Kit with a strange intensity he had not seen from him before.

"What?" Kit asked defensively.

"Well," said Sasha in a clear, controlled voice, which was at odds with his actions. "I was wondering what your day rate was going to be," he said finally.

"Day rate?" Kit asked, puzzled.

"Let me try another phrasing," Sasha said as he sat up straighter and looked at Kit properly. "What do you want from me?"

"I don't know," Kit said, thinking sluggishly. "We only have a few options with your leg. And we don't have any condoms or proper lube." Kit started to ask Sasha if he had any particular position in mind, when Sasha smiled. It was a proper smile and the first Kit had ever seen on Sasha's face. It took his breath away, literally, since his face lit up, coming alive in a second. For a moment Kit was completely floored and was glad Sasha did not smile like that often. It made it hard for Kit to think straight.

"You're here," Sasha said clearly, though when he tried to sit up he tipped backward. "I'll give you something for being here," he added. "So, what will it be…?"

"I want a pony," Kit decided, still feeling floored by the smile. Or was it the vodka?

"No," Sasha said as he leaned—fell forward. "Scare away cats, you know."

"You and your stupid cats," Kit mumbled, thinking seriously past his tumbling thoughts. "How about a TV," he said. "We can get a big TV and…."

"That all you want?" Sasha asked, looking puzzled. His mouth worked silently. He probably wanted to add a few more comments, but eventually words seemed to fail him and his eyes fluttered closed.

Too bad you need to be drunk to smile like an angel, Kit thought. Or maybe he said it out loud, since Sasha blinked in surprise. "You can't sleep here," Kit decided, and got to his feet. The floor tilted and he fell back clumsily to the sofa, making Sasha snort. "I'd like to see you get up," Kit challenged, but Sasha simply shook his head and sank down into the sofa, all loose limbs and tangled bedsheet.

Kit supposed he really should have left Sasha on the sofa, but he knew the bedroom was slightly warmer than the sitting room. Finally, he managed to drag both their drunk asses into bed without too many mishaps. He was sure he would have a doorknob-shaped bruise on his hip, but Sasha was still in one piece. In the bedroom, Kit hesitated, wondering if he should undress Sasha or let him sleep in his clothes.

Sasha opened his eyes and regarded Kit with drunken amusement. "Go ahead," he slurred, once again demonstrating his mind-reading powers. "You might as well undress me."

Wondering if this was a prelude to sex, Kit reached for his own T-shirt, but Sasha simply rolled his eyes at that.

"I'm too out of it to do anything but sleep," he told Kit. "But you might as well take a look. I know you want to."

Kit shrugged to show his indifference when in reality, he did want to have a look at the rest of Sasha's body. With that in mind, Kit decided to remove all of Sasha's clothes.

After all, His Royal Highness was simply dressed in slacks, and Kit had two good reasons for undressing him. One, Kit didn't think silk slacks were meant to be slept in, and two, he was curious. He wanted to know how far the injuries went and how bad they were. Kit knew how sensitive Sasha was about his scars, and he didn't want to flinch when he saw them. The best way to do so was by checking them out beforehand, and Sasha had given him permission to look.

He undid the belt and the fly button, pulled down the zip, and drew down Sasha's trousers easily. Sasha didn't wear tight clothes; he seemed to prefer loose ones that hid the shape of his body. Kit half held his breath as he undressed his roommate—or was it bedmate—and revealed his body to the light.

It was not as bad as he had expected. In fact, compared to the rest of Sasha's body, there was no extensive damage there apart from a long scar on his lower leg and some twisted flesh on his upper thigh. Perhaps it was more serious than it appeared on the outside, but to Kit's untrained eyes, it was not cringe-inducing. Sasha's legs were rather nice, unlike the rest of him. They were surprisingly well muscled—then again, Kit reasoned, Sasha probably did do a lot of leg exercises in the pool. Kit wondered what it would be like to have those long legs wrapped around his waist, and that drew his attention to Sasha's dick. Even limp, lying in a tangle of pubic hair slightly darker than the hair on his head, Sasha's dick was large, and Kit wondered what it would look like erect. Both of them were far too drunk to even contemplate doing anything, so Kit settled for pulling the covers over Sasha's nude form.

"Well at least I know what size condoms to get," he told himself and looked up guiltily, thankful Sasha had passed out. With a start Kit realized Sasha was wide awake, his eyes clear, watching Kit's actions the way a cat might watch a mouse before leaping on it. "Get some sleep," Kit said, blushing uncomfortably as he reached for Sasha. "We're both going to regret this tomorrow."

Then, on an impulse, Kit walked up to the head of the bed and kissed Sasha on his lips lightly before going to switch off the lights. As usual, he left the light on in the sitting room. It was becoming a habit.

When Kit crawled into the narrow space left for him between Sasha and the wall, Sasha shifted to make some room and drawled, "You're such a prize. Easy on the eyes, not afraid of kissing…. What more can a man ask for?"

Kit did not question the statement, though for some reason that last comment disturbed him. Kit didn't like whatever Sasha was trying to imply. Or maybe it was just drunk rambling.

Kit woke up in the middle of the night—or was it early morning—and reached for Sasha, then stopped. As usual, Sasha was fast asleep with his back to Kit, and Kit felt unusually hurt by the display of rejection.

CHAPTER
TWELVE

KIT stared hard at the brand new TV in the middle of the sitting room and then back at the movers who had brought it in.

"Are you sure it's supposed to be here?" he asked for the third time. "Maybe you got the wrong house."

"Nope," the guy replied as he walked to the door. "There's even a note to the house number and a scribble about how to recognize it from the overgrown main drive."

"Oh, okay," said Kit, wondering why Sasha had decided to order a huge flat-screen wall-mounted TV with a satellite connection. Not that it was a bad buy or anything, but it was hard to imagine Sasha as a TV-watching sort of person. Kit wondered if he should pay the movers or at least tip them or offer them a drink. Not that there was anything to offer other than the leftover vodka or tap water. Luckily for Kit, the men had another appointment and had to depart immediately, leaving Kit standing at the garden gate, trying hard to act as though it was an everyday occurrence for grown men to squeeze through the half-open waist-high gate.

He walked back into the house, wondering what to do. The answer was easy: watch TV, of course. But the question remained as to why Sasha had all of a sudden decided to buy one. Perhaps it was Sasha's way of letting Kit know something was about to change. He picked up the remote and sat down on the sofa. The men had also set up a cable connection and shown Kit how to use the multiple remotes they'd left on the mantle. Maybe....

Kit had expected sex—well, regular or semiregular sex from Sasha after they'd had the "talk" the other night. After all, they'd kissed, gotten drunk together, and would have proceeded to do more if they hadn't practically passed out together on the small bed. There had been nothing.

Sasha behaved the same as he always did—cold and distant. Not that Kit had noticed for about two days after their talk as he recovered from a vodka-induced hangover. He had expected Sasha to be angry at waking up naked, but he hadn't commented on that either. But Sasha still undressed in the bathroom, though he was a little relaxed in his dress code, and tended to wear a short-sleeved T-shirt and a pair of boxers to bed. A bed they shared but didn't do anything in, apart from sleep. Kit wondered if he should make the first move as he had done earlier, but amazingly enough it seemed Sasha didn't even have time to breathe.

He was either at his lawyer's office or at Cory's company when he was not at the gym and Kit could see just how much of a toll it was taking on Sasha's skinny ass. Kit knew enough to understand that Sasha was unsure of the whole issue, and he didn't want to worsen the situation by making a move while Sasha was distracted by other concerns.

As Kit opened the front door, eyes glued to the flat-screen monitor, he heard the house phone ring. Hoping it was either Eddy or Sasha calling him, Kit rushed to the phone and picked it up, to a "…get it," from Sasha.

"You know, people usually say stuff like hello, this is so-and-so speaking," Kit replied offhandedly as he perched on the side of the table close by.

"Did you get the home entertainment system?" Sasha asked, ignoring Kit.

"Just now," Kit answered, thinking Sasha spoke as if he'd heard the phrase "home entertainment system" from the salesperson and was simply repeating it, without much idea of what it was. He sometimes came across as more technologically challenged than Kit was, and that was saying a lot.

"Good," Sasha said shortly. "That should keep you busy for a while."

"So it's for me?" Kit queried in surprise.

"Of course it's for you." Sasha sounded frustrated. "You asked for it." Kit frowned, trying to remember when exactly he had asked for a TV. "About the time you asked for a pony," Sasha supplied, realizing Kit had a hole in his memories.

"Well," said Kit thoughtfully. "A pony is way cooler." Which probably meant Sasha remembered giving Kit permission to undress him as well, which was a relief.

"Whatever," snapped Sasha, and hung up on Kit so abruptly he was left holding the receiver, listening to the dial tone.

With a shrug, Kit put down the receiver and looked around the house, wondering why exactly Sasha had felt the need to give Kit a present—or a bribe. While Kit knew no house was complete without a TV, he still couldn't see the point of getting one, unless…. He smirked; Sasha wanted something in return. In Kit's experience, that something was what nearly everyone expected of him—sex, and Kit knew he had been waiting long enough for *that*.

Kit rushed to the bedroom and pulled open the second drawer where Sasha had stashed the cash, pulled out a couple of bills, and jogged to the convenience store. The store was usually manned by a part-time college student trying to earn an extra buck by working the till, and Kit wondered what the kid's face would look like when he tallied up the bill for Kit's condoms and lube.

WHICH was all for nothing.

Sasha came back at one in the morning, and fell into bed next to Kit with half-dried hair from the shower, and Kit wondered if he should have stuck the condoms on a flagpole and waved it under Sasha's nose for him to notice. Perhaps leaving them on the top drawer of the study table wasn't the most subtle of moves, but at this rate they would both die of old age before anything remotely sexual happened between the two of them.

The next morning Kit rolled over and opened his blurry eyes to see Sasha standing in the middle of the room getting dressed. Kit was far too sleepy to get up as he lay there, head lolling sideways, watching as Sasha pulled on his shirt efficiently and buttoned it up one-handed with practiced ease. Next he reached for his tie, something he had started to wear when going to meet his lawyer, when he noticed Kit watching him.

Sasha stopped what he was doing to scowl at Kit, which meant whatever was wrong was Kit's fault. "What?" he asked as he stood there, leaning against the table for balance. "I have a meeting with my lawyer again, and hopefully this will be the last of them."

"If you dress so fast, why does it take you ages to get dressed when you are in the bathroom?" Kit asked sleepily. "And that day at the gym, it took you forever to come out of the changing room...," he observed as he propped himself up on his elbows. He wasn't expecting a real answer to such a question, but when he looked at Sasha's face, he was surprised to see two red spots burning on either cheek as Sasha turned away with an expression of embarrassment.

"What?" Kit asked, sleepiness sliding away as he sat up curiously.

"Nothing," Sasha snarled, or attempted to snarl, though it wasn't very effective when he was also blushing like a virgin bride on her wedding night.

"What in the world did you do there?" Kit asked in surprise, feeling a little pleased that something was bothering Sasha to the point he looked uncomfortable. That did not happen every day, and he was enjoying the feeling of power that came with it.

"I...." Sasha swallowed, glanced away then, and grimaced. "Forget it," he said as he started to move toward the sitting room. "It's no big deal."

"I'm not the one who is acting like it is," Kit pointed out.

"I'm not either," Sasha snapped, obviously uncomfortable with the topic. "Let me just... get ready to go. I'm late as it is."

"You came in late last night," Kit offered, wondering if he sounded too domestic. "You don't have to go in early as well."

"It's not like I'm doing a job," Sasha replied, making a face. "You aren't exactly doing anything, but I suppose I can't expect anything from you. I, however, need to finish up this annoying business of clearing up the will and get a move on, so... now, if you'd excuse me...."

"Don't you say 'excuse me' when someone is blocking your way or something?" Kit inquired as he moved to intercept Sasha's way.

"I meant," Sasha said with mock patience as he maneuvered around Kit. "I am late and do not have time for this conversation with you."

"What conversation?" Kit asked, honestly puzzled. "I just wanted to know why you were taking so long in the bathroom to dress when you dress so fast when you are outside. Is it because there isn't enough room for you to move your arm or...?" He grinned as he thought of something else. "Were you jerking off in there or something?"

What he hadn't expected was the blush that took over Sasha's face almost like he were on fire or had some sort of flash fever. "What, wait," said Kit in excitement. "I was just joking. You jerked off at the gym," Kit said in surprise, coming fully awake. "With all those instructors and all and... and the changing room door is plywood... man...." He wondered why he was so surprised. Kit had had sex with people in the oddest places, so he wasn't one to throw stones, but the image of calm, collected Sasha masturbating was as alien as Eddy in a nurse's costume. Kit wondered why he was making such a big deal out of it—why they both were, when it was obvious the two of them were adults with plenty of hands-on experience in this sort of thing.

Sasha looked away, adjusting his tie one-handed as he moved farther out of the bedroom, and Kit could not help but follow him about. Kit winced as his bare feet came into contact with the unexpectedly cold tiles of the sitting room, and walked toward Sasha who, uncharacteristically, was backing away. Not that Sasha was obvious about it. He managed to look semi-occupied getting dressed, pretending to search for something and avoiding Kit's eyes. Kit was a master of such evasion tactics, and subterfuge was easy to see through.

Kit found the whole situation hilarious. The opportunity to see someone as calm and collected as Sasha squirm a little made him feel good. Kit walked up to Sasha until he was standing right under his nose and said, very carefully, "What's the big deal about"—he slid his hand down and cupped Sasha's groin, which was a rather large handful—"getting some action by *yourself?*"

"Quit breathing on my face when you have morning breath," Sasha said as he took a step back, though his voice was not as firm as it should be, and Kit knew he hadn't imagined the slight twitch from his handful of genitals. Sasha would have been dead or paralyzed from below the waist to ignore Kit's hand between his legs.

"Fine," Kit said, tilting his head to the side so he wasn't breathing on Sasha, though he knew his breath wasn't that bad. It was not like his mouth was dry or anything, and really, from the way Sasha was acting, he might not have shared a bed with a lover, ever. But then again, Sasha, being His Royal Highness, probably did not have bad breath or... whatever, Kit thought as he slid his hand upwards, really feeling Sasha's goods and giving them a good squeeze.

Sasha's breath hitched and his body spasmed slightly, the way a person would had he received a sudden electric shock. "What are you—" he started, and then gasped again. Kit pressed his palm hard against the growing bulge. The black silk slacks Sasha wore slid over, framing the semi-erection perfectly. Kit worked it with his hand for a while.

Sasha was breathing hard, his hand hanging by his side, unsure as to whether he should touch Kit or not. Then, making up his mind, he lifted it and put it on Kit's chest.

Kit continued to massage Sasha's crotch, expecting to be shoved aside; it wouldn't be long before Sasha came to his prudish senses or rediscovered his inner monk and pushed Kit away. Instead, Sasha closed his hand around Kit's ratty T-shirt and pulled him close until they were chest to chest and swooped down, closing his lips over Kit's aggressively. Kit needed no further invitation to dive into the kiss, his hand still between Sasha's legs, his free arm half winding around the other man, almost holding him up. Sasha seemed to have forgotten that, just a few minutes ago, he had been complaining about bad breath. His tongue plunged into Kit's mouth without any hesitation. Kit let him in, feeling a shiver of excitement run through his body as Sasha kissed him expertly, pulling him closer so they were pressed against each other. Kit knew Sasha could feel Kit's erection pressed against his thigh, and though Sasha did not break the kiss, the way he moved his leg was a sure indicator. Kit pulled down the zip of the black slacks, his lips still locked with Sasha's. His hand slid through to encounter silk underwear.

Kit pulled away reluctantly and pushed Sasha back until the back of his legs hit the edge of the sofa, causing Sasha to tumble backward with a definite lack of his usual grace. Kit half fell on Sasha, wincing as his knees hit the hard floor. He scooted forward, resting on his heels as he attacked Sasha's belt with some confusion.

"It's a clip-on," Sasha gasped, his voice almost gravelly with lust. "Under the buckle—there is a sort of lock…."

Kit followed the directions and found what he was looking for: a small latch, easily removable, designed for a one-handed man but apparently not for a desperate two-handed one. Kit almost broke a nail before he figured out he should pull it, not push it, and then the belt was off as he urgently attacked the top button. The trousers were off in a second, leaving only the underwear.

Sasha squirmed impatiently, his hand pulling at Kit frantically, and Kit broke off his ministrations to stand up and give a quick kiss before swooping down. He hiked up Sasha's shirt, feeling his stomach, wanting to explore more but not sure what it would entail. Anyway, he was eager to get to the "good stuff," and really, if Sasha was going to wear black silk boxers, he probably wanted to be molested.

Sasha's dick, when it was finally free of its confines, was erect, and Kit was slightly startled at its size. "Well, who's a big boy, now," he joked, shocked to realize his voice was none too steady.

Sasha mumbled something incoherent as Kit swiped at the head of his erection with his tongue, then leaned forward, his hand still under Sasha's shirt. He licked the head carefully before taking as much as possible into his mouth. Kit was practiced in the art of giving head, and his ability to suppress his gag reflex was well honed. Still, he had never tried deep-throating something as large as this. Not only was Sasha's penis long, it was also rather broad, and Kit was out of practice.

It didn't deter Kit much as he sucked in earnest, sliding his lips over his teeth, drawing back up only to catch his breath and nibble at the slit in a carefully practiced move that, he hoped, would make Sasha quiver. Kit was careful to hold Sasha's dick steady with a grip around the base and bob up and down slowly so he wouldn't choke.

After his initial vocal reaction, Sasha remained relatively quiet apart from a few grunts and several curses. His fingers closed around Kit's hair painfully, but he didn't push Kit's face in as some of his former marks used to. Kit used his tongue to feel the underside of his cock, pulling back, knowing from experience that if he did not give himself a break, his throat would get so sore afterward he would have trouble swallowing food.

Kit sat back a little and used his free hand to loosen the drawstring of his sweats and pushed his hand into the waistband. His erection was achingly hard, weeping clear fluid. Kit gripped it firmly, working himself as he resumed sucking Sasha. Sasha shouted something at Kit about him being close, which Kit ignored. He knew Sasha was close; he could read the signs and taste it on his tongue. He knew the moment Sasha started to come; his thighs locked on either side of his head. Sasha's hand pulled at Kit's hair so hard his eyes teared up, and his dick twitched on Kit's tongue. The next moment Kit's mouth was flooded with bittersweet fluid, which he swallowed hurriedly without giving it much thought. Still milking Sasha through the last of the aftershocks, Kit gave his own erection a few more pulls and came, gasping at the feeling.

Kit closed his eyes and rested his head on Sasha's knee, trying to catch his breath. He felt Sasha tug his hair insistently, and managed to scramble up the sofa on shaky knees until he was half lying on the other man. He tilted his head and looked at Sasha for a reaction, and was amused by what he saw. Sasha's face appeared to be more alive than at any other time he had seen it before, skin flushed, eyes shining.

Kit would never have pegged Sasha for a snuggler, but when he rested his head on Sasha's middle, Sasha didn't push him away. Instead he prodded Kit until he turned his head and bent down to capture his lips in a loose kiss. Kit could taste Sasha's come on his lips and knew Sasha could probably taste it too. However, His Royal Highness, who'd been complaining about bad breath not half an hour ago, didn't complain about the odd taste. In fact, he pulled out Kit's hand, which was still inside his sticky sweats, and experimentally licked one of his fingers clean.

Kit almost melted at the gesture; he loved getting his fingers licked, and for Sasha to do that was—sweet. He pressed his head against Sasha's chest and closed his eyes, listening to Sasha's heartbeat, feeling the afterglow. It was the sort of situation he loved to be in and didn't get to experience very often. As he was relaxing, however, almost drifting into a sleepy state, Sasha tapped him on the head, although not as hard as he normally would have done.

Kit sat up halfheartedly and blinked a little.

"I'm late," Sasha said, his voice softer. "Get off me."

Kit obliged so Sasha could get up, then dropped back onto the sofa and closed his eyes. He laid there while Sasha moved around, muttering something about having to change completely and being late, which he ignored easily. Kit continued to lie there comfortably despite his now-drying sweats as Sasha called a taxi and left. Half an hour later, Kit was contemplating whether to brush his teeth or go back to sleep, when the phone rang.

He sat up sleepily, wiped at his eyes to clear his vision, and stumbled toward the phone to pick it up. It was Sasha, and as usual, he had started to speak before Kit had placed the receiver against his ear. "… my briefcase," Sasha was saying when Kit finally figured which end went against his ear.

"Huh," he said intelligently.

"I said," Sasha said, sounding very impatient and a little pissed off, "I forgot my briefcase."

"Oh," said Kit, looking around, his brain refusing to process what he was hearing. "Okay."

"I want you to bring it to me," Sasha said.

"Oh," Kit said again, coming awake slowly.

"Are you high on something?" Sasha asked suspiciously. "On second thought, don't answer that. Now listen carefully, I'll tell you exactly what you have to do."

"Do I need a pen and paper?" Kit asked, only half joking.

"Can you write?" Sasha asked back sarcastically. "Alright, listen," he continued in the same tone. "I want you to bring my briefcase to my lawyer's office. Remember the building where you helped me down the steps? That one. Come to the ninth floor, office 170, and knock on the room that reads 'Conference Room'. Got it?"

"Yeah," Kit replied, already pushing down his sweats as he stood holding the phone with one hand. He didn't think Sasha would appreciate if he showed up in his nightclothes with dried semen stains on his crotch.

"And get a taxi," Sasha snapped. "Hurry."

Kit quickly changed into his outdoor clothes and rushed, taking the briefcase with him. He made it to the office in record time. He reached the door and gave it a brief knock, hearing raised voices inside. By the sound of it, there was an argument going on, and he was about to disturb it.

Kit tensed, hoping Sasha would not be in a bad mood when he opened the door. However, the person who answered the knock was not Sasha. It was someone Kit had hoped to never see again.

They both stared at each other for a moment, Kit feeling his blood drain from his face as he automatically held out the briefcase. Kit knew that in his lifestyle, there was always the chance he would run into one of his former marks in a social setting. However, he had not expected it to be that day.

"A—Andrew," Kit said, finding his voice first, thinking, *Of course, Andrew is still a stockbroker and still has shares in the company*. The last time he had seen Andrew, the middle-aged man had been furious, shouting at Kit to get out of his ruined car. A car ruined because Kit had given him a blow job while driving. Not that Andrew had been totally sober. Andrew had had a drinking problem, Kit remembered, not that he had minded at the time, though he'd had to put up with a lot of sob stories about family life while frolicking with Andrew in his inebriated state.

"Well, Sasha did say he was distracted when he left this morning," Andrew said, recovering as well. "I can see why."

"He doesn't know," Kit said sharply. "About us—" About any of them apart from Cory, his mind supplied, which he ignored.

"Fine," Andrew said, taking the briefcase. "I wasn't going to say anything." He shrugged. "I'm still married."

"Good," Kit said as he stepped back. "We've never met."

"Never," Andrew said with a nod before going back into the room. Kit stood there on the ankle-thick carpet, under the scrutiny of a suspicious secretary who luckily was too far away to hear anything, feeling the good mood of the day evaporate.

Kit couldn't remember how he'd exited the building; when he took in his surroundings, he was standing in front of Eddy's, staring blindly at the darkened shop. He could see his reflection in the dirt-smeared window, looking shocked and somewhat lost. Why Andrew, Kit wondered, why now? All his past sins seemed to be coming back to haunt him.

Kit had first met Andrew in a bar, nothing too seedy but nothing that screamed glamour either. Kit had spotted Andrew for what he was the moment the guy walked into the badly lit space.

Andrew was older than most of the clients who usually graced the place. Kit had estimated him to be in his midsixties, but had found out he was about a decade younger later on, during one of their "intimate" moments. Andrew had been dressed in a business suit, his wedding ring visible on his finger even from a distance, and had looked more relaxed than such a person normally would in a gay bar. Kit had watched him walk up to the bar and order a drink, then appraise the men and women dancing with frank curiosity.

Kit wasn't a person to pass up an opportunity; he had gulped down the last of his beer and slid over to the stool next to Andrew's without making it too obvious. He knew a mark when he saw one.

"Hi," he said with a smile. "Want some company?" That was suggestive enough without making him sound like a hooker picking up a john. Well, close enough.

Andrew had given Kit a once-over and nodded to show that Kit had met his approval. "Sure," he said. "Why not?"

"I'm Kit," he had said without any pretense. "I'm in between jobs." In the club, that meant Kit was out on the market for a new sugar daddy. He didn't know if Andrew understood the lingo, but it seemed Andrew was not all that naïve about the trade. Or he had done his homework before walking into the bar.

"What're you drinking?" Andrew asked as he signaled the bartender over.

"A Coke," Kit answered, knowing he needed to be sober from then on. Up close he could tell this drink was not Andrew's first drink for the night.

"A Coke for Kit." Andrew seemed to find the slight alliteration amusing. "And the same for me. Make it a double."

The bartender had looked like he was about to protest, then clamped his mouth shut. Waiting for their drinks to arrive, Andrew had turned around and given Kit a very pointed once-over. "So," he said conversationally. "Do you want to go out for a quickie?"

Kit hadn't choked on his drink, since he was used to such offers, but it had been close. "I don't put out on the first date," Kit told Andrew with a wink. "I'm not that easy." *Take a hint, you moron.* "Or that cheap." Kit knew from experience and from tips given to him by old pros that he should not be eager to act like a slut. After all, he was not an out-and-out hooker; he was just someone who picked up rich older guys from time to time. He also knew better than to duck into alleyways or backs of cars with people he had just met. The world was not that nice a place, and Kit was too street smart to forget that.

Andrew looked at Kit once more and apparently liked what he saw since he tossed back his drink and ordered another. And, Kit remembered none too fondly, Andrew had drunk consistently throughout their "relationship" and had talked nonstop in his drunken haze. Kit had learned more about the corporate world backstabbing and how fat and unappealing Andrew's wife was than he needed to know in a lifetime.

Finally, while it had been the disaster with a blow job in a car and dented hood that ended their agreement, it had been over for some time before then. Although Andrew was literally a bottomless pocket, his drinking had not made him an attractive catch. Still, Kit hadn't considered their agreement a bad thing; they had both gotten something out of it, Andrew a chance to explore his sexuality with a young boy while staying married, and Kit monetary compensation for putting up with him.

Until now.

Kit felt sick. Andrew hadn't questioned Kit about his past activities, and Kit hadn't told Andrew his life story. However, it was more than likely Andrew didn't expect Kit to be a sweet, innocent boy out for a good time. Kit didn't know what Sasha thought of him; true, Sasha had caught him in the act with Cody, but that did not confirm his lifestyle. He really shouldn't care about what Sasha thought of him, since Sasha was a cold bastard with a stick up his ass and an attitude that had people running away from him. Really, what was so great about Sasha that Kit wanted to stay with him?

Kit broke off his line of thought with a frown. *Stay with Sasha.* Since when did he want to stay with Sasha? As if that were a permanent thing. His Royal Highness would kick out his freeloading tenant any day now and....

"Aw, you're still closed, aren't you?" a girlish voice said to the right of Kit, and he whirled around in surprise. He looked down at the young girl with too much makeup, trying to jog his memory. Where had he seen her? He tried to remember as he took in her attire, a habit he'd developed since he worked in a clothing store. The black leggings and loose T-shirt were not familiar, but the belt she had looped around her slender waist was. She was one of those people who had bought a belt from Eddy's during their sale. Kit had even carried the packages up to her father's office. Kit narrowed his eyes, trying to remember her name....

"It's okay," she said with a nod. "I know you can't remember me."

"I never forget a good client," Kit said, slipping into his salesperson mode. "We'll be open soon, just closed for restocking."

"Hm," she said, unimpressed. "So what are you doing here, peeping through the window?"

"Just came by," Kit said with a shrug. "To... to see a friend, but he's got a meeting now." He indicated to the building across the road.

"Probably the same one as my dad." The girl rolled her eyes. "Those meetings take ages, I should know," she added. "So, you want to go to the arcade with me?"

Kit blinked down. Was the thirteen-year-old hitting on him? Didn't she know better than to go around talking to strangers? Despite her adult getup, she was either incredibly innocent about life or just very stupid. When he'd been her age, he had known better than to make suggestive remarks to older boys.

"Come on," she told him. "It'll be fun. You can play with me and we can come back when the meeting's over." She rolled her eyes. "It usually takes *hours*," she added.

Kit frowned. He did have the house key. However, he wanted a distraction, not time to sit on the sofa in front of the new TV and worry about Andrew.

"Sure," he said with a shrug. "Why not?"

He started to walk with her down town in the direction of his old apartment block. He knew exactly where they were headed. He was familiar with the area, having lived there for some time. The neighborhood was not exactly safe farther down, but just before the business district gave way to the squalor, there was an arcade, which was famous around the city for having some hard-to-find games and reasonable rates. "You are *paying*, aren't you?"

Two hours later, Kit was on the sidewalk standing next to Cassandra Nash, and yes, he could see why she hated her name, waiting for their respective men to come out.

"So what does your friend do?" Cassie asked.

"He's just gone to meet his lawyer," Kit answered evasively. Kit suddenly had a vision of Sasha walking out and ignoring Kit as he sat next to a little girl, dressed in what she considered to be the height of fashion. "Look," he said, trying to break the silence. "You should go up to your father's office. My friend—he might not come out just yet."

"It's okay," Cassie shrugged. "I don't have anything to do." Did she not even suspect Kit could be a psychotic killer preying on small girls? "What's his name?"

"Whose?" Kit asked absentmindedly. He gazed at the exit of the building across the street. The doorman had assured him no one matching Sasha's description had left the building; perhaps the meeting would take all day.

"Your friend's." Cassie sounded frustrated.

"Er—he's called Sasha—uh—Alexander, but…." Kit shrugged, feeling a little useless. "He's not exactly my friend," Kit added hesitantly, afraid Sasha would come out and be rude to his unexpected companion. "He's more like a…."

"Boyfriend," Cassie prompted.

"Landlord," Kit corrected.

"Oh." She looked disappointed. "I thought it was sort of like…." And then she looked up, her eyes lighting up as her father crossed the road to speak to them. Glad he had worn reasonably presentable clothes, Kit straightened up from his slouching position as Mr. Nash approached them.

"Mr. Nash," he said, noting the man relaxing as he came up closer.

"Kit, wasn't it," the man said, surprising Kit. "Works at the shop?"

"I'm surprised you remembered me, sir," Kit said cautiously.

"In my business, I have to remember all the faces I come across," Mr. Nash said. "Thank you for taking care of my daughter." There was an underlying threat to it, which was hard to miss. *Lay a hand on her and I'll kill you*, it said.

"I am waiting for a friend," Kit replied. "Ninth floor, lawyer's office." There, now he had a reason for hanging around, and a respectable friend who was at a corporate lawyer's office.

Mr. Nash gave Kit a cursory nod at that, but seemed more suspicious of Kit than his daughter was. Though annoying, Kit could understand parents being protective of their children.

"He's waiting for his boyfriend," Cassie supplied, probably catching on to her father's mood.

Mr. Nash flicked his eyes down to his daughter, then up to Kit again. "Why don't you go to the car?" he said as he handed over a key ring to the girl. "I'll be along shortly."

Kit was sure Mr. Nash was going to threaten him once Cassie was out of hearing range, but all he did was thank Kit for looking after his daughter. Politely, and in a tone that said he hoped it would never happen again.

"I've got to go," Kit replied with a shrug, seeing Sasha emerge from the building. Sasha flicked his eyes across the street, meeting Kit's gaze squarely. Kit nodded at the bristling older man and casually strolled across the street to Sasha.

Sasha appeared to be as composed as ever, though his eyes fixed briefly on Mr. Nash over Kit's shoulder. "What are you doing here?" he asked.

"Waiting for you," Kit answered, pulling his hand out of his pocket. "So, you finished for the day?"

Sasha did not bother to reply. Instead he turned around and started to walk along the pavement in his familiar shuffling gait. "There is a place around the corner where we can get something to eat," he said.

Kit smiled a little to himself, running to keep up with Sasha. When Kit had caught up, he slowed, walking so close his hand brushed against Sasha's.

Sasha turned casually and thrust the briefcase into Kit's hand. "If you want to hold something, you can hold on to this," he said.

It took Kit several seconds to realize Sasha was referring to holding hands, and he smiled at the thought. "Who said romance was dead?" he said as he passed the briefcase to his other hand and took Sasha's hand in his.

Sasha looked at Kit with a scowl, but he didn't pull his hand free. Kit decided not to think too much as they walked. He would not think of why he wanted to say things about romance and hold hands, even if it was only to tease His Royal Highness. He would not think about why he liked being around Sasha when Sasha was such a cold bastard.

He would just go with the flow for the time being, and see where it took him.

CHAPTER
THIRTEEN

"ONLY a few more days," Sasha told Kit as he sat at the kitchen table, watching Kit juggle two plates and a coffee mug.

Kit felt as if someone had doused him with cold water. He looked up, his chest tightening, unable to breathe as he forced himself to think. "I thought…." He tried to form a proper sentence. He had known whatever he had with Sasha was temporary. A blow job did not amount to much, and heck, Sasha didn't even like Kit very much, but still….

"I think we can settle this out of court," Sasha continued.

"Oh," said Kit, relief making it hard for him to speak. "Uh, that's good, right?" Sasha had been referring to his legal dispute, not to his unwanted tenant.

Sasha shrugged, looking more than a little tired. "I still have to figure out what to do and, like that damn woman said, I'm just not cut out for running a company."

"So you need to find someone to do it for you," Kit pointed out. "Someone you can trust."

Sasha gave Kit a glance that spoke volumes about what he thought of Kit's intelligence, which wasn't much, then moved his elbow off the table as Kit put his plate of toast and eggs in front of him.

"What do you intend to do after that?" Kit asked as he pulled his chair closer and sat facing Sasha. "Go back to your college or campus"— Kit wasn't sure if there was a difference between the two, but he mentioned both just to be sure.—"and finish up whatever you were doing?"

"I have an appointment for my next facial reconstructive surgery," Sasha replied. He took a sip of his orange juice and grimaced, then pushed away the glass with a look of disgust on his face.

Kit sipped from his coffee and shrugged. Sasha should have stuck to coffee like a normal person instead of drinking health stuff. It was not as though it would make his arm grow back. "Soon?"

"Soon enough—week after next I think," Sasha replied blandly. "I should be away for about three weeks."

"*Three weeks*," Kit exclaimed, then hunched over to draw less attention as his exclamation caused Sasha to raise an eyebrow, not that Sasha had two full eyebrows to raise, and look at him with displeasure. "You'll be gone for three weeks."

"Thereabout," Sasha replied. "Perhaps I can cut it down to two, but that depends on when the deal is finalized. I want to be back by the time the lawyers handle the small print."

"Uh," said Kit, and picked up his mug hurriedly. His mind was churning. He wasn't going to make a fuss, because if he did, Sasha might tell him to move out. He could just keep quiet and not make much of a scene, and things would settle down and Sasha would just forget that Kit was freeloading off him.

"What are you doing today?" Sasha asked abruptly, and Kit paused. He had gotten so used to Sasha getting dressed and going out every day that he had taken it for granted. But it was Sunday, and Kit assumed even Sasha had to rest.

"N-nothing… much," Kit stuttered. "Do the laundry and perhaps watch a movie." Did Sasha realize Kit was acting like a neglected housewife whose workaholic husband had suddenly gotten an unexpected day off?

"What movie?" Sasha actually sounded interested. Kit's thoughts came to a screeching halt. "Uh—I don't have a particular one in mind. You should pick. It's your home." After all, it was Sasha's TV; he had paid for it.

"I'm not sure I'm up to date on popular culture," Sasha said in a self-deprecating way as he stood up with his plate in hand. Though

Sasha ate more than he usually did, he still ate far too little in Kit's opinion.

"You talk like you're forty," Kit said instead.

"I feel eighty," Sasha said, shaking the leftovers onto the windowsill, though Kit very much doubted any of the cats ate plain toast. He held out his hand to Kit after keeping the plate down. "I'll do the dishes, you do the laundry, and then we'll see if there is a movie to watch."

It sounded so normal that Kit froze. He knew it was the sort of thing normal couples did, but did Sasha even know what he had said?

Mistaking Kit's hesitation, Sasha drew back. "Not done yet?"

"I'm finished," said Kit, handing over his plate, though he was hardly done. "I'll—just go load the washer," he added, walking out of the kitchen as fast as he could without making it seem suspicious.

Kit loaded the washer, set the timer, and then walked over to the sitting room and fiddled with the TV so he would actually look like he was going to watch a movie. He frowned at the movie he had settled on, unsure as to what exactly it was, when someone poked him from behind.

Startled, Kit jumped before realizing it was Sasha, who had approached him silently on bare feet. "Give a guy a warning," he said, knowing his sudden start had amused Sasha. The guy had a warped sense of humor anyway.

"Hn," grunted Sasha as he held out what he had poked Kit with.

Kit took it automatically, his eyes fixed on Sasha's face. "What's with you and shoes anyway?"

"After the accident, I had problems walking," Sasha replied. "Kept tripping when I tried to walk. It was easier when I could feel the floor so I gave up on shoes. I guess I got used to it." He dropped onto the sofa close to Kit, and held out his hand, palm down, fingers spread.

Kit stared at it incomprehensibly before something clicked, and he looked at it. Sasha had handed him a small nail clipper. He supposed it was hard to keep one's nails short and neat with only one hand. He grabbed Sasha's wrist and studied the hand closely; the fingers were long and slender, the wrist slim, fragile-looking. The nails were long, bitten on by the looks of it, and one was ragged, and he realized it was at odds with the implacable image Sasha projected. Bitten nails and Sasha just did not seem to fit together. He looked up, and his eyes met Sasha's. He could see into the pale-green irises of Sasha's eyes, the faint outline of hair growing on his upper lip, and the scars on his face running into each another like roads on a map. They were sitting so close that he could smell the soap and fabric softener from Sasha's clothes.

"How short do you want them?" Kit asked as he adjusted his legs so he was seated facing Sasha.

"Short."

"That's nice," Kit muttered as he started on the pinkie. By right, it was not a difficult thing: just snip the nail and get it over with. However, Kit's coordination seemed to have gone to hell. The first cut was at an angle and the next simply made it worse.

"Oh crap," Kit muttered as he tried to rectify the situation but wound up even more uneven. This was fun. On TV, someone swore, and from the corner of his eye, Kit saw a vehicle flip over. He could feel a bond forming between him and the driver on-screen.

The next nail was an equal disaster, and it didn't help that Sasha wordlessly snorted at Kit's attempt to even the edge. Finally Kit put down the nail clipper down, and then picked up the hand and guided the finger into his mouth. Feeling the edge with his tongue, he nipped at it with his teeth to even it out, and held it up for inspection.

"That's better," he said as he looked up at Sasha, who had gone still all of a sudden.

"Yes," agreed Sasha, though it came out in a large gasp. He'd probably been holding his breath. His hand shook slightly just as Kit started on the third finger, and he cut through the edge. Sasha did not even flinch as a drop of blood bloomed at the corner of the fingernail.

"Oh shit, I'm sorry," said Kit automatically as he set the clipper down and glared at the blood, wishing it would go away. He held on to Sasha's hand while he looked around for something to clean it up with.

"Relax," Sasha said dryly. "I'm clean." Which was not what Kit had expected to hear. And why was Sasha bringing up the issue of

STDs after he'd swallowed Sasha's come? And why hadn't he thought of it before!

"What!"

"After the accident, I had to have a blood transfusion, and Cory was anal retentive about getting an AIDS test. Did it every six months in case we missed something in the first test, and nothing's shown up so far. And Cory was always clean—he got tested every time I did and—" Sasha stopped frowning. "I suppose you're the only person he...."

"I'm clean," Kit interrupted. He wasn't going to discuss Cory. The mood was just right, and he didn't want to bring up the ghost of lovers past. He didn't want to mention that he got tested regularly since his lovers demanded it of him as well, and he did use condoms. He'd never fucked anyone without a condom, ever.

Sasha shrugged, pulled his hand free, and stuck his injured finger in his mouth. "You obviously are terrible at this. If I had wanted someone to bite off my fingernails I would have done it myself."

"Sorry," Kit said apologetically, while on-screen a violent shooting decapitated a scantily dressed woman. "I'm just not used to it."

Sasha accepted the apology as his due and leaned back, looking at the screen, where two men argued in highly colorful language. "Is there anything more—" He seemed perplexed as he search for the proper word. "—toned down we could watch?" he asked. The wording was polite, though the tone implied Sasha expected Kit to follow his instructions. Kit scrambled for the remote and turned off the TV.

"Let me bite off the other two nails," he offered without really thinking.

"No need," Sasha dismissed Kit's offer, holding out his hand, palm up. Kit, not knowing exactly what object Sasha was demanding, held out both the remote and the nail clipper. Sasha took the remote from Kit, switched the power back on, and started to change the channels rapidly. "Is there anything like Discovery here?"

"Guh," said Kit, wondering what to say to that. As far as he was concerned, Discovery was boring and repetitive. Kit could see this would be one painfully boring day unless he did something fast.

He leaned toward Sasha and bit his earlobe gently. Sasha froze, his finger still on the remote, and the programs skipped across the screen far too fast to see as random bursts of sound and words filled the room. Kit licked the bite carefully and drew back a little. "I have condoms and lube in the room," he said softly, letting his breath brush against Sasha's now-sensitive earlobe.

Sasha shivered slightly but, to his credit, didn't turn around. Instead he hit the power button on the remote, turning off the television. Kit could hear the cars on the road and the yowling of a distant cat in the vacuum of noise.

"Then, by all means, let's go see," Sasha said dryly, though his voice did not sound all too steady. Kit stood swiftly and held out his hand. He was sure Sasha would refuse and was surprised when his hand was taken. Sasha let Kit pull him to his feet and lead him to the bedroom in a show of docility that had Kit worrying a little.

Once Sasha was seated on the bed, Kit scooted down to his knees and started to root around the bottom drawer for the stuff he had discreetly put aside. He finally found what he wanted and turned around triumphantly to find Sasha sitting exactly where Kit had left him, looking like a wax statue.

"Is something wrong?" Kit asked slowly, though he had a feeling Sasha had changed his mind and was about to tell Kit to get out.

"So." Sasha actually hesitated, pausing to swallow. "How do you want to do this?"

"Did you…?" Kit almost asked, "Did you and Cory plan ahead?" but in the last moment saved himself. "Do you have anything in mind?"

"I mean," Sasha said carefully. "There are certain positions I cannot—I'm not comfortable with."

"I'm not really into pain or any of that crap either," Kit reassured him.

"I mean," Sasha said, sounding slightly strangled. "My body—after the accident, isn't as flexible as it once was."

Oh! Kit thought it over. He had had sex with people with all sorts of body types, a few with problems like diabetes and high blood pressure, but he had never fucked with a crip—oops, disabled. While he didn't actively think of Sasha as damaged, he did remember all the scars and the missing hand and—the bum leg and....

"You can lie on your back and I'll ride you from the top," Kit offered. It seemed the best solution to the problem. Though he had gone out with a few people who stated specific positions they wanted, it seemed a little odd to be with someone who not only had less experience than he did, but was older and in more control of the situation.

Kit sat on his heels and looked up at Sasha, whose face was blank apart from two spots of red burning on his cheeks. Kit could see Sasha was feeling self-conscious and would withdraw into his shell unless Kit did something to prevent it. He dropped the sachets of lube and condoms onto the floor and fell to his knees. The room was small enough that he was able to fit himself between Sasha's knees with only a few movements, since he knew, no matter what, crawling would not work for His Royal Highness. Kit reached up as Sasha leaned down, and their lips met in a comfortable kiss. He wound an arm around Sasha's shoulders, pulling him down while keeping his other arm on Sasha's knee for balance.

The kiss was slow, almost sensual, as Sasha leisurely explored Kit's mouth, nibbling at his tongue. Kit groaned at the sensation, pushing himself up to get a better feel, and Sasha stiffened all of a sudden, drawing back with a wince.

"What...?" Kit asked before realizing where his hand was, pressing down on Sasha's upper thigh. "Oh, damn, forgot about your leg, sorry."

"It's fine," panted Sasha, looking as though he was really sorry he had made a fuss about his leg. "It didn't hurt, just a reflex."

"You have been working on it at the gym, haven't you?" Kit inquired, more to make himself feel better. "That is, I hope you have."

In reply, Sasha scooted back and hooked his arm under Kit's, pulling him up. Kit let himself be lifted as Sasha leaned back, almost knocking the top of his head against the wall.

"Need a bigger bed," Kit observed as he half-laid on top of Sasha, one of his hands inside Sasha's T-shirt, the other cupping the back of Sasha's head so he would not end up with a concussion before they finished making out. Sasha grunted in response and pulled Kit down so they could pick up where they had stopped.

Kit carefully placed a knee on either side of Sasha's hips, straddling Sasha to avoid accidentally putting pressure on his injuries (not that he had any idea if they still hurt or not), and started to place small kisses on Sasha's face. He kissed down the scars, working his way down from the temple to the corner of his mouth, sucking lightly, careful not to leave marks. Kit knew just how bad it could get if he left any hickeys behind, and he didn't want to piss off Sasha the next day. The scars felt funny against his lips—not rough, almost smooth and hard; Sasha twitched a little but did not protest to the treatment as Kit expected him to.

Knowing just how body-shy Sasha was, Kit did not break off from the kiss as he started to roll up the loose T-shirt. However, he had to draw back just enough to pull it off before resuming his ministrations, this time concentrating on Sasha's neck. Sasha had a sensitive neck. Kit licked and nipped his way down as Sasha gave a low moan and arched upwards, throwing his head back, baring his throat to Kit.

Kit sat back on his heels and stared down at Sasha lying there, panting, flushed, his chest bare. The scars looked as Kit remembered them, but at the same time not as bad as he had feared. Sasha had put on a little weight too, and it helped with his overall appearance.

Aware of being scrutinized, Sasha opened his eyes and looked at Kit warily. "What," he said, sounding both breathless and pissed off at the same time. "Don't like what you see?"

"You've put on weight," Kit told him.

Sasha lifted his head and glanced down at himself with a grimace. "Yeah, mostly around my middle," he said.

"It's not bad at all," Kit replied, rolling his eyes. "Looks good on you, not seeing all those bones stick out."

He crouched forward, supporting most of his body on the arm placed above Sasha's shoulder, and licked one of Sasha's nipples lightly before blowing on it. He shuffled back on his heels to get into a more comfortable position, and paused when his crotch brushed against the hardness in Sasha's pants. Kit hooked a finger around the waistband of the sweats and pulled it down. Sasha helped by raising his hips just enough for the material to slide off.

Sasha's erection sprang free, proud and bobbing, and Kit groaned at the sight. Though he had had that in his mouth, the thought of it fitting inside him made him pause.

"That is huge," he said softly. He leered at Sasha, who was blushing lightly while smirking at the compliment. "Going to be a little difficult getting that in me."

The blush deepened as Kit had anticipated it would. "Actually," Sasha started. "I was hoping you would…."

"What?" Kit asked suspiciously.

"Top." Sasha managed to make it sound like a swearword.

Startled, Kit's supporting hand slipped, and he fell face-first onto Sasha's chest. He lifted his head and looked at Sasha's face, which was now very close. "You want me to top?"

Apparently Sasha was able to go from embarrassed to annoyed in about two seconds. "I said…."

Kit slid forward over Sasha's bony chest and sealed his lips with a quick kiss, then rolled over and off the bed and grabbed the condom and lube he had deposited there a few minutes ago. He stood up, pulled off his T-shirt, and shimmied out of his sweats before crawling back to bed.

There really wasn't much room in the bed, but he was not that concerned about it. Kit resumed his earlier position above Sasha, on his heels, looking down at his Sasha spread below him, but farther down the bed. The bed that was far too short and narrow, and if Kit were to lean back, he would be in danger of falling off backward. Sasha appeared to be tense but not uncomfortable. Kit held out his hand for the spare pillow. Sasha passed it over wordlessly and lifted his hips for Kit to slip it under him.

"Would you prefer facedown?" Kit asked, and Sasha rolled his eyes at that.

"I am hardly a virgin," he spat out. "I prefer this." Then, thinking of something, he added, "I might not be able to lift my leg. The muscles are stiff, but if you lift it for me, it won't hurt."

"Right," said Kit, opening the sachet of lube carefully, making a note to treat Sasha's injured leg with care.

Kit was more nervous than anticipated, since he squeezed the tube far too hard and half the contents squirted out, missing his hand and landing on the bed. It seemed to have a positive effect on Sasha, since he snorted and the lines around his mouth softened a little. Emboldened, Kit took the lube in his fingers and reached down. Even as he did, he couldn't help but press a quick kiss to Sasha's knee.

Sasha raised his eyebrow at this action. Apparently no one had admired his knee before. Kit gave up on scraping the lube off the bedcover to scoot down until his ass was practically hanging off the bed, and decided to give Sasha's leg the attention it was due. After all, Kit had found those bare feet fascinating, not that he was going to suck on Sasha's toes or something disgusting like that, since really, the guy did walk around without shoes on. Still, the idiot had nice legs, and Kit started to work his way up from the knee. He started off with Sasha's good leg, nibbling at the back of the knee and then up the sensitive inner thigh. Sasha moaned quietly before remembering himself and biting it back, his legs falling open, and Kit decided it was as good a chance as any to slide the first finger in. Sasha didn't even stiffen at the intrusion.

Kit managed to find some more lube off the bedsheet as he buried his nose in Sasha's pubic hair and inhaled deeply. Sasha said something that sounded suspiciously like a good thing, then again was silenced midword. Really, Kit would have been pleased if His Royal Highness just relaxed a little instead of trying to maintain iron control over everything.

Kit licked along Sasha's erection lovingly as he scraped another glop of lube off the bed and worked in the second finger. There was a little resistance, muscles tightening from lack of practice, but even as he scissored his fingers, Sasha relaxed, practically impaling himself on Kit's fingers. Kit didn't hesitate to work in the third finger, even as he sucked on the flared head of Sasha's cock. He managed to get the third finger in without much trouble when a condom hit him squarely on his forehead.

He looked at Sasha and scowled. Really, here he was trying to give Sasha some oral… er… attention, and the Princess was giving orders. However, Kit sat up, making sure his lips made an obscene wet sound as Sasha's cock sprang free, and smirked as he picked up the condom and broke it open. He slid it over his neglected erection and squeezed the last of the lube on himself and smiled at Sasha, savoring the moment.

Sasha practically growled with impatience, and Kit had to bite back a laugh despite the situation as he carefully guided his erection to Sasha's prepared entrance. He slid in slowly. Sasha was warm and tight, though he made a conscious effort to relax and welcome Kit—his head thrown back, eyes closed, lower lip caught between his teeth.

"Damn it," Kit cursed as he sank into Sasha all the way to the hilt. "Just let go, scream if you want to. It's just you and me and I'm fucking you in the ass so you really can't be that repressed."

Sasha didn't open his eyes, but his mouth relaxed and his lower lip sprang free, red but not quite bleeding.

Kit started to thrust slowly, rocking back and forth minutely, searching for the perfect angle to make Sasha moan. He found it on his third try, a place that made Sasha buck and curse like a two-dollar hooker. Sasha lifted his good leg and wound it around Kit's waist in a fluid movement. His other leg twitched, and then suddenly it, too, wound itself around Kit, pulling him closer.

"Faster," he spat out. "You move like an old woman with a walker and an overstuffed shopping bag."

Kit started to speed up, taking care not to be rough. Sasha proved he had more control over his inner muscles than Kit had given him credit for as he clamped his legs tightly around Kit. Kit threw himself forward, letting his arms, placed on either side of Sasha's head, take his weight as he started to thrust in earnest.

Sasha's body arced upwards, mouth open in a moan of pure pleasure, his blunt nails scrabbling at the bed for a grip. "God, Kit," he moaned, his hips thrusting down, his erection bobbing between them, red and weeping. "Yes, yes…." Then his words turned into an incoherent babble as he practically mewled, and Kit smirked. Cory was a fool if he had only let Sasha top for him.

Kit concentrated on maintaining a steady pace until each thrust made him feel as though he was on the verge of exploding, as though he was on a rollercoaster about to hit the steep incline. He managed to find a free hand, pushed away Sasha's, and started to work Sasha's cock none too gently in time with his thrusts, which were becoming more and more erratic. Kit moved his hips faster and faster, forcefully, pushing Sasha up until his head was knocking against the wall with every thrust, but Sasha didn't seem to care. Sasha was incoherent, his mouth spewing words Kit would have been shocked to hear in any other circumstance, his body tensing as he neared his climax.

Sasha came first, his head thrown back, mouth open in a silent scream, his eyes open, fixed on Kit's face, which was much better than shouting his name. Kit managed a few more thrusts, but the way Sasha clamped down on his cock was enough to force him over the edge, and he was coming, falling down as the arm holding him up gave way and he sprawled inelegantly onto Sasha.

When Kit managed to control his breathing, he was still on top of Sasha, who was also breathing deeply, his face turned to the side, hair stuck to his forehead with sweat. Kit pulled himself free and carefully took off the condom, then, cursing Sasha for not having a trash can near the bed, walked over to the table and deposited it carefully into the proper place. No matter how lust-addled he was, Kit knew from past experiences that stepping on discarded condoms on the floor didn't endear him to people. He also plucked a few tissues from the dispenser on the table before walking back to bed. Those he threw at the basket after wiping Sasha down. He was not about to get out of bed twice, not when his legs were still shaky.

Sasha didn't move, so Kit scrambled over him to his usual place on the bed and Sasha sleepily pulled him closer for a hug. The position was slightly uncomfortable, but Kit was still feeling the effects of very good sex after a long time, and didn't move as he closed his eyes. He must have fallen asleep, since the next time he woke up, Sasha was asleep in his usual position, his back to Kit. The warm glow left over from their activities faded fast, and Kit glared at his back.

CHAPTER
FOURTEEN

KIT awoke to the feeling of someone groping him under the sheets. He was flat on his back, one hand curled behind his neck, the other draped over the side of the bed. They really needed a bigger bed, Kit thought as he spread his legs for easy access without even opening his eyes. He grinned sleepily and opened his eyes to find Sasha watching him through half-closed eyes. Kit worked some saliva into his mouth and swallowed hurriedly in the hope he would not have a bad case of morning breath before reaching over to kiss Sasha. Sasha was being rather mellow about things that morning, so it couldn't be all bad.

Sasha accepted the kiss as his due, stilling his hand between Kit's legs to fully appreciate it; Kit placed small kisses up Sasha's throat before finally latching onto his mouth. Sasha's mouth tasted fresh, and Kit wondered if His Royal Highness ever suffered from any human failings like bad breath. After a few seconds, Kit broke away to trace a scar running down Sasha's cheek with his tongue.

"There isn't much feeling there," Sasha said softly, and Kit was too distracted by the hot breath against his cheek to realize exactly what Sasha had said until a few seconds later.

He pulled back, propping himself on his elbow so he could look down properly. "You don't feel anything?" he asked quietly.

"I do," Sasha said with a frown. "It just feels—different." He sighed and pulled his hand from its current position of cupping Kit's balls to wind his arm around Kit's waist and pull him closer. Kit let himself be dragged down until he was resting partially on Sasha's chest, appreciating the advantages of having two arms. He palmed Sasha's damaged cheek, not looking at it directly, just mapping the marred skin by feel.

"I can feel the pressure but not all of the… sensations." Sasha paused, searching for the right words. "The nerve damage was extensive, and I've had three surgeries to glue my face to this level of public acceptability." Kit continued to stroke Sasha's face, letting him talk. It was very rare of Sasha to speak—or cuddle—and Kit was going to get the most of it. "The doctors are going to fix it in the end so I will have a suitably blank expression," Sasha continued. "That side of my face is not going to have much movement."

"That's not going to be very noticeable," Kit said before he could help it, and then tensed, wondering if he had just spoiled the mood.

Sasha snorted and pinched Kit's side almost playfully. "I should be thankful for small mercies," he said agreeably. Then he slid his hand lower, and his fingers dug into Kit's butt.

"Want to top?" Kit asked softly, grinding his semi-erect cock against Sasha's bare thigh. "I think it's your turn."

"Yeah," agreed Sasha softly. "About that—" Kit tensed. "—it was acceptable, wasn't it?"

"What?" asked Kit, honestly confused. What was Sasha asking?

"The only other person I have been with was C—Cory and…."

Sasha was asking for reassurance from Kit about his sexual performance. Kit wondered if he was dreaming. No one he knew, or slept with for that matter, had ever asked him about their performance; they all assumed they were good, and anyway, aware they paid Kit to tell them what they wanted to hear, even if it was something as inconsequential as "faster" and "harder."

Kit knew he had to handle the situation just right or he might push Sasha away, making him revert back into that cold half person. Kit liked Sasha the way he was right now, without his blank expression and snide, clipped comebacks. "Would you believe me if I told you it was the best sex of my entire life?" Kit quipped.

"Not really," Sasha replied, weary but composed.

"If I told you it was the best sex I've had in a long time and wouldn't mind having some more," he said carefully. Sasha didn't reply to that, but he did pull Kit closer. "I enjoyed it and I wouldn't mind a repeat." Sasha huffed softly, sounding not exactly displeased but almost amused. "So, do you want to top?"

Sasha twisted his body completely and looked around. "Where is the lube—and the condoms?"

"Somewhere around," said Kit, reluctantly pulling free so he could feel around the bed, not that there was much space to feel around. He bumped his elbow hard against the wall and winced at the sudden pain. "Ouch."

"Hurt your brain much?" Sasha asked, sitting up and pushing aside the bedcover, apparently comfortable with his nakedness.

"Funny," Kit mumbled under his breath, rubbing his elbow with his other hand.

"I know," Sasha said after a few seconds. "We really should move to the rest of the house instead of living in the visitors' room."

"Visitors' room?" Kit asked, confused.

"This part of the house we use," Sasha said. "Separate entrance, the bathroom in the sitting room, were all designed for a visitor. The rest of the family lived in the other rooms. When I came here, I just settled in the closest room, since it was the most convenient. Didn't expect to be here for so long."

Sasha was being particularly garrulous, and Kit wondered if it was the sex or the lack of clothes.

"I've got a contractor coming over to look at the house and do some much-needed repairs." Sasha continued to speak. "Do some interior decorating and clearing up.... The roof leaks in the main bedroom and the attic is a mess."

Kit's first reaction was "Why didn't you tell me before?" but he bit back his response. He and Sasha had been lovers for a short while, enough to get used to each other's nudity but not much else, and that did not amount to anything. It didn't mean Sasha had to discuss his decisions with Kit—not like they were together or anything.

"I expect you to supervise them while I'm gone," Sasha added almost as an afterthought. Apparently he had included Kit in the equation, just not the way Kit would have wanted. But that meant Sasha expected Kit to stay on in his absence and trusted him with the house.

"Well then," said Kit as he triumphantly pulled out the flattened lube from its hiding spot between the mattress and the wall. "We could...."

The phone rang.

Kit groaned as Sasha swung his legs off the bed and stood up with his back to Kit. Sasha was not at all slowed by his leg when he moved without much thought and was not aware of anyone watching him. Kit, apparently, did not count as anyone in Sasha's opinion. Kit watched Sasha's bare ass as he walked to the telephone, comfortable with his nudity. It surprised Kit that Sasha was a different person when he was relaxed, amazingly touchy-feely (for a guy with only one arm), and overall not as much of an asshole as before. It did not mean Sasha had had a complete personality overhaul, and there were times he commanded and Kit obeyed.

Kit got off the bed as well, scowling at the interruption, and picked up his discarded shorts off the floor of the bedroom. He pulled them on and strolled to the front of the house, where Sasha was speaking calmly to someone on the phone.

"Of course, I'll be there," he was saying, though his face said otherwise. "Formal wear—yeah, I think I can find something in the closet." Kit knew Sasha didn't own a whole lot of clothes, since most of what he owned had been left at Cory's place. Sasha had made a few purchases: ties, dress shirts, and such, as it was expected when he went to meet the lawyers, but there was a lot of empty space in his closet. Formal wear probably meant it was business related and definitely not something that concerned Kit.

Knowing Sasha the way he did, Kit knew he wouldn't crawl back into bed; biting back a yawn, Kit decided to put a few things together for breakfast before taking a shower. Then he needed to do the laundry. At least the bedsheets, and afterward he was going to watch the midday special on TV. He was completely housebroken. Perhaps he should do his nails while watching the hero of the day kick some monster ass, which would be perfect.

He was mixing the pancake batter when Sasha walked in, dressed in sweats and a shirt, unbuttoned down the front, looking pensive. "I have a dinner to go to tonight," he said in reply to Kit's inquisitive glance. "Ken wants to formally introduce me to the department heads to cement the new ownership."

"Ah," said Kit as he gave the bowl a more vigorous stir.

"Ken says it's just a show of power," Sasha added, glancing out the window, where a large tabby was sunning.

Kit didn't see where the conversation was going. Ken was Sasha's trusted lawyer who had won back the company for him. Though it was not finalized and there were so many loose ends to sort out (at least according to Sasha), Kit knew the worst was over.

"Even when I was with Cory, he—" Sasha paused and then continued. "—didn't take me to these company functions...."

And Kit understood. Sasha was torn about inviting Kit to go with him. No one Kit had ever been with had even considered taking him out on an official capacity. That Sasha even considered taking him meant a lot to Kit. He gave the batter one more decisive stir and pushed it away. "Go shower," he said. "I'm going to do the laundry once I'm done with this."

Sasha seemed grateful that Kit had not pressed the point, not that there was much expression to see on his face. He straightened up and was about to leave when the phone rang again. Sasha rolled his eyes at the disturbance and disappeared, presumably to answer the phone. Kit picked up their one and only multipurpose frying pan, switched on the stove, and kept it over the flame, wondering if he should get an apron to go with his domestic streak when Sasha shouted, "Don't ever call again," followed by the slamming of the receiver.

Kit looked over his shoulder, startled. His Royal Highness did not raise his voice for anything. In fact, the rest of the world toned down to match Sasha, not the other way around. He poured the batter into the pan and turned down the heat before he walked to the sitting room, just to be sure there was only one other person in the house. By then Sasha had confined himself to the bathroom and the phone was ringing insistently.

Kit stared at it for a while, gave a shrug, and returned to the kitchen before he burned breakfast. Whatever that was, it was none of his business. Kit made two pancakes and managed to feed a large tabby on the windowsill with the previous night's leftovers. The phone continued to ring. It was distracting him. Kit served the next cat a plate of pancake batter and decided to answer the phone or switch it off or something before the continuous ringing drove him mad. On his way to the phone, he glared at the bathroom door, which was shut firmly, and debated the wisdom of letting His Royal Highness deal with the whole thing; it certainly sounded personal, if nothing else.

Kit frowned at the phone, which refused to stop ringing, and finally picked it up. "Hel—"

"I knew you were there," the voice at the other end snapped. "What's the big deal about hanging up before I could even...."

"Um," said Kit intelligently. "This isn't Sasha."

There was a pause, and finally the voice said, "I suppose you're a friend of his if you're calling him by that annoying nickname."

Kit frowned. He had no idea how Sasha was addressed outside of his house. He did acknowledge Sasha was a cross between a dog and a girl's name, but Sasha had never corrected Kit or told him any other name to call him by. Then he realized the voice at the other side was waiting for him to confirm the suspicion.

"Um," he said intelligently. "Who is this?"

"I'm his brother." Kit tried to connect the voice with one of the faces in the photo that sat over the fireplace mantel, and failed. Those faces had been young and carefree; this voice was harsh and grating.

"Hi," said Kit before he could bite his tongue. That, he was sure, would come across as really intelligent.

"I only found out today that Alex's—uh—friend had killed himself," the brother said. "I just wanted to know if he was all right."

"That was some time ago," Kit said, a little peeved that Sasha's brother seemed to be reluctant to accept the relationship Sasha had had with Cory. Not that it was any of his business. And calling Sasha "Alex" was so unreal.

"I found out accidently from an old newspaper." The brother sounded harassed. "It's not as if Alex ever calls us or anything."

"Uh," said Kit instead of saying, "Why don't you call him?" The intricate subtleties of family life were beyond him.

"I suppose he's fine now that you are there." Kit could see someone washing their hands of responsibility even if Kit was not too bright when it came to interpreting family situations.

"Yes," said Kit, feeling slightly mean. "I have to go finish making breakfast so I can join him in the shower." Then he put the phone down in the deafening silence, feeling pleased, and turned around to find Sasha standing just behind him, regarding him with a blank expression. "I—" He paused. "I just—well, it was annoying and—thought—breakfast...."

"So you were going to join me in the shower," Sasha said, sounding pleased.

"Breakfast—"

"Can wait," said Sasha smugly.

It was perfect, Kit thought.

Little did he know it would all fall apart that day.

KIT gave the inside of Eddy's a perfunctory look and scowled. After Sasha had left for the day, gym bag slung over his shoulder, briefcase in hand, Kit had received a call from Eddy asking him to come to the shop.

Kit had gotten dressed hastily and run out, only to find he had beaten Eddy to the shop. Disgruntled, Kit tried to appear busy as he slouched at the doorway when there was the sound of running feet behind him.

"Help." A small body slammed into Kit hard, and they both staggered before regaining their balance. Kit looked down quickly and identified the person clinging to him. It was the girl, Cassandra

"Cassie" Nash, all-around nice kid who liked to dress up with very little fashion sense. The kid was scared, Kit realized; she was trembling, her face buried in his middle.

Looking up to confront whatever had scared her made Kit wish he was elsewhere. It was the type of man Kit wished to avoid. Though dressed decently enough in clean but old clothes, the man had a nose that had been broken once too often to be fixed straight and the scarred fists of someone who got into frequent fights. He stood head and shoulder over Kit, feet apart, hands clenched, clearly ready to strike out. His shoulder muscles bulged, his cheeks quivered with barely restrained anger, and Kit wondered just how fast he could run with a girl attached to his hip.

"Cassie," Kit asked the girl hanging onto him like a leech. "Is this man bothering you?"

The man in question snarled. "What do you mean, bothering her?"

"H—he's chasing me," Cassie managed, voice teary. The tough-kid act was just that, an act. "He was going to...."

"You her pimp?" the man asked Kit. "All I did was ask her how much."

"Hey," Kit said wearily. "She's just a kid, perhaps you should leave her alone."

"Well excuse me," the man said with exaggerated politeness. "She's the one who's selling ass on the pavement."

Cassie didn't respond, refusing to even turn around and look at the man.

"I'm very sorry for the trouble she caused," Kit said without making eye contact. He just wanted the man to move away without a fight.

The man stood for a moment, probably weighing his options. It was close to midday, and there were people around, and their little altercation was drawing the attention of passersby. The man relaxed his fists with an annoyed grunt, and Kit breathed a little more easily.

"If she's not for sale, tell her not to dress like a slut," the man said in parting before turning his back to them dismissively and retreating the way he had come.

"Hey—Cassie," Kit said gently. "He's gone. You're safe now."

The girl looked up with a strangled sob, though she didn't let go of Kit. "Thanks," she managed, sniffing loudly.

"You can go now," he said with a pat on her shoulder as he tried to break free. The girl clung to him with the tenacity of an octopus, and he had to work her hands free one by one slowly.

Her mascara had run and her lipstick had smeared, making her resemble a clown. Then she stepped back and kicked him hard on the ankle. The only thing that prevented Kit from serious injury was her wedge heels didn't give her much power behind the kick.

"What the fuck was that for?" Kit snapped. "I just saved your ass."

"You apologized to him, for me," Cassie told him. "I didn't do anything wrong."

"What should I have done?" Kit asked, puzzled.

"You should have told him I wasn't selling ass and told him to back off, politely."

"Like you're being polite with me?" Kit retaliated.

"It's different." Cassie pouted. "You're a friend, and you should have—"

"I'm not going to apologize," Kit told her firmly. "I know it's not your fault, but I'm not the guy to defend your honor. I'm your basic coward who just wants to avoid a confrontation. If saying sorry got that guy off my back, I'd do it again."

"Hm." Cassie looked at him with a disappointed look. "You mean you'd have ignored me altogether if I hadn't run into you."

"Trust me on this," Kit told her firmly. "If you were on the other side of the road screaming for help and that guy was there, I'd look the other way."

"You don't have that many friends, do you?" Cassie scowled at him.

Kit saw little point in chastising her; he was neither her father nor her boyfriend. If she wasn't smart enough to figure out he wasn't the type of person she should hang out with, who was he to interfere? Kit wondered if she had problems—after all, a kid her age probably should be at school, but it wasn't as if his childhood had been trouble-free.

"Cassie." Oh shit, the protective father who was always there at the wrong moments. Kit stiffened waiting for the inevitable blowup.

"Daddy!" Cassie broke free of Kit and ran toward her father, who looked more confused than angry. There was a brief pause as Mr. Nash felt his daughter carefully to ensure that she hadn't been harmed physically. Shrugging free of his grasp, Cassie scowled. "I'm fine," she snapped. "Kit saved me. Where were you, I was waiting for you for ages."

"There was a last-minute call—" Mr. Nash said in an apologetic voice. "What happened?"

"There was this *bum*... he was bothering me." Cassie actually sounded more shocked that a bum had tried to pick on her, rather than the fact she had been propositioned like a hooker. "He pulled at my top and tore it." The material of her top was flimsy and transparent; a strong wind could have torn it off. "Luckily, Kit scared him away." Yeah, right!

Kit wondered if Cassie had always skimmed the truth, and how her parents could be so blind as not to notice. Still, it was none of his concern....

"Why don't you go and wait in the car," Mr. Nash said firmly, and for a moment Kit was sure Cassie was going to argue. "You're eye shadow thingy is running." Mr. Nash was clearly used to dealing with his daughter in such situations. Cassie made a dash to the car, hand half covering her face as though exposing her makeup-smeared face to the world was a crime. Kit waited until she was out of earshot before turning toward Mr. Nash. He had to say his piece before there was any misunderstanding.

"He thought she was a whore," Kit said bluntly.

"I know," Mr. Nash said in a small voice. "Isn't the first time."

"Then you should—" Kit broke off. None of his business, he told himself. Don't get involved.

"I know." Mr. Nash sounded broken. "I'll talk to her mother, this really can't go on." He looked over at where his car was parked, where they could both see Cassie reapplying her makeup using the rearview mirror. "Wait—can I—" He took a deep breath. "—ask you to keep quiet about this." He fished out his wallet and pulled out a fifty. "Think of it as a thank-you."

Even as Kit reached for the money, he wondered just how many people Mr. Nash had paid off to make sure Cassie could live in oblivion. In Kit's opinion, the girl's father deserved a good slap and Cassie needed to spend some time clothes shopping with a person with some dress sense. Also some time playing with some kids her own age instead of people like Kit.

"Kit." Kit whirled around, the fifty curled in his fist at the sound of the familiar voice. Sasha stood on the pavement a few feet away from them, dressed in his business getup of shirt, slacks, and tie, wet hair combed back, looking exotic as always.

"I thought you were at the office," Kit said, sounding almost defensive.

"I went to the gym first," Sasha replied. "I…." He scowled at Mr. Nash and then turned his attention to Kit's fist, where a corner of the note was visible. "Am I interrupting something?"

"No… not at all," Mr. Nash said, looking embarrassed as he backed away. "I was just leaving." He turned around and walked to the car as quickly as possible without running, ignoring Sasha, who was glaring at him through narrowed eyes.

"I've seen him before," Sasha said with a thoughtful frown.

"I think he has an office in the same building as your lawyer's," Kit offered.

"What are you doing here?" Sasha demanded as he kept his briefcase down and swung his gym bag at Kit. Kit caught it automatically, grunting under the weight.

"Eddy called and said he was opening the shop today," he replied reluctantly as he tried to juggle the gym bag while stuffing the money into his pocket. "Just some restocking and cleaning up before opening." Kit wondered if Sasha would expect him to move out now that Eddy had returned and Kit was once again employed. The topic of when Kit was planning on moving out hadn't come up in a while, though he had overstayed his one-week welcome by some time. While Kit was pleased with the prospect of being employed once again, he was wary as to how Sasha would perceive the change.

"Keep the bag," Sasha said, ignoring Kit's prattle. "I don't need it anymore. You might as well hang on to it."

"What's in it, bricks?" Kit asked as he slung the long handle over his shoulder.

"Wet clothes," Sasha said blandly. "I'm going to be late tonight, office party."

"I know," Kit groused. "I'll be here until late as well, I think. There's a lot to do."

Sasha looked at the grime-coated shop window and pointed at the phone number with a nod of his chin at the letters in the right-hand corner. "Is that the phone number?"

"Y... yes," Kit said slowly, unsure if the phone line was still connected.

"I'll give you a call when the party's over," Sasha said. "It shouldn't take too long; it's just some congratulatory drink in the conference room. We can share a taxi home."

Home! Kit liked the sound of that. "Yeah, sure," he said, trying hard not to grin like an idiot. He hoped the party wouldn't drag on for long. He was sure he'd be able to wrap up the restocking before six, as long as Eddy showed up anytime soon. He couldn't wait to go back "home" with Sasha.

KIT was wrong. By the time the last shawl was draped on the rack and the new dummy squeezed into the new cocktail dress, it was past ten at night.

"That's the last of it," Eddy said as he shoved aside the empty boxes. "Kit, can you just put these in the storeroom?"

"My back is killing me," Kit grumbled as he stooped to pick up the boxes. He'd been surprised by just how many items Eddy had picked up in his absence. He was sure some of the dresses were going to be big hits. And the comic-themed ties would interest at least a few lighthearted paper pushers.

"You've grown soft," Eddy said, not unkindly. "Move it, boy."

"Slave driver," Kit snapped back as he balanced the boxes on his hip to toggle the light switch for the storeroom. He managed the feat with some difficulty and blinked as the dark room lit up. The storeroom was a closet located at the rear of the store, small and cramped, one wall fully shelved. It was where Eddy kept unsold items that were far too expensive to be thrown away. As Kit dumped the boxes onto a lower shelf, he knocked against one of the crates stacked above, causing it to topple over with a crash, spilling its contents onto the floor.

"You okay in there?" Eddy called.

"Yeah, just knocked over a crate," Kit called back. "Give me a sec...." He stooped down to pick up the clothes and paused. The first item he had picked up was a green, shiny shirt—the very shirt that had drawn Cory into the shop. A shirt meant for Sasha. Slowly, Kit sat on his heels and looked at the shirt Sasha had rejected.

Oh, Cory, he thought. *You really didn't know Sasha, did you?* Now, after getting to know Sasha, Kit could see the shirt was all wrong for him. Dark colors made Sasha seem washed-out, and the cut would have emphasized how skinny he was. Sasha wouldn't have been seen dead in it. Spurred by the thought, Kit hurriedly put the fallen crate back in its slot and walked out, looking at the new items in a new light. Sasha would look good in gray, he thought. The new shirts with the high collars would be perfect for Sasha, along with the—

Kit jumped when the phone rang and, even though he knew it could be Sasha, held back as Eddy answered it. Instead he moved out of earshot, back into the storeroom, and flattened a few empty cardboard boxes to be sold to the recycling plant's collection point down the block.

"Kit," Eddy called, and Kit stopped stamping on empty boxes to peer out. "Message for you." Eddy looked and sounded curious. Kit never got calls at the shop—never once during his entire career. He'd always kept his personal life separate from work, making sure all his sugar daddies called his cell phone until it was damaged in a bar scuffle.

"What?" Kit demanded impatiently.

"Someone wants you on the fifth floor of the Cinnamon Crescent, now," Eddy said with a smirk. "Didn't leave a name, just sounded pretty pissed."

"That's new," said Kit sarcastically as he moved to pick up the gym bag he had stashed under the counter. When had Sasha ever sounded happy with the world in general? "We done for the day, Eddy?"

"Sure," Eddy replied with a shrug. "You can leave. Just remember to come early next Monday. We'll be having our grand opening."

"Yeah, right." Kit rolled his eyes.

"Hey, I'm paying you, remember," Eddy called as Kit pulled open the door. Biting back a retort about how late his monthly pay had been, Kit stepped onto the pavement, lit only by streetlights. There was barely any traffic as he jaywalked across the street with ease and entered the building he had mentally dubbed "Sasha's lawyer's." The party had better be over, Kit thought as he jogged across the foyer with a nod to the dozing night watchman. He was sweaty, covered in lint and dust, and had a scratch on his palm from a complimentary shoulder pin that came with a red sundress. He didn't want to meet anyone apart from Sasha.

Kit brushed at his clothes ineffectively until the elevator doors pinged open, and Kit stepped inside before the watchman came fully awake and questioned him.

The fifth floor was brightly lit, and the sound from behind the large wood-paneled door indicated there were several people inside, all of them talking loudly. Kit could smell the alcohol from the elevator lobby; he was sure the whole place would go up in flames if he were to strike a match. He walked forward uncertainly and pushed at the door. With the noise inside, no one would have heard if he'd screamed his head off.

The room turned out to be a brightly lit conference room, a large wooden table in the center with comfortable operator chairs around it, expensive-looking jackets draped across them. Several briefcases were piled on top of a tightly closed filing cabinet. On the center of the table was a collection of liquor bottles and empty glasses that would have put a well-stocked bar to shame. The only edible items to be seen were some bags of chips and popcorn, probably from the vending machine Kit had noticed in the lobby.

The group inside the room was a mixed bunch. Some Japanese or Chinese Asian-looking man (not that he could tell them apart; they all looked alike to him) in a three-piece business suit danced to an invisible beat while another attempted to do some odd wall-climbing maneuver. A couple of females in stern business suits chattered in high-pitched voices, their makeup intact despite the late hour. Kit spotted Sasha immediately in the far corner of the office, leaning against the wall, half-empty glass in hand, in a deep conversation with another man who was drink free.

Kit backed up slowly; it was obvious he didn't belong in the room. He'd wait downstairs until the party broke up or until Sasha decided it was time to leave. As he stepped back, he bumped into another man who was entering the room.

"Sorry," Kit said automatically as he moved to a side.

"No worries," the guy said with a shrug. "You got the pizza we ordered."

"Uh, no." Kit shook his head. "I'll just wait outside...."

"Hey, Paul," the Asian guy called out, catching sight of the new arrival. "Did you get him a taxi?"

"I had to practically carry him down." Paul sounded disgusted. "Andrew was so drunk I paid the cabby extra to make sure he made it inside."

Andrew, Kit thought with a jolt; at least that guy was out of the picture. Funny, Kit had forgotten about the presence of Andrew in

Sasha's office completely, which was unlike him. He took another step back, almost out of the room.

"Kit," Sasha called, having turned his head at the sound of the conversation. "Just the person I was waiting for." He pushed off the wall, staggered, caught his balance, and wavered toward Kit as though walking across an obstacle course.

"You're drunk," Kit declared flatly.

In reply, Sasha reached Kit, almost falling flat on his face at the last step, and slung his arm around Kit's shoulders in a friendly gesture. The glass he had been holding tilted to the side, and a dash of Johnnie Walker sloshed onto Kit's shoulder. Kit froze. Sasha was beyond drunk; he was pissed, and there was a strange gleam in his eyes Kit had never seen before, but made him feel wary.

"Had fun today?" Sasha asked conversationally.

"Yeah, if you can call arranging all those...," Kit started to answer nervously. Sasha had never been prone to "how was your day?" types of questions.

"Got paid?" Sasha interrupted.

"Eddy paid me—finally and...." He broke off, unsure of what to say. "Sasha...," Kit started to say; he didn't know what. Anything to disperse the tension he was feeling.

"Everyone," Sasha called out. The conversation broke up, and the occupants of the room looked at Sasha expectantly. Maybe he did call the shots here, Kit thought hysterically, knowing something was about to go down. "I want to thank you all for coming and all the help you've given me these past weeks... months...." He didn't sound drunk, Kit thought. Sasha sounded so much in control that Kit would have found it believable if the only thing propping him up hadn't been Kit's hip. "I propose a toast," Sasha continued, holding up his glass. The group turned expectantly.

"To all of you, not just Ken." Sasha nodded toward the Asian-looking man who had stopped dancing. "And also to Cory." Kit didn't know what to think. "As you all know, he left me everything. His company, his house...." Here Sasha suddenly burst out laughing, though Kit could see little humor in the situation. "And his toyboy...."

Kit felt the world collapse around him as he stood there. Kit imagined he was standing at the end of a tunnel and listening to everything being said around him from a distance. Someone laughed shrilly, as though Sasha had said something funny, and he could see Ken move toward them hurriedly.

"Kit here is something of a prize, as Andrew told me, passed on from...."

Kit shoved Sasha aside, not caring if the other man fell. He took a step back, dropping the gym bag to the floor. Another step and another, and the next thing he knew he was out of the room and running down the step, unwilling to wait for the lift. He paused once on the sidewalk to retch into the gutter, and then he was up again, running blindly.

Absurdly, Kit wondered why it wasn't raining. It should rain, he thought. It always rained in the movie when someone died. It felt as if he had died.

CHAPTER
FIFTEEN

THREE weeks. *Three fucking weeks*, thought Kit as he pulled open the shop door savagely. The chimes made a disconcerting sound and fell to the floor with a clang. Grateful that Eddy wasn't around to see his display of misplaced anger, Kit scooped up the chimes, letting the door swing shut.

He automatically turned the "Open" sign to "Closed" and flicked off the display lights while studying the chimes closely. The base had shattered and the little bells were cracked in places. *Just like how I feel*, Kit thought as he tossed it in the general direction of the cash register. He would see if the chimes were salvageable with a bit of super glue the following day. He just wasn't in the mood for any fine pasting after an entire day of dealing with difficult customers all by himself.

Kit knew his anger would burn out soon, and by the time he'd walked back to his apartment, he would be so lethargic he would nibble at his dinner and try to sleep—"try" being the key word. He felt he was missing something in his life, as though he'd lost a limb. Kit straightened a rack he'd pushed aside, wondering how he would have been able to manage everything if he'd really lost a limb like Sasha had.

Which brought him to the problem at hand, the one he was unable to avoid thinking about: Sasha. It was strange how much of his time he'd spent trying hard not to think about His Royal Highness. It was a little like the meditation exercise he had been forced to perform at one of his better foster homes. The moment someone told him to empty his mind, his mind got cluttered by trying hard *not* to think. Idiotic of him, Kit knew, but he missed the asshole.

The more Kit tried to forget, the more he thought of Sasha. It wasn't as though he'd tried to push him aside at first; he had actually gone back to their... Sasha's home the morning after the declaration. He'd spent the entire night walking the streets, reeling from the shock of Sasha's calculated cruelty. Thinking back, Kit realized he'd been very lucky not to have been mugged as he'd blindly stumbled through the night.

So Andrew had told Sasha about his time with Kit. Andrew had known Kit wasn't some nice boy out for a good time; he'd even known a little about Kit's other lovers, since Kit had taken to frequenting the same bar for some time. Kit also knew Andrew told *everything* to everybody the moment he was drunk. He had little discretion. Kit had heard all about Andrew's ex-wives in graphic detail when he was drunk, something Kit could have done without.

He had decided to give Sasha time to cool down and let the alcohol work out of his system before confronting him. Kit had no idea what he wanted to tell Sasha, but he realized he didn't want to lose what they had. Kit didn't give up easily. He didn't have many options in life, but those he did have, he fought tooth and claw to hold on to.

Determined to work it out with Sasha no matter what, even if it involved groveling and begging, he'd made it to Sasha's home around midday to find the front door closed. On the front door step was a duffel bag, and inside were all the clothes Kit had ever owned or worn while he was with Sasha. For a moment it had floored him, and he had stood at the doorway staring stupidly at the cats that had come to investigate the visitor. After five minutes, his shock had turned to anger, and Kit had started pounding on the door in earnest.

Sasha might have finally decided Kit had overstayed his welcome, but this was no way to throw him out. After all, he'd cooked and cleaned for His Royal Highness. They'd sat and talked. They'd also fucked, but Kit knew better than to put weight into that. Sex didn't cement bonds, this he knew for sure—it was all the other small things that counted. He had thought the two had formed a connection.

He tried to reason it out. He had given no cause for Sasha to get that mad at him. True, Sasha had discovered he'd slept with Andrew. But it would have been extremely strange if Sasha had expected Kit to be some sainted virgin at the age of twenty-two, and really, after all those innuendoes and hints, Sasha must have realized Kit's sexual experience came from somewhere. And as for Cory….

"Sasha," Kit called out loudly, grateful for the lack of nosy neighbors. "Open the stupid door and talk to me."

The silence was not unexpected. He knew Sasha was one of the most stubborn people around, and it would take a lot of door pounding for him to come out.

"Sasha," Kit tried again. "You'd better not be sitting on that skinny ass of yours just listening to me on the other side of the door." He leaned against the door and kept his ear against the grainy surface in case he could hear Sasha shuffling on the other side, the familiar leg-dragging sound he half imagined he could hear. He rested a little, eyes half closed, as the events of the night before caught up with him, and he realized he was exhausted, both physically and mentally.

He was about to call out again when something brushed against his leg, and he jumped before looking down. A large cat was staring at him with an expression of pure loathing. Kit wondered if Sasha had somehow turned into a cat. He then laughed at his stupidity as he slid down the door until he was sitting on the doorstep, his feet resting on the duffel bag, shooing the cat away. He tilted his head back until it rested on the door and closed his eyes.

Sasha was probably inside, sleeping off his hangover from the night before, and all Kit had to do was wait it out. Sasha would have to leave the house one way or another, and Kit was going to catch him as he did. After all, Sasha wasn't the only person in the world who could be stubborn, and Kit had perfected the art of waiting in uncomfortable spots since he was a child. He closed his eyes and decided that perhaps it was time to take a nap. He'd know if the front door opened.

It was just a silly misunderstanding. He'd explain it to Sasha the moment he opened the door, and everything would be fine. Stupid Sasha, always overreacting.

When Kit opened his eyes, dusk was falling, and his lap had been taken over by a large cat who was digging its claws into his balls like its life depended on it. "Ouch, you mind?" Kit yelped as he came fully awake. "Those are some sharp claws."

The cat gave him an unimpressed stare, jumped off his lap, then walked away without a backward glance. Kit scowled at the retreating cat's back and got to his feet, wincing as his legs broke out in pins and needles. The door was still firmly shut. He stepped up and gave it another knock.

"Sasha, you in there?"

He had been on the doorstep the entire day, and he hadn't seen Sasha. What if—for a moment Kit felt his heart sink—what if Sasha had fallen down somewhere, what with the slippery bathroom tiles, or because he was too drunk and his bum leg couldn't support him and he couldn't get up. The thought spurred Kit into action, and he ran around the side of the house, tripped over a rosebush in his hurry, and tried to peer in through side windows of what he'd dubbed their bedroom. The bed was neatly made, something Kit didn't remember doing the previous morning when they'd both left the house, and the pillow and the bedcovers were folded neatly in the middle like a statement, a final "fuck off." The room was bare—none of Sasha's clothes were visible, and his shoes, which he usually toed off the moment he walked into the room, were also gone. Sasha had packed his bags and walked out.

Perhaps there were clothes in the cupboard, Kit reasoned. He tried to wedge his fingers under the window pane to tug it open, but it was secured too tightly, and he gave up after a couple tries. He didn't bother breaking the window. From the looks of it, Sasha was not at home. He really didn't think Sasha was lying in the bathroom, fully clothed.

He could have gone out before Kit had arrived on the front doorstep. Perhaps to the gym or to meet the lawyers, Kit decided. Then Sasha would return, if nothing else. All he had to do was wait. Since he was already on the side of the house facing away from the road, Kit emptied his bladder into a rose bush—it needed watering anyway—and decided to sit on the front step until Sasha came home.

A few hours later, cat-scratched, hunger gnawing at his stomach, Kit decided Sasha was probably having another late night. He got up, finally, walked to the closest shop, bought a few snacks, and returned, hoping Sasha had arrived during his absence. It was absurd; if His Royal Highness was having some hissy fit and wasn't talking to Kit, or just outright avoiding him, he should just get home and get it over with.

As he sat, Kit started to plan out what he was going to tell Sasha. Andrew had been someone he'd picked up—or in this case, he had picked Kit up—a long time ago, and that was it. They'd had sex and Andrew had paid for Kit's expenses, and then they'd broken up. No big deal. End of story. Nothing to fuss about.

He really couldn't see why Sasha was making a such a ruckus over it.

Kit woke up the next morning, shivering in the cold wind, hugging the duffel bag to his chest, being gnawed on by two half-grown cats who hissed and spat at him when he moved his legs. He sat up with a scowl and decided Sasha was avoiding him by crashing at someone else's place. Short of breaking into the house, there was nothing for Kit to do. His butt was sore, he was cold, and the morning dew had soaked into his clothes. He was hungry, cold, and in desperate need of a shower. Sasha could have at least had the decency to leave a note. Angry at himself for sitting there pathetically on the doorstep, waiting for some insensitive jerk, Kit decided to make a move.

He got up and picked up the bag. He would show Sasha he had places to be other than sitting on his doorstep. Anyway, he was starting to smell from wearing the same clothes for almost three days, and he had to meet up with Eddy for the opening of the shop. He had places to be and things to do.

KIT had held back for a week, busy with starting work at Eddy's and finding a place to sleep (same old shitty apartment, different room) before going back to the house—this time with cat treats. The cats were happy to see him—as happy as cats could be—but Sasha had not been at home. It was as though Sasha had run away from his problems, something he'd accused Cory of doing.

Which brought Kit face-to-face with a problem he'd been trying very hard not to think about: Cory!

He had to acknowledge Sasha wasn't really angry at him for sleeping with Andrew. It was Kit's relationship with Cory that had shocked him, the information about Kit that Andrew had given to Sasha. Perhaps the understanding that Kit had seduced Cory in a predatory manner for money, the same way he'd approached Andrew, not that Andrew had needed much persuading. The old Kit would have scoffed at this thought. It was survival of the fittest, and Sasha had definitely not been fit. He'd been unable to keep his man, and Kit stepped in. But Kit knew he'd changed; Sasha had no idea how bad Kit had felt because of the outcome of his actions—about Cory's death. Surely he didn't think Kit was unaffected by all that. He just had to get to Sasha and tell him that, though Cory had started off as just a mark, there had been more. And Kit was not hanging around anyone for money anymore. Why hadn't Sasha simply asked him instead of reacting the way he had?

Perhaps it was time Kit simply let Sasha cool off. Or not.

He returned to Sasha's house, and as usual, it was deserted. He'd even kept his nose to the doorway to make sure nothing smelled funny inside, and had used Eddy's phone to make a couple calls, all of which were rerouted to the answering machine.

Two days later, emotionally exhausted, Kit had knocked on the St. James mansion door—his last resort. The St. James clan had barely spared him a glance before dismissing him as unimportant. They'd all been busy supervising the men packing up their things, and some of the mansion's original furniture as well. None of them seemed to remember Kit from before, for which he was grateful. No, they hadn't seen Alexander, and no, they didn't know where he was.

It had been then that Kit simply gave up. He'd run out of options. He didn't know where else to look for Sasha. It was as if he had fallen off the face of the earth. There was nothing Kit could do about it apart from picking up his life and moving on. Only it seemed he didn't want to move on. He didn't want to go to a bar and pick up another mark. He didn't want to—do anything. He just wanted to stay in one place and be fucking miserable over some cripple with an attitude problem.

Kit sighed; he still had a job to hold on to. Perhaps he would take down the blue dress on the display and put on one of the leather skirts instead, play it down with a long-sleeved flared blouse so, instead of looking trashy, the skirt would simply make a statement. It was better than going back to his shitty room and staring at the wall.

After all, Sasha had done the same thing as every other guy Kit had gone out with: dumped him on his ass on the pavement.

He walked to the front window and peered out to make sure there were no potential customers. He also looked out at least five times a day to make sure he wasn't missing a glimpse of a slender figure with an odd gait making his way to the building on the other side of the road. As usual there was no Sasha in sight, but what he did see made him pause.

"Oh shit," Kit said, stepping back, a part of him wanting to leave it alone. It was none of his business really. On the sidewalk on the other side of the road stood Cassie, dressed scantily as usual, with the man she'd had problems with before looming over her threateningly.

Let it go, Kit thought. He really didn't have the energy to deal with other people's stupidity and… and…. Kit saw Mr. Nash come hurrying out of his car and run across the street, narrowly missing being run over by a bus in his haste to reach his daughter. There, problem solved—Kit deliberately turned his back to the street and started walking toward the storeroom, stubbing his toe against a clothes rack, when there was a sound of a distant female scream. Kit groaned—so much for remaining uninvolved.

The most intelligent thing to do was to call the police, but Kit had survived by avoiding the law since he'd run away from his fifth foster home. Taking a deep breath, he walked to the front of the shop and pulled open the door, missing the broken chimes already as he stepped out.

Once he'd decided to act, there was little use of hanging out. Kit rushed across the road, taking more care than Mr. Nash had, and reached the front of the building where the larger man was beating the shit out of Mr. Nash. A screaming Cassie was trying to hang on to her father, only to be pushed aside. Kit examined the onlookers, a handful of office workers unlucky enough to be leaving their place of work at six o'clock on a Saturday, clearly unwilling to be involved.

"Has anyone called the police?" he asked in general. The police might question the caller if needed, which was fine with Kit.

A lady in a blue pinstripe suit nodded, looked at her watch while pocketing her cell phone, and hurried away, probably late for some important appointment due to the brawl on the pavement.

"Kit," Cassie screamed, having spied him. "He's going to kill Daddy."

And Kit could see some truth in the statement. The larger man had Mr. Nash by the throat and had lifted him clean off the ground. Mr. Nash's mouth worked soundlessly as his cheeks turned blue. It really didn't look good. *Why me*, Kit thought before stepping in.

"You're killing him," Kit said loudly enough to be heard, but not so loudly that the angry man might let go of his potential victim and turn on him.

The man turned his head slightly to glare at Kit, who belatedly realized that, apart from Cassie, he was the only person to directly address the madman. Kit could see the eyes of the assailant—wide open, pupils dilated—and thought, *Oh shit, hope he's not stoned*. But from experience, Kit decided to assume the worst. The stoner blinked once slowly and then turned fully to face Kit, letting go of Mr. Nash.

"I've seen you before," he said, and Kit was surprised by the tone of his voice: calm and conversational.

"Nice to see you again," Kit mumbled, stepping back and—blinked. For someone over six feet tall and probably as high as a kite, the man moved fast. He was in Kit's space in a second, and the next moment Kit was lying flat on his back, looking at a blurred sky. It took another few seconds for the pain in the back of his head and his jaw to register. "Ow," Kit mumbled, propping his upper body up on his elbows and folding his legs under him. He gazed hopefully at the audience to see if there was anyone willing to step in and save him.

There was none apart from Cassie who looked as battered as he felt, trying to help her father to his feet. From the corner of his eye Kit could see the familiar red-blond-haired slender figure he had been hoping to see for the past month. Kit turned away quickly; it wouldn't be the first time he'd imagined he'd seen Sasha in a crowd. He just hoped it was his mind playing tricks again since he really didn't want to meet Sasha in such a situation.

The stoner moved forward, intent on kicking Kit now that he was down, and Kit scrambled aside fast before the metal-studded boot could tear a hole in his side. As Kit got to his feet, shaking his head to get rid of the dizziness, his attacker stood, regarding him. Kit didn't dare to take his eyes off the madman to glance over his shoulder to confirm whether Sasha was behind him or not. It struck him as odd, how quiet the confrontation had gotten. The crowd around them, if it could be called that, was strangely silent, Cassie's sobs were muffled by her fist in her mouth, and Mr. Nash looked out of it. Their attacker was also silent, sniffing into the sleeve of his jacket, watching Kit with hooded eyes.

Kit backed away slowly, trying hard to keep his movements steady and unthreatening. If he could just reach the road, he would make a dash to the shop, rubberneckers be damned. He had done all he could, and he really couldn't remember if he'd locked the shop before he stepped out, which gave him a valid reason for hurrying back. He almost made it to the outer circle of rubberneckers when his attacker suddenly charged. There was no way to avoid being hit, Kit realized. He brought up his left hand to block the punch and hoped he'd be able to walk away from it once everything was over. Even as he braced for the pain of a direct hit, there was a crack, and the attacker reeled away looking shocked.

"What?" Kit said in surprise, staring behind him to where the rescue had come from.

"The police are coming," Sasha said softly, swinging his walking stick threateningly with all the confidence of a master swordsman handling a blade. "I'd be running if I were you." He glanced at the stoner and gave him a level look, appearing surprisingly steady on his feet, and right on cue the distant wail of sirens could be heard.

Typical, thought Kit. *He hasn't changed at all.*

ONCE the police had taken away the stoner, there was a little awkward pause as Mr. Nash pulled out his wallet with an embarrassed smile. He pulled out more bills than Kit could count at a glance—perhaps four or five—and handed them over to Kit. "I seem to owe you again," he mumbled through a fat lip.

Kit managed a smile through his swelling jaw, and pocketed the money without looking too closely. He had been given less for doing more, and who was he to complain.

"It might be better if you use that money for therapy for your daughter," Sasha said with a scowl from just behind Kit, and Mr. Nash reached for his wallet again. "Oh, don't pay me as well," he said in impatience and glared at Kit in exasperation, angry that he had taken the money. Kit studied Sasha, standing a little more comfortably than he'd ever seen before, walking stick held loosely.

The prosthetic arm was firmly in place, appearing a little stiff but not awkward. Sasha's face looked worse, swollen along the bad side and with scar tissue raised like welts. He had small plasters over the bridge of his nose and his eyebrow, which did not hide the reddening around the areas.

"What," Kit snapped back, feeling defensive. "I earned that money, so don't you make me give it back." Mr. Nash, mindful of the atmosphere, backed away hastily, leaving the two of them glaring at each other angrily.

"Tell me that is how you always earn money off him and...." Sasha broke off with a look in the general direction of Mr. Nash.

"I forgot to lock the shop," Kit swore to himself. "Why don't you come over and we can talk there."

"I really don't have the time," Sasha said evasively, moving back. It seemed as though he was having second thoughts about talking to Kit, or even coming to his rescue.

All of a sudden, Kit snapped. The anger at Sasha for humiliating him at the party, the closed-up house, the entire month of silence, all came together in one big ball of pure emotion. "Don't you dare run away," Kit snarled.

"I...." Sasha seemed to brace himself, taking a deep breath and pulling himself together. Kit reached out and grasped his hand above the elbow; it felt warm, solid, familiar, and Kit smiled despite the gravity of the situation.

"I'd ask you to come with me to my apartment, but I don't think you want to walk up eight stories to smell boiled cabbage."

Sasha seemed too stunned by Kit's verbal spillage to actually comment. He also let himself be maneuvered to the end of the sidewalk and across the street with very little resistance. There was hardly a limp to Sasha's walk despite the walking stick he held, Kit noticed. He seemed to have at least hit the gym regularly and stuck to his therapy although living in hiding.

Sasha stood in the middle of the shop, looking around as though it was the most fascinating thing in the whole world. He inspected the partially dressed dummy, the coat racks, the sundresses, and everything other than Kit.

"So...." Kit cleared his throat nervously. "You look...."

"Worse," Sasha filled in dryly, fingering the bad side of his face with a grimace. "The doctors assure me the swelling will go down in a couple of days, and it will be an improvement to before." He shifted his walking stick from one hand to the other in a practiced gesture, and regarded Kit, assessing him silently.

Kit watched Sasha closely, noting the way his clothes fit him. Sasha had gone and gained weight while Kit had been starving himself, pining away like some moron. "You've put on weight," he said, voice muffled with hurt.

"Yeah." Sasha actually sounded embarrassed. "They put me on a diet at the clinic, said I was dangerously underweight. The doctor wasn't even willing to anesthetize me until I'd put on some weight."

"You are all right now?" Kit asked cautiously. He knew Sasha had been underweight before, and inquiring about his health kept the conversation going.

"I'm getting better now," Sasha said with a shrug. "Looks worse while healing. Just have to be careful about staying out of the sun and not getting an infection. That's the reason I was out late, wanted to avoid the sun."

"So you didn't come looking for me...." For some reason, Kit wanted Sasha to have been out searching for him. To have missed Kit the same way he had missed Sasha.

"Kit...."

"You could have called me, you know," Kit said through gritted teeth. "I looked for you, fucking everywhere. I went to your house, I went to Cory's place, I... I...." He leaned back and closed his eyes in despair. "I know I didn't mean anything to you, who am I kidding."

"It's not that," Sasha said softly, as though afraid to startle Kit. "You mean too much to me. If you hadn't, I'd have laughed at what Walker said and continued to... to fuck you. I didn't want to face the fact you might have been with me for money—hoping to get a part of Cory's funds. I mean, the first time you kissed me in the kitchen was after one of those horrible sisters had visited me and told me I was getting all the money. I made jokes about you being a slut—I... had my suspicions then, and when Walker told me those things about you, it was—I was drunk. I shouldn't have accused you in public...."

"Where were you?" Kit asked while trying to process what was being said. He needed to tell Sasha about his other job and his former lifestyle before Cory, but he needed the time to find the right words. He also wanted to tell him how much he'd changed, and that the reason Sasha had walked away, the suspicion that Kit was after him for money, wasn't true. The funny thing was, Kit had never even thought of Sasha as a mark, in the beginning because Sasha was nothing like the usual picks (rich and old), but also because he'd never thought of money when approaching Sasha. He'd felt guilty about the part he'd played when it came to Sasha's predicament and he'd thought to pay his dues, not to collect anything from it.

He'd had enough time to think it over in the past few weeks, and he realized he'd changed more than he'd given himself credit for. A part of Kit didn't want to admit to looking for Sasha, to waiting for him to come home, or to how much he'd missed him—afraid of sounding needy.

"I made an emergency appointment at the clinic and flew out that morning," Sasha said softly. "I needed time."

"You ran away," Kit accused him. He didn't ask which morning he was referring to.

"I...." Sasha walked over to the counter and poked at the broken chimes. "I'm back."

"Really," Kit said sarcastically. "And the first thing you did was accuse me of... of having something on with Mr. Nash."

"After I saved your ass," Sasha snapped back defensively.

Kit scrambled to get away, but Sasha stopped him by grabbing his hand. His grip was iron hard, and he pulled Kit closer to him. "I wasn't finished," he said. "I wanted to call you," Sasha admitted. "I told myself I'd call you after a week, then I said after the surgery and then the surgery got delayed—I stalled because I didn't want to know the truth about you."

"What do you mean by 'truth'," Kit said coldly. In reply, Sasha let go of Kit's hand abruptly, realizing he had been holding it all along. He walked to the counter and picked up the broken chimes lying there, looking at them intently.

"You mean you aren't... sleeping with that guy I saw you with today," Sasha said quietly, letting the chimes fall to the counter and turning around slowly. "I've seen him in your company three times, and twice now he has given you money. From what Mr. Walker told me, that is how you make a living."

"Walker...?" Kit searched his memory. "Oh, Andrew," he said, then wished he hadn't said it.

"You didn't even bother denying it," Sasha said, sounding tired. He made to push his hand over his face and stopped, as though remembering his surgery.

"Which part do you want me to deny?" Kit asked, feeling tired as well. He pushed aside the dummy he had been fiddling with and sat on the floor beside the rack, his legs incapable of supporting him. "I fucked Andrew for money," he said slowly, meeting Sasha's eyes squarely. "I do hang around rich old guys who need a little arm candy and some young stud to fuck, and I do get paid for it." He thought over what he'd said, rubbing at his throbbing jaw. The back of his head was developing a nice bump to go with it. "Relatively young," he said with a shrug. "I don't think twenty-two counts as young anymore."

"And this Mr. Nash is your latest catch," Sasha ground out between his teeth. He picked up his walking stick and swung it in an arc, catching the edge of the rack of nightdresses. "Did you fuck him while you were living with…?"

"No," Kit shouted, scrambling to his feet. "Don't you dare make up stuff. I never ever slept with him." He remembered Sasha mentioning he'd seen him in Mr. Nash's company, and thought back to the few occasions he had been with him. "He's a customer, he came with his daughter, and I go to the arcade with her once in a while—you saw her today."

"The kid with the annoying father," Sasha said wearily. "Oh, yes, I saw her. I think everyone there did."

"Well." Kit smiled at that. "The last time that guy tried to grab her, I scared him off and Mr. Nash paid me for it."

"You scared him off," Sasha said in disbelief.

"He wasn't high then," Kit said defensively. "He was reasonable."

"Well, I'll give him that," Sasha said. "From what I overheard him telling the police, she's been walking around, calling him names."

Kit thought it over; was Cassie that stupid? "She might have done that," he concluded. "She's used to her father paying off people every time she does something stupid."

"And this Mr. Nash paid you to… so you… because you saved his daughter," Sasha said a little skeptically. "I've seen him pay you twice."

"Don't you think if I'd been fucking him for money, I'd take the money before I put my pants on," Kit snapped back, angry at Sasha for not believing him. "Not take money off him on the street. Really, that isn't how it works."

"Fine," said Sasha abruptly. "I owe you an apology on that." He sounded so formal when he said that. "I was too hasty in calling you out. I saw you a couple of times with that old guy on the pavement, and based on the things Walker said about you at the party…."

"He could never keep his mouth shut when he was drunk," Kit observed viciously.

"True," Sasha agreed. "I jumped to a conclusion...." He let his head drop onto his chest, sounding tired but not very sorry. "Just tell me, did you and Cory... did he... what kind of...." He broke off, stuttering, unable to form the question, and Kit felt as though he had been punched again.

Kit took a deep breath and looked at Sasha, who was staring directly at him. For a moment he wanted to push everything aside and run—run out of the shop, out of the road, anywhere but there. He could understand the reason people ran away from difficult situations. They were so fucking impossible to talk about.

"I...." His mouth was dry. He swallowed and tried again. "I.... When I first met Cory, I thought he was some rich prick with a twink. I mean, who the fuck has a name like Sasha... it's as...."

"Terrible as Kit," Sasha said dryly. There seemed to be no malice in his voice, but it was hard to tell.

"I've fucked married men before, the type who want a little fun on the side, I've fucked men with partners before, I think it was expected...." Kit struggled with what he wanted to say. "At first, Cory was the same. I wanted him 'cause he was rich and gay and I... I...."

"He talked about you," Sasha said softly. "Not much, but he'd mention sometimes that he'd taken you out to dinner or a drink." He moved a little toward Kit, then stopped, looking unsure. Aware of the walking stick and the potential weapon it represented, Kit stayed still, unwilling to provoke Sasha.

"He didn't cheat on you," Kit said softly. "Not because I didn't try, but because he was obsessed with you." He gave a wry laugh, mocking himself. "I liked him, you know. He treated me like a human being, not some idiot like certain people do. He took me to restaurants, he talked to me like I mattered instead of some hole to be fucked, and it was like having a—" He groped for a word to describe his relationship with Cory. "—friend. Maybe a little older than usual but, well, nice, and then I had to go and fuck it all up." He could feel his eyes tearing up as he looked down. "It's all my fault in the end," he admitted bitterly. "He didn't want to but I pushed him, forced him... and it killed him." There, he'd said it. His little secret he had been shielding for so long. "I messed up your lives."

"Are you kidding me," Sasha said loudly as he lurched forward until he was almost touching Kit. "Cory and me... we were together because he felt guilty of how I ended up. When I saw you with him, the first thing I thought was, 'Finally, I can leave him.' Cory hated being with me, we didn't love each other, there was nothing there. He was the happiest when he was out with you, and I was just holding him back. I know I should have said something before leaving the house that day, I... I didn't know." He shrugged. "I was afraid I wouldn't have anyone if he left me.... That was the only reason I hung onto him."

"He thought the world of you," Kit said slowly.

"Once, maybe," Sasha agreed. "But after the accident, every time he saw me, he was reminded of his incompetence. He was depressed, he had mood swings. I should have paid more attention to him. Gotten him a shrink or something. I sometimes wish he hadn't left me everything. I didn't deserve it."

Kit didn't know what to say, so he studied the floor carefully for cracks in the tiles.

"Can I ask you something," Sasha said at last.

"Sure," Kit admitted, glancing up at Sasha. His eyes were tearing up, but there was nothing to do but continue to talk.

"Why did you come to my home that day?" It was not the question Kit expected him to ask. "When you got thrown out of your apartment, why my home? Why not anywhere else...?"

"Because." Kit had to think hard to find the correct way of saying it. "I knew there was space, but most importantly, I thought, when I read Cory had died, that there was no one to take care of you. I mean...." He tried to correct himself. "That's what Cory did, he took you to the gym, the pool... everywhere, and you looked terrible when I saw you...." He waited for Sasha to contradict him, but there was only silence. Either Sasha was keeping quiet, waiting for Kit to finish talking, or he had fallen asleep. "I thought about you all the time after Cory died. You were kicked out of the house, you had nowhere to go, and when I got kicked out of mine, I thought of you. I know I'm not making much sense." He stopped and waited for a comment, but there was none. "Why did you let me in?' he asked finally. "You hated me."

"Remember what you said to me when you helped me down the steps when the elevator broke?" Sasha asked.

"I said a lot of things that day," Kit said, wondering if it had been anything particularly nasty.

"You said you needed Cory more than I did," Sasha supplied helpfully.

"I didn't mean it like that," Kit said, blushing despite his tears. Had he said something so crude to Sasha?

"When I opened that door, you looked like a drowned rat," Sasha went on, ignoring Kit's comment. "You had your clothes in a bag and you might as well have been half dead." He looked at Kit, his expression unreadable. "Cory might have been dead, but you meant something to him. I just couldn't let you...."

"Fuck Cory," Kit exclaimed loudly, shocking Sasha. "So we meant something to him... big deal. He shouldn't have killed himself. Thousands of people have cheated on other people, and it's not worth killing themselves over." Thinking over what Sasha had said previously, Kit added hastily, "I know you said he had problems, I should have seen it also"—which he should have noticed had he not been so preoccupied with the thought of seducing a potential mark—"but sometimes, there's only so much you can do, and... and I do care about you. If there'd been any way to save Cory, perhaps... but it's too late now. And we're still here, alive." There, he'd said it. He wasn't over Cory's death, but at the same time he was tired of the dead man coming up every time he was with Sasha. By dying, Cory had seemingly made sure none of them would be truly happy. It was time to put that ghost to rest.

Sasha gave a bark of a laugh, though he didn't seem particularly amused. "That's the Kit I know."

"I... you think...," Kit stuttered, afraid he had said the wrong thing again. It was obvious Sasha still cared for Cory, no matter what.

"No, no," Sasha said with a wave of his hand. "Without people like you around, people like me would be going around in circles." He gave a wry smile. "I needed that," he admitted. "You always did have a way of stating the obvious and moving on to the next step." He held out his hand.

Kit reached forward and touched Sasha's hand, and when he wasn't pushed away, he snaked his arms around Sasha and hugged him. "I missed you," he said, his face buried in Sasha's chest. Sasha smelled the same, down to the stupid aftershave Kit was becoming fond of. He felt solid, no longer just skin and bones.

"I missed you too," Sasha admitted softly, his breath fanning the top of Kit's head.

"I missed you every fucking time you turned your back to me when we slept," Kit mumbled into Sasha's shirt, feeling needy.

"I what?" Sasha sounded surprised as he drew back. He didn't let go of Kit, but gazed down at him with a frown. "I never turned my back to you in bed...."

"But...."

"I sleep on that side," he explained. "I broke my ribs on the other side, it hurts to sleep that way."

"Oh," Kit said numbly.

"You idiot," Sasha said in fond exasperation. "I guess we both are."

"THE frame comes apart," Sasha said as he stepped over a cat. "It'll fit through the doorway, one way or another."

"You sure about this?" Kit asked cautiously. They had discussed it several times over, and in the end decided the best option was to remain at Sasha's house. The St. James mansion was too large, too full of bad memories for Sasha. He had refused to even step into the bedroom where Cory had killed himself when they went to visit. Instead, Sasha had arranged to have the remainder of his clothes and some of the furniture moved to his, or rather their, house.

"Yes," Sasha said abruptly, and Kit tried hard not to smile. The invitation for him to move back into Sasha's house had been nonverbal, but in a way very clear. Sasha had told him to bring his stuff back, and that had been that. "Think you can manage the movers?" he asked, interrupting Kit's train of thought. "I have to meet up with Lux soon."

Kit grimaced at the thought of Sasha meeting up with one of Cory's sisters. Sasha had left the day-to-day running of the company to Candela and Lux, though he had the majority of shares under his control. He was also under the tutelage of his lawyer, Ken, on how to run the company, but it was a slow process and someone needed to take charge in the meantime. According to Sasha, it helped maintain family stability, though he had not given back the house to the St. Jameses.

Instead, Sasha had arranged to have some of the furniture moved to his house and to rent the mansion out to a wealthy couple that was, according to the rumors, in the business of making pornographic films.

"Going to the mansion as well?" Kit asked as he sidestepped another cat. At this rate they were going to give up the house to the cats and move to the garden shed.

"Not today," Sasha said distractedly, pulling out his cell phone. "Unless you want to meet them for a job offer."

Kit took a deep breath and looked at Sasha pointedly. "Ouch," he said carefully.

Sasha glanced up at that and managed a grimace of a smile. "I didn't mean it like that, it was a joke."

"I'm the one overreacting now," Kit managed with a self-deprecating smile. He knew he and Sasha had more rough edges to smooth out. There were points where they would snap at each other, or when Sasha's razor-sharp tongue would scornfully point out Kit's shortcomings—both knowingly and unwittingly. Sasha sometimes regarded Kit as an idiot, especially when he spoke of certain subjects, such as the geographic location of major cities or politics. Though recently Sasha had hinted there were night classes at his college he thought Kit might find interesting. Kit had dismissed higher education out of hand before, but he was thinking on it now. Not just because Sasha wanted him to, but because he did want to be something other than what he was now. If Sasha was happy with the result, it was a bonus.

Kit smiled at the thought as he reached forward and kept a hand on Sasha's bicep. "If you say something really, really mean, I'll tap you on the head with your walking stick," he said.

Sasha managed a snort at that. "I'll hold you to it," he said firmly. "I mean it."

"It'll be like a love tap," Kit said, then wished he hadn't said it as Sasha froze, his phone held between loose fingers. The L word was something they never said between the two of them. *We eventually might*, Kit thought optimistically. Sasha still had an assload of issues to deal with, but they were slowly getting there. His Royal Highness just needed the time to get used to it all.

"I...." Sasha looked away as they heard the moving truck up the road, and Kit sighed in relief. The mood was broken and he was safe.

"They're here," said Sasha, pocketing the phone. He swung his walking stick neatly, and handed it handle first to Kit with a small, shy smile. "You're going to need this, then," he added, then limped off, leaving Kit standing at the doorway with a wide smile on his face.

SANDRA BARD started writing when she was quite young because there was always a story inside her head, but never thought of writing for an audience until recently. She only decided to try her hand at writing for the sake of being published after a series of events left her with some free time and in between jobs.

She grew up travelling the world from Africa to Asia and, though she now lectures full time at a university, dreams of having a job that wouldn't tie her down to one place. She enjoys reading books, watching anime and, occasionally, visiting a fan-fiction site. She also dabbles in tai chi and yoga in the hope they would keep her flexible and help lose weight. She lives with her pets (fish, cats, and dogs) and has been a volunteer for an organization that takes care of stray dogs (there are many, where she lives) for over ten years. She would love to hear from her readers and can be found at her Tumblr, http://sandrabard.tumblr.com, or e-mailed at sandrabard123@gmail.com.

KEEPING
SWEETS

Cate Ashwood

Also from DREAMSPINNER PRESS

STATE OF MIND

LIBBY DREW

http://www.dreamspinnerpress.com

www.ingramcontent.com/pod-product-compliance
Lightning Source LLC
Chambersburg PA
CBHW060057260626
47160CB00005B/1699